# Jacob's Journey

# Jacob's Journey

MICHAEL HADLEY

' To Debbie, if I hadn't of met you 'Diss' story may never have been written.'

'To my children, thanks for believing in me. And may your 'journeys' take you to wondrous places.'

'And to anyone who has any self doubt. Stand tall, be strong and just go for it.'

# Chapter One



The rain battered against his face as a torrid downpour was being driven in every direction by a strong wind. As he trudged along the sodden muddied path that would lead him to the tavern off in the far distance, he struggled with every heavy footstep, battling against the horrendous weather that cut through his entire body. He had been walking for miles since his trusted steed had broken its leg when losing its footing, snapping the poor creature's front left shinbone and rendering it lame and helpless.

Unable to put the poor beast out of its misery and pain due to the gunpowder being soaked with rain in the small purse he had upon his person, he had no choice but to unsheathe the large knife and slit its throat.

The night was black as coal, the wind howled like a banshee, and the rain fell heavy and hard while he knelt next to his trusted steed, his head bowed and hand upon its head.

This journey would have to continue on foot, and now alone.

Gathering what he was able to hold, Jacob took the carry sack of water and placed it around his neck and over his right shoulder. The satchel which held the breadcakes and dried beef was placed over his left shoulder. He took the overcoat off the horse's rear and put it on. The rain was now heavier, and the wind colder.

Placing one hand on the head of his horse, he said in a low voice, "Sleep well, my friend …"

Grabbing the musket, Jacob stood up and, with a deep breath, started to walk.

There were a good few miles in front of him. The rain was now pouring down and, being whipped about by the bitter wind, Jacob pushed onward, leaning forward, every step an effort. He clutched at the collar of the overcoat with his closed fist under his chin, his head dipped down, fighting through the weather. Crossing the field, Jacob came across the road - a water-logged uneven dirt road that was thick with wet mud. The road would lead him to the tavern, his destination, and to his friend, Tobias.

Jacob had been walking now for about a mile. The road, so thick with mud, had forced him to walk along the verge, and the thorns and brambles were catching at his clothes. He was tired, soaking wet and hungry. As he approached a bend in the road, the brambles and bushes thinned out, opening up holes, and he saw a big tree with an overextended canopy of branches thick with leaves. This would be an ideal place to rest up and get out of the rain.

Jacob stepped further up the verge and made his way to the tree, only twenty yards or so set back from the road. The ground was dry underneath the canopy of its leaves. He placed the rifle up against the trunk and sat with his back to it, his legs feeling heavy. A huge sigh left his lips, and with it, his breath could be seen in the cold air. The rain was so heavy that no other noise could be heard over it, but now at least, he wasn't feeling it. Now was the best time to eat without the food getting wet, so Jacob pulled the bag around from his side, took out the breadcakes and dried beef and started to eat. The noise from the rain belting down over the tree sent Jacob's mind adrift, and he remembered the time he and Tobias met each other …

# Chapter Two



It was the year of our Lord, 1711. Jacob, just turned 21, was sitting at the table by the window of the old inn just on the outskirts of the village where he lived. A young barmaid by the name of Josephine brought over a jug of ale and placed it in front of him.

Jacob smiled and said, "Thank you, miss."

She smiled back but in a rather coy way that Jacob noticed, which made his smile turn into a grin. Embarrassed by this, Josephine hurried back to behind the bar, trying desperately to look busy and hide the fact that she was attracted to Jacob. This made him grin even more.

Looking out of the window, he noticed a horse being hitched up by a rather large man with a very noticeable scar running from the top of his right eye, just above the brow and down past his cheek. He looked around the same age as Jacob but bigger with broad shoulders. The man entered the tavern and sat on the opposite side of the room in the corner. Jacob nodded to the man, and the man, holding the rim of his hat, nodded back.

The man beckoned to Josephine with his hand in a gesture, imitating a drink. "A jug of yer finest ale, please," he shouted across the room.

Josephine replied, "Yes, sir. Would you like some food with that?"

"Yeah, I'll 'av one of them there meat pies I can smell."

Josephine nodded and said, "Be right with you …"

Meanwhile, Jacob was watching out the window when five men on horseback gathered across the way from the tavern. The horses were snorting and breathing fast. One of the men dismounted his horse and walked over to the horse that was hitched up outside. He checked the saddle and then went back across to the other men. The man spoke to the others, and Jacob could see he was speaking aggressively by his arm movements and pointing towards the tavern. The hairs on Jacob's arms and neck raised straight up, tingling his skin and warning him that something was about to happen. The men rode their horses over to the tavern and tethered them to the posts. Jacob could now hear them as well as see them.

The man who had checked the horse's saddle was telling two men to wait outside. "Wait here in case the bastard gets past us and makes a run for it."

Jacob's mind was racing but in a calm way. His eyes were searching for possible weapons to use if he needed to. This was not his fight as he didn't recognise the men but, as had happened to him before on several occasions, 'trouble' had a habit of involving him.

Like many other men of his time, Jacob's father was a farmer, but he was also a 'bare knuckle' fighter, and a very good one. Farming was an arduous living and presented hard times, so more often than not, men would fight for money. A very hard and brutal way to earn some extra coin, but it could also be fairly quick if the man was good at it. Jacob's father, Henry, was such a man and had brought about quite a reputation amongst those that participated. Because of this, Henry ensured that Jacob had been raised being able to fight and fight well.

Pugilists of the time were often all brute force and punch. However, as Jacob had grown up, he had seen far too many with broken noses and cauliflower ears: lumps and bumps on faces. Therefore, he had adapted his own style to an equal defensive way, moving and parrying punches, plus launching counter-attacks which proved to be very successful as he had never lost any fight that had come his way.

The other three men entered; one remained standing at the entrance, and the other two were walking towards the table on the other side of the room, where the man with the scar was sitting.

"Tobias Johnson," said one of the men.

Looking up from under the peak of his hat, the man answered, "Who the fuck wants to know?"

"You gave my brother a beating, and now I'm gonna do the same to you …"

At that moment, Josephine had brought over the food and jug of ale that Tobias had asked for and, upon hearing the conversation, said, "Please, sirs, I don't want any trouble in here. My father and brother will be back at any moment."

No sooner had the words left her mouth, the man shouted, "Fuck off, wench," and backhanded Josephine across her face.

Tobias launched himself up, knocking the table up and over and smashed the man straight in his jaw, sending him flying across the room backwards and knocking him out cold.

On seeing Josephine clutching her face, Jacob jumped up and hit the man standing at the entrance with such force that he sent him smashing through the door and outside. Tobias had grabbed the second man at the table, and spun him around, holding him by the collar and the back of his trousers. He proceeded to run with him across the floor and threw him out the door, passing Jacob through the air on the way out. Both Jacob and Tobias ran outside to confront the other two men, and the one sprawled at their feet.

Punches were thrown from both Jacob and Tobias, knocking the two men over and out. The last man who Tobias threw out jumped to his feet and ran.

Jacob and Tobias turned to each other, and then, realising Josephine was still inside, Jacob ran to see if she was alright. She was slumped to the floor, holding her face.

Jacob helped her to her feet and asked, "Are you alright, miss?"

"Fucking bastard," Josephine replied and, looking to where the man who hit her was out cold on the floor with his arms outwards and his legs apart, ran four steps and kicked him right between his legs.

"Bastard, bastard!" she screamed.

Tobias, who had been standing in the doorway, gently grabbed her by the arms and said, "That will do, little missy. I think he's had enough."

Josephine kicked him one more time, then, cocking her head to one side, looked into Tobias' eyes and said, "I need a drink!!"

Going behind the bar, she set up three jugs on the bar and poured out the ale, spilling froth over the counter. "Drinks are on me, boys."

"I think we all need one," Jacob said as he approached the bar, picked up one of the jugs and took a drink. Then, looking at Josephine, he apologised for the fracas that had just occurred.

Tobias had walked over to the upturned table and set it back upright and into place again. "Me too, missy," he said.

As Tobias turned, walking to the still unconscious man on the floor, Jacob asked, "So, what was all that about then?"

Picking the man up and placing him over his right shoulder, Tobias answered, "Fucked if I know, mate. I just came in for a drink as I was passing through."

"Well, they seemed to know you by name. Is that indeed your name ... Tobias?"

Leaning forward with his left hand stretched out, Tobias said, "It is indeed. Pleased to meet you ... I didn't catch your name, mate."

Reaching out and shaking his hand, he said, "Jacob ... and I'm not sure it is a pleasure under such circumstances."

Both men stood for a few seconds, hands grasping each other's and laughed.

Tobias walked towards the door and said, "Well, we can't leave these men here. Gotta clean this mess up. If you don't mind helping me, Jacob, we can shackle these men to their horses and send them on their way."

Both of them picked up the bewildered, half-conscious men, put them on their horses and tied their hands up with the reins. They then slapped the hindquarters of the horses, making them run off in all directions.

At that moment, Josephine stepped outside and said, "Well, I know both of your names, so … I'm Josephine."

# Chapter Three

===== October 1713, Back on the road =====

Jacob awoke, shivering and to the sounds of the bird's morning chorus. He had fallen asleep quickly, exhausted from the journey he had started out on earlier the day before. Sitting up and rubbing his eyes, he stretched and then took a drink from the water carrier, a leather flask, around his right shoulder. It was morning; the rain had stopped, but the sky was a dismal dark grey. Dawn had broken, but the light was still slightly dark. Using the trunk of the tree, he pushed himself up to a standing position, let out a yawn, and shook out the tiredness in both his legs and arms. He stretched his arms skywards and lifted both heels as high as he could on tiptoes. Grabbing the musket and readjusting the hat on his head, he walked back to the road, which was still sodden and thick with mud but now also with small pools and puddles.

With a sigh, he said to himself, "At least it isn't raining."

Jacob still had a few miles to go before he would reach Josephine's tavern, where he would be meeting up with Tobias. A few weeks earlier, both had received news from Josephine via messengers that she needed their help. She had written them both a letter saying that her father had been robbed and killed in a struggle when he had gone to the nearest village to acquire some items that he needed for the tavern. Her brother, Gabriel, had returned with their father's dead body on the back of the cart they had gone to the village in, and he told Josephine of the robbery that had occurred. He was set upon and had been knocked unconscious. When he awoke, Gabriel found his father by the side of the road, covered in blood and dead from his wounds. The money they had with them had also gone.

Josephine had requested their help to find her father's killers. Since that first meeting between the three of them over two years ago, they had become close. And Jacob and Tobias had both realised, after fighting those five men in the tavern that day, that they had a skill set that could make them money. They were fearless and could fight, which would bring up many opportunities to earn coinage for them both. They would become 'hired men.'

===== February 1711 =====

When they met, Jacob was 21, Tobias was 24, and it was the year 1711. Josephine was 18 but mature for her age. She had to be since her mother died when she was ten years old. She had taken on the duties of the lady of the household: cleaning and cooking and washing all the linen. Her father, George, had rooms above the tavern that he would rent out for a night to weary travellers, traders and the occasional gentleman who would be passing through.

The tavern had been in George's family since his father and his father's father. It was old; the roof leaked, and the wood shrunk and swelled throughout the seasons. This would bring about a howling through the gaps in the doors and window frames when it was windy and cold. But at both ends of the tavern were huge fireplaces which kept the old place warm at least. Josephine's brother, Gabriel, one year younger than her, would be made to do chores. This was a family business, so everyone had jobs to keep it that way.

George was a clever man. He had been schooled by his mother and could read and write and so taught his children the same. The world had changed in the last thirty years; trade had boomed and people had gotten richer. Merchants had the run of it by buying at low prices and selling high. England was moving forward, and an educated mind was a better mind. Rich people owned land and profited greatly from the produce grown on it. These were generally of noble birth and had never dirtied or soiled their hands in their lives. Yeomans also owned land but would work it alongside the men they employed for labour. George owned a tavern. He was not rich but also not poor, and he did not want his children to be lacking. So they would work, study, observe and learn.

Tobias had an altogether different upbringing. He, too, lost his mother, Elizabeth, at a young age. She died of pneumonia when he was just seven years old. His father was of Irish descent, a drunkard and a brawler. More often than not, Tobias would have to look after his father in his teenage years. Luckily, he was a big young lad, and with that came enormous strength, which came in handy in picking up his drunk father and carrying him home.

The priest of the small village where Tobias lived as a child had a room in the back of his parish and had allowed them to live there after his mother died. Father Almand had a lot of time for Tobias' mother and so took them in when Edward, Tobias' father, fell to pieces when his wife passed away. This was his duty, as a man of God, to take in Edward and his young son at such a terrible time. Or at least until Edward could stand on his own two feet again.

The deal Father Almand had with Edward was that he could take lodgings in exchange for any jobs that needed to be done around the small church and its grounds. Alas, as time went on and the more drink he consumed, these jobs would fall to young Tobias to fulfil. Poor Edward could never get over the death of his beloved wife, and the only solace he found was at the bottom of a bottle. As it was a small village and parish, Tobias would often find his father drunk and face down. He would then carry him home and put him to bed.

By the time Tobias had reached the age of twelve, he was as big as most of the men in the village. And stronger. The other children were cruel to him, calling him names and throwing stones and small rocks at him. He may have looked bigger than his age, but he still felt hurt and pain as a child would, in his heart, at least.

One day, as he went looking for his father, he saw three men fighting another man up ahead in the road. As he got closer, he could see that it was his father the men were beating on. He ran as fast as he could, shouting and hollering at the men.

"Oi! oi, stop …! Stop it … Please stop! That's my father."

As he reached them, Tobias grabbed at one of the men and spun him around. The man had a knife in his hand, and as he turned, his hand came up, and the blade caught Tobias in his face, cutting him down from his eye. Tobias screamed out loud, clutching his face; blood streamed from his hand and through his fingers as he slumped to the floor onto his knees. The man froze, not knowing what to do, while the other men pulled at his clothes shouting at him to come.

As they ran off down the road, Tobias heard one of the men say, "Fuck him; he's just the son of a drunk."

# Chapter Four



Jacob took Josephine's hand, kissed it and said, "It's a pleasure to meet you."

Tobias took off his hat, held it against his chest and said, "Sorry about your table, miss."

Josephine wished them both a good day, spun on her heels and went back inside.

Tobias turned to Jacob, smiled and said, "You fight well for a skinny runt."

Jacob laughed and said, "So do you, for a girl."

They both laughed and shook each other's hands again.

"Listen, I can see you have a very useful talent there, Jacob."

"As do you," Jacob replied.

"Well, I could use a partner like yourself in my line of work. That's if you would be interested, Jacob?"

"And what exactly would your line of work be, mate?" asked Jacob.

"Well, let's just say I'm hired to do the things that the people who hire me can't do themselves …"

"You mean persuading people to do what you want them to do … violently? And because of what has happened here today, you think I could join you in such work?"

Tobias looked up, blinked, looked back at Jacob, smiled, and said, "Well … yeah!"

"Why not? I'm no good as a farmer," Jacob answered.

"Meet me here tomorrow at midday, Jacob, and I will take you to a man who will give us some work and pay us handsomely," Tobias said as he mounted his horse and pulled the reins to the left, turning the horse.

"Midday it is. I will be here," Jacob confirmed.

Tobias kicked his heels into the horse and trotted off down the road, turning his head and shouting, "Until the morrow, my friend ..."

As Jacob stood in the road and watched him ride away, the dust kicking up from the hooves catching the last of the sun's light as it was slowly setting, he thought about the day's events that had unfolded. How quickly they had turned and how he had ended up where he now was.

Only this morning, Jacob had helped his father on the farm until he had a disagreement with him. Jacob wanted more out of his life than to spend it breaking his back by working on a farm. Henry, his father, had scoffed at this idea and told Jacob that good, hard, honest toil would make him a man. Jacob had argued that Henry could have made much more money with his particular skills in fighting.

"I fight because I 'av to, boy, not that I want to!!!" his father had told him. "The extra coin comes in handy, but at the cost of hurting another man sits uneasy with me."

Jacob argued that God had given him these skills, the power to knock a man over with one blow, so it should sit just fine...

Henry replied, "Your life is your own, boy, as has been mine. Do with it what you will."

At that point, Jacob said, "I will, father, I will," and he turned and walked away.

He continued to walk and walk, thinking over and over in his head about his father's words. Kicking at the stones and dust on the ground, his mind was going round and round. Jacob had a deep yearning within him for a different life.

He walked for a while until he came upon a tavern ...

Jacob shook his head and smiled to himself. The day's events certainly had turned around. In the morning, the argument with his father had led to an opportunity now set in front of him: one that was riding off into the distance.

Jacob said to himself out loud, "Maybe this is God's plan for me."

"Maybe it's your own," said Josephine.

Jacob turned to see her standing in the doorway, a small coin purse in her hand.

"Is this yours?" she asked, holding the purse out and shaking it in front of him.

Jacob checked the right side of his belt with his hand and, noticing nothing there, replied, "Yes, it would seem so. It must have come loose during the fight. Thank you."

Josephine stepped forward and, giving him the purse, said, "You don't want to be losing that, Jacob. You're going to need it when you meet Tobias here tomorrow. I've already let you have a drink for free - can't be making a habit of it."

Taking the purse from her hand and lashing it to his belt, he laughed and said, "Why, yes, of course. Maybe I could buy you a drink back?"

Josephine smiled. "Maybe you can. See you tomorrow, Jacob."

The light now fading as night approached, Jacob dipped his head and said, "Goodbye, miss."

He turned and started the walk back to the farm, smiling.

# Chapter Five

===== October 1713, Reuniting with Tobias =====

Jacob, refreshed and fed, continued up the road to the tavern. The verge had now disappeared, so he had no choice but to walk in the muddied road. His feet were slipping with every step, and he was trying to gain some grip so as not to lose his footing. The sun had come out now and reflected off the puddles making him squint as the sun's light danced off his face. He had walked about a mile since leaving where the tree stood. The sun, now offering some heat, was warming Jacob up and making the walk harder. He stopped for a minute, removed the overcoat, rolled it up and tied it to the satchel carrying the breadcakes, wedging the hat between them. He breathed deeply, and then, letting out the air that filled his lungs, he continued onward.

It had been exactly one week since he and Tobias had seen each other. They had both received Josephine's letters at the same time and were staying at the same board and lodgings. Their business always put work their way. Tobias had received news about his father some days before from Father Almand. He was not well and had been bedbound for a few days now. After Tobias had teamed up with Jacob, their reputation had grown as well as their coin stack. This enabled Tobias to take better care of his father and to seek lodgings for them both, moving him out of Father Almand's small room in his small church. So after receiving the news, he told Jacob to meet him at the tavern while he visited Edward's bedside.

Jacob was walking and thinking of his horse. He was missing him. He had bought the horse a year ago from a man who owed a debt he was to collect. He offered the man a small price knowing that he wasn't in a position to decline it. It was a handsome brute. Black as night with a long mane. And fast. Not only had it speed but endurance as well. He asked the man what its name was.

"Ain't got no name," said the man.

"Then that's what I will call him … Noname," Jacob answered.

While Jacob was walking and thinking, he heard a horse galloping behind him in the distance. He turned around to see a figure a way behind. He carried on walking, turning his head every now and again. The horse was getting louder and nearer. Another minute or so passed, and as he turned, he could see a large figure with a hat on, and the head dipped. As the rider got nearer, he could see it was a man, and not just any man. He could see it was Tobias.

As the rider passed, Jacob he threw his arms up in the air and shouted out, "Tobias … Tobias!"

The horse came to a halt; its hind legs lowered, and its head was up high as Tobias pulled hard on the reins and lent back as far as he could. The horse let out a loud whinny, and Tobias an even louder, "Woah!!!"

Turning the horse, Tobias said, "Jacob! Why are you walking? Where's yer horse?"

Jacob explained what had happened and told him how far he had been walking. Tobias thrust out his left hand and pulled Jacob onto the back of his horse.

"I'm sorry to hear that, Jacob; he was a good horse," Tobias said thoughtfully.

"I know, I know. Anyway, how's your father?" Jacob replied, keen to change the subject.

Tobias twisted his body to face Jacob and just said, "He's dead. He died before I could get to see him, Jacob."

"I'm so sorry, my friend; I really am."

"Thank you, Jacob."

Tobias took a deep breath and told Jacob that he had buried Edward in the grounds of the small church and that only he and Father Almand had attended the funeral. He had sent for a stonemason to make a headstone at his father's grave. Tobias had instructed him to write the words: "Here lies Edward Johnson, loving father and husband."

Father Almand had the grave dug next to Elizabeth's, Tobias' mother and Edward's wife.

"At least they are with each other again," said Tobias.

"Forever," said Jacob.

With a quick dig of Tobias' heels, the horse stepped into a canter and headed towards their destination. There were still at least two or three miles to go, but at least now Jacob was on horseback again.

# Chapter Six



It was the morning after the fight at the tavern, and Jacob had woken to the sound of the cockerel, as he did every morning. But this particular morning, he awoke with vigour, excited about what the day would bring. As he washed his face in the bowl at his bedside, he noticed a cut on his right hand just above the knuckle of his third finger - the outcome of the previous day's events. He placed it in the bowl and left it for a few minutes, opening and clenching his fist, the cold water soothing the bruising and stinging the cut for a few seconds. He felt good inside, like he had gained a sense of power from the fight and from discovering that he had the ability to knock a man down with such ease and so quickly.

He looked out of the window across the field where his father was working. The sun was already high in the sky, and Henry was hard at work. He admired and respected his father for getting up every day and working, but Jacob didn't want the same for his life. He would look around him growing up and see people working hard with very little to show for it. This never sat well with him. He would tell himself that a man should be able to reap the rewards from his toil. As much as he admired and loved his father, he also resented the fact that Henry didn't put his pugilistic talents to better use: to better his life and earn more money. This, decided Jacob, would not be the mistake he would make.

After the argument with his father the morning before and the events that unfolded leading right up to the fight, including meeting Tobias, Jacob felt that maybe it was all meant to be. Everything had fallen into place. The way he felt with his father, then walking until he saw the tavern, going inside for a drink, then Tobias appearing and the men, and the fight. And now, all leading to meeting Tobias again later back at the tavern.

To go and see a man about some work that would earn him the coin that he so desired.

Was it luck? Or meant to be??

Whatever it was, he was elated, excited and looking forward to a new chapter in his life. In just a few hours, he would meet Tobias … and Josephine.

Tobias had woken in a room above the old alehouse in the village, a few miles north of the tavern, that he had been renting out for the last couple of days. Either side of him were the two women he had paid to stay the night. Both were buxom and curvy and lying naked next to him. They looked small against his large frame. As he woke, rubbing his eyes and moaning, he sat upright and looked around the room, sighing heavily from the night's cavorting. He placed both hands on the women's behinds and slapped them. The women woke with a start.

"C'mon ladies, up yers get! I've had me fill, and now you's can be about your way."

Tobias moved to the end of the creaking bed and stood up, kicking an empty bottle of rum, spinning it across the floor and into his trousers heaped in the corner. Naked, he walked over to the basin and filled it with water from the jug. Cupping his huge hands together, he plunged them into the cold water and threw the water over his face and down his chest, which was covered in thick black hair. He let out a loud belch and turned back to the bed. The two women were still half asleep and a bit worse for wear from the night's shenanigans. Tobias grabbed an ankle of each of them and pulled them towards him.

"Come on, my little darlings, get up, get up. I've things to do."

Both women got up from the bed and searched around the floor for their clothes.

They were grabbing at garments as Tobias, standing at the doorway, opened it and bellowed, "Let's be 'avin' yer."

The women scurried out the door, half-naked, with one saying, "He's no gentleman, he ain't."

Tobias laughed loudly, saying, "And you two ain't no ladies ..."

He stepped back into the room and shut the door behind him. Still naked, he found the chamber pot and began to take a long piss, scratching his chest and up to the back of his neck. He yawned so long and hard that he heard and felt his jaw crack. He finished pissing and turned to see his trousers. He bent down to pick them up, and as he did so, the empty bottle that had nestled there earlier spun on the spot and then stopped at the wall. After putting his trousers on, he then sat on the bed and pulled on his left boot. Scratching his head, he looked around the room for the other one. He saw it on the other side of the room.

"How the fuck did that get over there?" he mumbled.

Taking two steps and picking the boot up, he tried to put it on but fell backwards, straight into the basin filled with water knocking it over the wall and onto the floor.

"Arrggg, ye bastard!" he yelled, picking up the basin and slamming it back down in its place. He sat back on the bed and put the boot on. His shirt was on the floor, and his coat was under the bed. On his way out of the room, he took the satchel from where it was hanging on the peg, threw it over his shoulder, and closed the door. Tobias said his farewells to the innkeeper and collected his horse from the stable. He walked the horse out, grabbed an apple from the saddle bag and gave it to him.

Patting its neck, Tobias whispered, "Good boy ... Good boy."

The horse lifted and shook its head, snorting gently.

Tobias mounted his horse, tapped the heel of his boots into the underside of its belly and trotted out onto the dirt road that led through the village. The sun was shining bright and high in the sky. The people of the village were milling around, going about their daily business. Chickens were running in every direction as he rode past, children were playing, and he saw two boys with big sticks sword fighting. That reminded Tobias to sharpen the blade of his small axe. He had always preferred an axe to a blade or sword if his life depended on it. An axe was easily hidden and carried. It was perfect for close combat but could also be thrown with great accuracy. He would often practise throwing it into trees hence why the blade needed sharpening. An axe, thrown with intent, could stop a man at twenty or so paces easily. And used at close quarters, it was lethal if the right blow was struck.

As he rode, there were little stalls along the way selling such things as bread and vegetables, fish and meat, both fresh and dried. The village was growing in size and population, and all around, new wooden houses were being built. Sometimes, small-time merchants would pass through selling their wares on the backs of donkeys or some with horses and carts. Times were changing; small towns were being built all over, the population was growing, and merchants and traders were appearing more and more. England was moving forward and fast.


Jacob walked outside to his father, bringing him a plate of food: meat and bread, and a jug of ale. He placed it down on a big old tree stump and whistled to Henry to come over and eat. The sun was now high in the sky as it was about mid-morning.

Walking over, Henry said, "Is that for me, Son?"

"It is, Father. I'm off to meet a friend of mine, and I won't be back till much later."

"You be sure to take care, my boy, and stay away from any trouble."

Jacob took a few steps backwards, turned and said as he did, "I will, Father, I will."

He went over to the small stable, saddled his horse and set out to meet Tobias.


Tobias left the village and rode along the road to meet Jacob. He flicked at the reins and took the horse into a gallop, thundering along the road. Jacob had reached the tavern and could see a young woman feeding the chickens outside. He dismounted his horse and walked it up behind her and could see it was Josephine.

"Morning, miss."

Upon turning around and seeing Jacob, a huge smile spread across her face, and her cheeks flushed red.

"Jacob. Good morning. It's good to see you again."

Seemingly out of nowhere, Tobias' horse appeared and came to a shuddering halt, dust and stones flying up.

"So you made it here then, Jacob." And then, tipping his hat, he said, "Good morning to you, little missy."

"Good morning to you, Tobias."

After tipping his hat to Josephine, he turned to Jacob and said, "Well, my new partner, we have a man to see about some business. So mount up, and let's be on our way."

Jacob said goodbye to Josephine, mounted his horse and took off after Tobias.


They rode south for a few miles until they came upon a rather large house set back in its grounds. A wide pathway, almost as big as most roads, led down to the house. Cart tracks could be seen set deep within it. The two trotted down, and Tobias told Jacob to let him do the talking when they met the man of the house, whose name was Jeremiah.

"What's the job gonna be?" asked Jacob.

"We won't know 'til we get in there and speak to him, but the last job I did was for a debt owed, and it paid some nice coin to boot."

The truth, in fact, was that the last job had indeed earned him some coin but had also not gone totally as he had planned, and he proceeded to explain why to Jacob.

Tobias had been given the job of retrieving a gambling debt from a man named Arthur. He had lost a large amount of money at cards and had agreed to settle up in a week's time but failed to do so. The man he owed the money to had sold on the debt to Jeremiah. This was the business, and it paid rather well. It was usually quick and easy. Sometimes, all it took was gentle persuasion and, other times, the taste of a boot or fist. This particular time, gentle persuasion did not work, so Tobias had to use his fists. And his boot ... several times. He had retrieved the money owed but had also left Arthur in rather a bad way: a few less teeth and a broken nose kind of bad way. As far as Tobias was concerned, this had been a job done well and nothing more. The unfortunate thing was that Arthur's older brother Archie did not see it the same way. The way he saw it was that his younger brother had been set upon by a much larger man with a scar down his face. Arthur, on the other hand, had not mentioned to his brother the game of cards. Or losing the game. Or indeed the debt.

All he mentioned was being beaten black and blue by Tobias. Now, because of his size, scar and the fact he had been doing this type of work all around, it wasn't that hard for Archie to find out more about Tobias. Like where he frequented and the places he would drink.

So, after a couple of weeks, Archie finally found and caught up with Tobias. Due to his size and reputation, he had brought along with him four other men. Together they had tracked Tobias down one afternoon - to a tavern!!!

Jacob pulled hard on the reins and said, "So you mean to tell me that those five men-"

"Yes," said Tobias. "But to be fair, I did not know who they were at the time."

"So how the devil do you know now?" asked Jacob.

Tobias proceeded to explain that after he had left the tavern, he doubled back around and followed the horse with Archie on its back. It had taken him straight back to Arthur's house, and by the time they arrived, Archie had now fully woken up from being unconscious. He had gotten off the horse and gone into the house. Tobias hitched up his horse and confronted the two men with his axe in one hand. Waving it in both the brothers' faces with anger in his voice, he got Arthur to explain the beating to Archie.

He had left the men with a simple warning: "If I ever see yer faces again, you will both end up in shallow graves!"

"And does this happen often?" asked Jacob.

"No, no, no, never. First time ..."

Jacob shook his head and shrugged. The fact was that he and Tobias took on five men, and beat them all, easily. And if truth be told, he enjoyed it.

They came to the end of the path, which opened up to a small stony courtyard and then the house. They both dismounted and walked towards the door. Tobias knocked three times.

A middle-aged silver-haired man opened the door. He greeted Tobias and said, "Good to see you. Who's your friend?"

Jacob introduced himself, and they walked into the big house, down a hallway and into a large room.

"Sit, sit," said Jeremiah. He poured out two brandies and gave both men a glass.

"Now, let's get straight down to business, shall we?" said Jeremiah. "I'm sure, as you are aware, gentleman traders and merchants are making a lot of money nowadays, and I would very much like to get my hands on some of it. There is a trader by the name of 'Dupree' who has an unpaid debt to me, and I need you to reclaim it. I will pay you half of that debt owed if you bring me the money … and something extra."

Tobias drank the contents of the glass in one go, tipping his head back and then he leant forward, putting the glass on the table in front of him. "What do you mean, something extra?"

Filling up Tobias' glass, Jeremiah said very calmly, "A finger …"

Jacob, while taking a drink, coughed and spluttered and then said, "A finger!!!!!"

Tobias placed a hand on Jacob's shoulder to steady him, looked at Jeremiah and said, "Why a finger? He owes you money, not his flesh."

"It's simple. I run a money lending business and not a charity. Every now and again, I have to prove that I will not be made to look weak by people who think they can withhold payments to me. Now, do you want the job, or shall I pass it on to another …?"

Tobias looked at Jacob and winked. "There's no need to pass it on; we will take the job. Where will we find this 'Dupree'?"

"Every second Monday, he travels along the Norwich road with his cart of supplies to trade at local markets. You can catch up with him there."

Tobias stood up, grabbed the glass of brandy, gulped it down, and then grabbing at Jacob's arm to stand him, up said, "Consider it done. We will return in a week's time."

He then shook Jeremiah's hand, and both men left, mounted their horses and trotted back up the pathway.


Jacob's mind was all over the place. He blurted out, "A finger? A fucking finger!"

Tobias turned to him. "Look, I have had to beat up a few to get a debt off them. Most only require a threat of it, but I myself haven't had to cut off a finger as part of that debt, but a job's a job."

Jacob winced and then told Tobias that he had slaughtered chickens and pigs and chopped them into different cuts of meat and that blood and guts never bothered him. But a man's finger ... it didn't seem right.

Tobias stopped his horse and took out the axe from his belt. He held it in front of Jacob and said, "This isn't for show. I have had to use it many times to defend myself. This business can be bloody. I thought after seeing you fight yesterday that you could be a useful partner. If you are having second thoughts or don't feel up to it, then I'll understand."

Jacob's brow furrowed. "Listen to me. I will fight any man that's put in front of me; I'm no coward."

"Good," said Tobias. "Then first thing in the morning, let's go and find this 'Dupree.' But first, let's stop at Josephine's tavern to get some food drink some ale, and I will rent a room for the night."

They arrived at the tavern and hitched the horses to the pole outside. As they entered, Josephine wasn't there, but her father was. There were also people sitting down, eating and drinking. George introduced himself, told them to please sit down and asked what they would like.

"Two of yer jugs of ale, please," Tobias said, "and a bowl of stew."

"Certainly, and will you be eating as well?"

"I'll have the same," said Jacob.

George poured the two jugs of ale, placed them on the table and told them their food would be out in a little while.

"I'll be wanting to rent a room for the night as well," said Tobias.

"Yes, of course. We have a room available. Just let me know when you would like to go up."

A few minutes later, Josephine came out from the back room behind the bar with their food.

"Jacob, Tobias ... How are you both?"

The three of them talked for a while. Josephine asked them not to mention anything about the day before to her father as she didn't want him to know anything. They both agreed that would be best. Josephine was called back by her father and told to go upstairs and prepare a room. They both said good night as she went and then drank some more before Tobias went to his room and Jacob went home to his father's house.

# Chapter Seven



===== February 1711, The first job =====

Jacob had woken early and was in the small stable, putting the saddle on the horse. He didn't know how long this job would take. He packed food and water, plus his father's rifle, along with gunpowder and shot. He also filled a saddlebag with oatcakes and a few apples for the horse. Upon returning home, Jacob explained to his father that he would be gone for a couple of days or maybe longer. The sky was grey and overcast, and it was colder than the day before. Jacob grabbed his coat and led the horse out. He then opened the gate and mounted the horse. He turned back towards the house to see his father feeding the chickens. At that moment, a thought crossed his mind that gave him a small shiver down his back. What if this day goes wrong? What if it turns into bloodshed, and this is the last time he sees his father? He knew nothing of this man, 'Dupree,' or what he might be capable of. A knot formed in his stomach, and he found himself just staring at the floor. Then the horse snorted, shook its head, and Jacob snapped out of it. He was about to venture into the unknown, but he knew his own capabilities. He knew he wanted a better, richer life, and this feeling of fear was also a feeling of excitement about the future. He looked back at his father to see him looking back and waving. Jacob put his arm high in the air, gave a short wave, then pulled the reins around, turned the horse, and rode off towards the tavern.

Upon reaching the tavern, he could see Josephine hanging out clothes to dry and her brother Gabriel chopping up wood. Josephine was lucky that she could wash out clothes as nearby was a small brook. Soap was expensive, but her father had acquired some from a trader that had passed through.

Jacob rode up to the tavern, tethered his horse and said, "Good morning, Josephine."

Josephine had already heard and seen Jacob and was walking towards him.

"Morning, Jacob, although be it a grey one."

They stood and spoke for a while, and then her father, George, came out and told Gabriel to fetch some of the wood he had been chopping and stack up both fireplaces. As he instructed the boy, he saw Jacob and walked over to him.

"Ah, good morning, young man. Your friend is in the stable, tending to his horse. He tells me you are both off this morning on quite a long ride."

"Yes, sir, we are," said Jacob.

"Well, a safe journey to you both then."

George walked back to Gabriel and clapped his hands, telling him, "Come now, boy. Let's get this wood inside. Hurry up." He then turned to Josephine and said, "There's work to be done, my girl. It won't get done by itself."

Josephine said goodbye and walked towards the door. Just before walking through it, she turned back and waved. Jacob returned the wave and smiled.

From behind him, he felt a slap on his shoulder and, spinning around, saw it was Tobias.

"Well, Jacob, are you ready for your first job?"

"Ready as I will ever be," said Jacob.

"Good, good. Then let's get going. It's a fair ride from here."

Both men mounted and rode off towards Norwich road.

The wind was blowing leaves about in the fields on either side of the road and brought with it a chill that was enough for both men to have the collars of their coats up around their necks.

"How far is the Norwich road?" Jacob asked.

"It's about thirty miles or so. A good day's ride - maybe a day 'n a half."

Tobias told Jacob that about five miles up ahead, there was a small marketplace where they could stop to buy provisions for themselves and the horses. He also said that there was a very skilled blacksmith who does a sideline in rifles and pistols.

"I already have a rifle," Jacob replied.

"Yes, I see, but that is a 'matchlock' rifle, and for the last five years or so, a more advanced rifle has been around, called the 'flintlock.' They also make pistols, which I am hoping to acquire from him."

"I've never fired a pistol before," said Jacob.

"Fear not, my friend. You will have many an opportunity to shoot at a tree or two on the way."

"So, do you think we will need a pistol?" asked Jacob.

"Well, I would rather have one than not, Jacob," said Tobias. "And besides, we don't know who or what we are dealing with here, so it's better to be ready than to be sorry ... or dead!"

They had travelled for about five miles, and just up ahead was the small road that led to the marketplace. It was set back from the main road about two hundred yards and could be seen easily enough. They trotted into the market, tied up the horses and then went on foot to look around. There were stalls set up all over. Local people had fruit and vegetables for sale, plus bread, eggs and chickens. There were also traders, including butchers, bakers and sheep farmers. All sorts of goods were sold by legal vendors. Tobias bought some bread, turnips and a half dozen apples. He put them in the saddlebag hanging from his shoulder and walked around to find the blacksmith he knew.

"There he is, over there, Jacob. Come on, this way."

Joseph, the blacksmith, had a stall set up selling tools, hammers, farm tools, knives, nails and horseshoes, among other things.

"Joseph …!" bellowed Tobias as he approached the stand.

Stepping out from the stall with both arms out, Joseph embraced Tobias. "Hello, my friend, how are you? Ain't seen you for months."

The two shook hands with a grip that could ring the life out of a large goose.

Tobias introduced Jacob, and Joseph grabbed his hand and said, "Any friend of this big lunk is a friend of mine."

Turning back to Tobias, he said, "So what can I do you for, Tobias? Shoes for your horse, perhaps?"

Tobias answered in a soft, quiet voice. "I'm looking for any 'other' wares you might be having about you … Like the pistol sort of kind."

"Ah, of course, I have indeed, but not here with me. Follow me back to my cart, and I'll see what I can do for you."

Turning his head, Joseph beckoned to a young lad sitting on a sack of oats. "You stay here for a bit, boy. I'll be back shortly, and watch out for anyone who's looking to steal."

The two men followed Joseph out of the market to a big cart attached to a large horse. Joseph had built an iron cage on the cart with a lock. He unlocked it, pulled open the iron door and lifted up two loose pieces of wood in the floor of the cart. There, within, were five flintlock pistols, gunpowder, balls of shot and lint.

"How much for two pistols, powder and all?" asked Tobias.

"Well, seeing as you're a good friend and the fact I still owe you for getting back my two shire horses that were stolen, you can have them both for five pounds. I'll throw in the shot, lint and powder."

"That's a good price, Joseph. It's a deal."

Tobias handed over the coin, wrapped up the pistols and everything in two sacks and tied them together.

He placed the sacks over Jacob's shoulder and said, "Here you go, you can carry them. Now, wait here while I get the horses and meet you back here."

Joseph and Tobias walked back into the market and said their goodbyes.

"It's good to see you again, Tobias. Maybe next time you're around these parts, we can get drunk like old times."

"Yes, yes, sounds good to me. Well, take care of yourself, Joseph, and I will see you soon."

Tobias returned to the horses, mounted his and grabbed the reins of the other and slowly rode them to where Jacob was waiting by the cart.

"Well, we have the pistols, food, and just up the way, there is a small stream so we can fill up for the journey," Tobias explained.

Jacob gave one sack to Tobias, mounted his horse, and they both set off again.


They had been riding for a few hours and stopped to rest the horses and themselves. This would be a good time to practise with his pistol, thought Jacob. There were plenty of trees around to shoot at. He took the pistol out of the sack, loaded the shot and gunpowder and placed the piece of lint. Tobias did the same as he wanted to try out the 'flintlock pistol' as well.

"Now, listen, Jacob. You don't need to be far away like with your rifle, so just point and pull the trigger. At this range, you can't miss."

Jacob lifted his arm and pointed at the tree. As quick as he had aimed, he took the shot. The hammer slammed down, causing a spark, which lit the flint, lighting the powder, and the shot slammed into the trunk of the tree, sending small pieces of bark everywhere.

"There you go. I told you, you can't miss."

With a huge grin on his face and punching the air, Jacob let out a 'whoop' and then said, "I think I like pistols, Tobias."

"I thought you might, but pointing at a tree and pointing at a man is a very different thing, Jacob."

And then, swinging himself around to face the tree, Tobias pointed and shot.

"You have to be as quick without hesitation, Jacob, or it could be you with the hole or worse - dead."

Jacob was silent for a few seconds, nodded and said, "Let's eat."

Tobias took a loaf of bread from his saddlebag, broke it in half, and put the other half back. He then halved it again and gave a piece to Jacob, along with an apple. They both sat and ate, and then Tobias took off a leather flask he had hanging from his saddle and threw it at Jacob.

"Get that down your neck."

Jacob caught the flask and said, "What's in this?"

"Open it and take a swig."

Jacob pulled off the top and sniffed at the neck …

"Ale!" he cried and took a big swig of the contents. Wiping his mouth with his hand, he outstretched his arm to Tobias, who took an even bigger swig.

"Ahhhh, now that hits the spot, don't it?"

Jacob, breaking the apple in half and feeding his horse, said, "It sure does, my friend."

Tobias tied the leather flask back to the saddle and mounted his horse.

"Well, we should be on our way if we are to make it to the Norwich road by the morning."

"Yes, yes, of course, Tobias. If we can make it to within a few miles by tonight, we can set up camp and leave again at first light."

"Exactly, Jacob."

Tobias knew that Dupree would be going towards the docks at Ipswich to buy from the traders that had landed there selling their

wares. And also knew he would have money to buy with, so it would
be the ideal time and place to reclaim the debt he owed Jeremiah.
He knew that Dupree was a middle-aged man who had a black
beard with a white patch on the chin. He was of French descent and,
on the side of his cart, was written "DUPREE TRADING," so he
would be easily recognised.

Hours had passed riding, and the sun had been replaced by the
moon. It was almost too dark to be able to see, even with the lanterns
they had lit. Both men were tired and aching from the journey. To
their left across the field was a clump of trees, so they rode across to
set up camp and rest until morning ...

The sun slowly began to rise, burning a deep red colour. The
early morning chorus of the birds stirred Jacob awake. He stretched
on the ground and rubbed his eyes. Yawning, he got up and rolled
the blanket up and put it on the horse. Tobias was asleep, snoring.
Jacob kicked at his boot. "Tobias, wake up. It's morning."
Tobias grunted and turned over onto his side.
Jacob kicked at his boot again. "Come on, wake up."
Tobias stretched one arm up towards the sky and let out a loud
yawn. "I'm awake. I'm awake."
He sat up and held a hand out to Jacob. "Help me up then, man."
Jacob grabbed his hand and pulled Tobias to his feet. "Good lord,
you are heavy!"
"Aye, I'm a growing lad," said Tobias, laughing.
Both men took the horses by the reins and walked out of the trees
and into the clearing of the field.
"I reckon we have a couple of hours riding, and then we will be
at the Norwich road, Jacob. Now, before we get there, we need a
plan to stop this Dupree. We know he will be heading to Ipswich
dock to buy his goods. So we need to get ahead of him and block

him off. When he stops, we will pull out the pistols and get the money."

Jacob just nodded and said, "Sounds good to me."

After a couple of hours, they reached the Norwich road and could see quite some distance along it.

"This will do fine," said Tobias. "Now, we wait …"

They positioned themselves just off the road about fifty yards back to have a clear sight.

They waited for a while until they noticed something in the very far distance.

"There … I think I can see something," Jacob said.

Tobias took out a small spyglass from his saddlebag and looked down the road. Sure enough, he could see a horse pulling a cart but couldn't make out who was in the cart.

"Do you see?" asked Jacob.

"Yeah, but I can't make out if it's him."

"Let me look, Tobias."

Jacob took the spyglass and looked through it.

"Well?" asked Tobias.

Jacob pondered for a few moments until the image became clearer.

"Yes … Yes, I think it's him."

"Give it 'ere. Let me see," Tobias said as he took it from him.

As Tobias looked down the spyglass, he could see that the man had a black beard with a white part on the chin.

"Right, let's get ready, Jacob."

Both men loaded their pistols ready and hid them inside their coats. They waited until they could see with their own eyes and then positioned the horses side by side in the road so that the cart could not pass.

"When I say, Jacob, pull out the pistol and point it at him. Let me do the talking."

The cart came to a stop about thirty yards away from them. A man dressed in furs with a black beard that was white at the chin held the reins in his hands. He grabbed a musket, stood up on the cart and pointed it straight at them.

In a French accent, Dupree shouted, "Out of zee road!"

Jacob, thinking quickly, grabbed the reins from Tobias and said, "Please, sir, we need help. My friend has been shot; he is losing too much blood ..."

Under his breath, he instructed Tobias to lean forward onto the horse's neck.

Jacob slowly rode his horse in front, holding the other's reins and said, "Please, sir. Can you help him? We mean you no harm."

Dupree shouted, "Stop! Don't come any further, or I will shoot!"

With that, Jacob got off his horse and began to walk towards Dupree with his hands spread out in front of him. "Please, help my friend," he said. "Please, sir, I don't want him to die ..."

Dupree, seeing the desperate state Jacob was in, climbed off his cart and walked towards him. "Keep your 'ands in zee air," he said, pointing the musket at Jacob.

Tobias was groaning with his face in the horse's neck, and Jacob was still pleading for help.

Dupree, now next to Tobias' horse, looked at Tobias and said, "Where 'as he been shot?"

Suddenly, Dupree felt Jacob's pistol at the back of his head and heard the click of the hammer being pulled back.

"Put down the musket," Jacob demanded.

In one move, Tobias sat up with his pistol in hand, pointed it at Dupree's head and said, "NOW!"

Jacob grabbed the musket from Dupree and threw it behind him. Tobias jumped down and put the pistol's barrel right into Dupree's right eye.

"You have a debt to pay, and we are here to collect it."

"Monsieur, I don't know what you are talking about. I have no debt …"

Tobias pulled back the hammer and said, "Your name is Dupree, and you owe a debt to a man called Jeremiah. Now, pay what you owe, or I leave you here with a big fucking hole in your head and just take it from you."

Dupree, scared and desperate, said, "I swear I have paid the debt. I owe Jeremiah nothing."

Tobias quickly hit Dupree up the side of his head with the pistol, causing him to fall to his knees, holding his head.

Dupree screamed out in pain.

Tobias put the gun to his head and said, "Now give us what you owe or die."

Dupree fumbled at his side and pulled out a purse with coinage in it and held it up, saying, "Ok, ok. Please, just take it. Don't kill me."

Tobias grabbed the purse and opened it. "That will do," said Tobias.

Jacob was astounded at what had just happened. "What the fuck is wrong with you?" he said to Dupree as he pulled him up off the floor. "Why lie and risk your life?"

Dupree was very shaken and now bleeding from the blow to his head. "That's all zee money I 'ave, and I need it to buy goods so I can sell zem at the market."

Dupree explained that he had fallen on hard times and had been robbed a few months before. He had no choice but to borrow money from Jeremiah, and the interest was very high. He said that he had every intention to pay but just needed a few more weeks to get the money.

"Tough shit," bellowed Tobias. "You pay your debt. That's how it works."

Seeing a great opportunity, Jacob said, "Hold on a moment." He leaned into Dupree's face and said, "You trade for goods and sell them at market, yes?"

Dupree nodded. "Oui, yes, yes ..."

"Ok, I have a proposition for you."

Tobias was about to say something, but Jacob waved down his hand and said, "Hold on, hold on."

Jacob looked back at Dupree and told him that if they paid Jeremiah half the debt and told him that's all the money Dupree had on him, in return, Dupree would partner up with both of them in the trading business.

"Woah, what the hell are you doing, Jacob?" asked Tobias. "This isn't the job. We get the money, take a finger, and return with both things to Jeremiah."

Duprees eyes widened. "Sacré bleu!" he cried out loud. "A finger ...? What do you mean 'a finger'?"

Jacob grabbed Dupree by his arm, "Don't worry, we ain't gonna take your finger."

Tobias pulled his axe from his belt and said, "We fucking are, Jacob. I made a deal: the money and a finger. If we don't bring both to Jeremiah, then we won't be paid ... and I intend to be paid!"

Jacob grabbed at the handle of the axe and said, "Listen to me, big man. We will be paid, but we will also be in a position to set ourselves up in business as merchants. Do you not see? There is far more money to be earned in trading goods and selling than in just debt collecting. You need to think bigger. Trust me, my friend, we will own our own business a few years from now. This is a great opportunity that has presented itself to us ..."

"I know nothing of traders or merchants," said Tobias. "I know how to fight and get debt back; I know how to make people give me what I want."

Jacob took Tobias aside. He explained that this was a good idea and that they could make some real coin from this endeavour. To look forward into a possible future where they could be rich.

Tobias stood there for a few minutes and said, "What about the finger?"

"We don't need the finger," said Jacob. "All we need to tell Jeremiah is that we took all the money and thought it wouldn't be a wise thing to take a finger while money was still owed, in case Dupree did a runner and set up somewhere else in the country because he was scared of what else would be cut off him."

Tobias agreed it would make sense. "Ok, then, Jacob, I'm with you on this. The question is, is he?"

They both turned and looked at Dupree. Tobias stood right in front of him, towering above him.

Jacob stood to the side of him and said, "So, are you in agreement?"

Dupree brought both hands up and nodded his head. "Oui, oui, gentleman. I will gladly partner with you both and show you the business of trading in goods."

"Then we have an accord," said Jacob.

# Chapter Eight



Tobias rode with Jacob holding on at the back until they reached Josephine's tavern. It was now mid-morning, and as they approached, they could see Gabriel scattering chicken feed. There was a chill in the air as the sky was blanketed in dark clouds. A deep rumble could be heard off into the distance as thunder rolled and crashed in the sky. Tobias pulled his horse up to the hitching post and wrapped the reins around it as they both got off.

"Looks like it could rain again, Jacob. This damn weather of late is beginning to piss me off."

"Seems so. Let's get inside and see Josephine."

They walked over to Gabriel, and Tobias put his big arms around him. "It's good to see you again, little man. Sorry to hear about your father. How are you holding up?"

"Ease up, big man; you're crushing me," said Gabriel.

Tobias let go of him and ruffled his hair with his hand. "Let's go see your sister," he said.

Jacob put out his hand and shook Gabriel's while placing the other hand on his shoulder. "We are here now, Gabriel, so come; let us talk."

All three entered the tavern, and Gabriel walked straight to the bar where his sister was serving a jug of ale to a man.

"Josephine, Josephine, look ... Look who is here."

She put the jug on the bar and looked up to see the two men standing just inside the door.

"Tobias, Jacob. It's so good to see you both," she said, coming out from behind the bar and walking towards them both. With her arms wide, Josephine hugged and kissed both men on the cheek.

"Come, sit, sit. I will bring you something to eat and drink. Gabriel, can you fetch some food from the pantry," she asked, "while I get some ale for us all?"

Tobias and Jacob took the table in the corner and sat down facing the door. Both men placed their pistols on their laps. This was a habit that had served them well in the past and was something they just did when inside any building. Second nature to them both was better to be prepared than dead.

Josephine brought over the ale and sat down. She preceded to tell them both what had happened on that fatal day nearly two months ago now that led to her father's murder.

She explained that her father had prepared the horse and cart and had written a list with her of what goods to buy in the local town. He had left with Gabriel that morning as they did every time to buy supplies. A few hours later, she said that Gabriel had returned with a cut on his head and with their father's dead body in the back of the cart - he had been stabbed and shot.

Tobias stood up and slammed his fist down onto the table. "Bastards, bastards!"

The man at the bar and a man and his wife eating turned to look at the table.

"Please sit down, Tobias," Josephine said gently.

"Yes, sit down," said Jacob. "A calm head is needed right now."

Gabriel put three plates of food on the table and put his hand on Tobias' shoulder. "Eat something; you must be hungry."

Gabriel sat down and started to tell them what had happened.

"I helped my father put the harness on the horse and then shackled the cart to it. We set off towards the town, and I took the reins. We headed up the road for about a mile just before the bend in the road by the big tree. As we went around the bend, four men on horses were blocking our way. My father asked them to move. One moved to my side of the cart and one to my father's. The other two were in front. Father asked them what they were doing and could they let us pass. Then the one on Father's side pulled a musket. I panicked and pulled up the reins. The horse reared up, and I felt a blow to the side of my head, which knocked me out. When I awoke, my father was lying by the side of the road. I stumbled to him and turned him over to help him ..."

Gabriel put his head in his hands and shook his head from side to side.

Jacob leant across the table and put a hand on his shoulder. "It's ok, Gabriel. Please continue."

Gabriel took a deep breath and said, "His eyes were shut, and he was covered in blood. He wasn't breathing. I cried out to him to wake up. I also shook him. But ... he didn't."

Josephine put her arms around with tears in her eyes, "It's ok, brother. It's ok."

Tobias leant back on his chair and brought his hands to his face pushing back his head.

Josephine looked at Jacob and said, "This is why I sent for you. To find my father's killers. To find them and to bring them to justice."

Tobias rocked forward and said in a deep low voice, "Justice ... justice. Oh, have no fear; there will be justice. I'm gonna find them and tear their fucking arms off!"

Jacob was quiet, sitting back in the chair, his lips pursed and eyes rolling around the room.

"Can you remember anything about them?" asked Tobias. "What were they wearing? Did they have any scars?"

Gabriel sat up. "The one who hit me - he had a patch over his eye. His left eye."

"The left eye?" Tobias asked.

Nodding, Gabriel answered, "Yes. Yes, definitely, the left eye. He was right next to me."

"Good, good," said Tobias. "That's a start; something we can work with. There can't be too many men with a patch over their eye."

Jacob leant forward and took a huge swig of his ale. "Is there anything else you remember? Anything at all?"

"An accent," said Gabriel. "A Scottish accent. I remember the one who pointed the musket at Father said, 'Your money or your life,' in a Scottish accent."

"Are you sure?" said Jacob. "If you're sure, then we have two things that will help us find these bastards."

"I think so. I mean, I took quite a blow to the head, but I'm sure he was Scottish."

Tobias grabbed at the plate in front of him, cut a thick slice of the beef, broke off a chunk of bread, and took a bite out of both. With a mouthful of food, he said, "Good, that's good."

He then took a large swig of ale, emptying the jug and spilling some down the side of his mouth and chin. Wiping it away with his coat sleeve, he said, "We need more ale."

Josephine filled a large jug and put it on the table. Then excused herself to tend to the bar.

Outside, it had started to rain. Gabriel stood up and said, "I've left the wood for the fire outside. I won't be long."

Jacob and Tobias sat and discussed what they had just heard. They both agreed that the best place to start looking for these men would be the village a couple of miles or so down the road. Maybe someone would remember seeing them around the time. Perhaps someone had seen the murder but fled, not wanting to be involved.

Tobias grabbed the large jug and filled his own. Picking up his jug, he stopped halfway to his mouth and said, "Hold on a moment. Why?"

"Why, what?" asked Jacob.

Tobias drank from the jug. "Why were they there? The four men. Why then? At that time?"

"I see," said Jacob.

"They must have known Gabriel and George were on the road at that time. Or they had robbed others on that road."

"Drink up, Tobias. We need to ride to the town and ask around the locals."

Tobias picked up the large jug on the table and, holding it with both hands, brought it up to his mouth and drank. He gulped and slurped, froth coming out the sides of his mouth, down onto his neck and chest, tipping his head back until it was empty. He banged it back onto the table and, with one hand, wiped away the froth whilst letting out an enormous belch.

"Lord above ..." said Jacob, shaking his head.

"What? You said drink up!"

Jacob stood up and walked towards the bar.

He told Josephine they were leaving to ride to the small town to see if any of the locals could remember anything of that day. If any had indeed seen the four men.

Josephine nodded and said, "I will make up rooms for you both. You can stay here for the night, or as long as you want."

Jacob leant over the bar and cupped both of her hands with his. "We will try our very best to find these men. I cannot promise that we will, only that we will never stop ..."

Josephine leant forward, kissed Jacob for a few seconds and said, "I know you will, thank you."

Tobias cut off another thick slice of beef, grabbed the rest of the bread and walked to the door. "Come on, Jacob. We have people to see. We will see you later tonight, sweet Josephine, hopefully with some news."

He opened the door. It was still raining, and now the wind was picking up, making the fallen leaves dance and tumble across the ground.

He took a bite of the beef and stepped outside.

Jacob placed a gentle hand on Josephine's face and said, "We shall be back later."

He turned and walked outside to where he saw Tobias standing by the horses, rocking backwards and forward on his heels. As he got closer, he could see Tobias was taking a piss.

"You piss like a horse, Tobias."

"It's the rain and wind, my friend. Made me want to go," said Tobias.

"Really? Not the entire large jug of ale then ..."

Tobias laughed. "Well, it may have helped."

Jacob mounted his horse and could see Gabriel sitting under the roof of the small log shed he had built to keep the logs dry from the rain. With his head in his hands, Gabriel just sat there.

Jacob pulled around the horse towards the road that led to the town and said, "Let's go ..."

Tobias mounted his horse and turned towards the road.

Jacob was a few feet in front. He turned to look back and said, "Look over there ... the log shed."

Tobias looked behind and saw Gabriel. "What am I looking at? I only see Gabriel."

"Exactly," said Jacob. "Do you not find that odd? He's just sitting there on the logs ... in the rain."

The two horses trotted onto the road, now side by side and snorting, their ears twitching from the rain.

"Perhaps he wants to be alone," said Tobias. "I mean, he just went over his father's murder again. He's probably upset."

"I don't know," said Jacob. "Maybe ..."

Tobias kicked his heels into the horse's underbelly and sped up. "Well, let's get to town and see what we can find out."


As they rode along the road, the rain eased up, but the wind stayed. A mile or so down the road, they came to the bend where the large tree stood – the exact place of the murder. Jacob pulled back the reins and came to a stop. He looked around and imagined what had happened. Tobias stopped about fifty yards past the bend, noticing Jacob had stopped. He turned the horse around and rode back.

"Why have you stopped, Jacob?"

"This is where it happened," he said. "I'm just getting a feel. You know, playing it out in my head."

Tobias pulled his pistol and shot at the large tree. Jacob's horse reared up and whinnied at the sudden gunshot. Jacob held on and pulled on the reins to steady the horse.

"What the hell are you doing?" yelled Jacob.

"Oh, I'm just playing out in my head what I'm going to do to those bastards when we find them. Now, let's get to the fucking town!!"

Half an hour later, the two men rode into the town. The sun was peeping through a grey sky, its light hitting the horizon. The horses were brought to a slow trot, passing by stone and wooden houses. Up ahead was an alehouse.

Tobias pointed to it. "That looks like a good place to start, Jacob."

They stopped outside and hitched their horses. As they did, they could hear music and laughter coming from inside.

Tobias held Jacob's arm for a second and said, "We get some ale and then ask if anyone knows of any men with the descriptions Gabriel gave us."

Jacob nodded, and both men opened the door. The music grew loud as they stepped inside. The laughter filled the rafters as people danced and drank. Jacob asked the bartender for two ales. As Tobias made his way to the bar, a large woman with an ample cleavage danced in front of him. With a drink in one hand, she took Tobias' hand with the other and danced around him. Tobias put his arm around her waist, lifted her off the floor and danced her towards Jacob. As he reached the bar, he swiped the jug of ale out of Jacob's hand and took a swig. Then, putting the woman down, he gave her a kiss and laughed wholeheartedly. The woman let out a loud 'whoop,' refilled her cup at the bar and then danced back to her table to clapping and cheering from the group sitting there.

Tobias, now standing next to Jacob, drank the rest of the ale, throwing his head back. He slammed the empty jug on the bar and said, "Fill it up, my good man."

Jacob nudged Tobias in his ribs. "'Ere, we're meant to be finding out stuff."

"And we will, my skinny friend, we will. Now drink up and enjoy yourself."

Tobias took another swig, spilling some ale down his coat, and wandered over to the table where the woman came from. Mimicking a French Dandy, he thrust his right leg and right arm out and bent forward. "May I have this dance, my lady?"

The woman smiling and laughing, curtsied and said, "You most certainly may."

Jacob leant against the bar and took a swig from his jug. His eyes studied the room as his ears filled with music and laughter. Three men were playing instruments in the corner by the fireplace - one a lute, one a violin and the other a flute. People were clapping and stamping their feet, drinking and laughing. A merry old time was being had by all. A woman stood up on a table and danced while others cheered her on. The owner of the alehouse was shouting at her to get down. Jacob noticed an old dog next to the bar curled up with its head on the floor, its ears down and eyes open.

"That dog must be deaf," he said to himself.

As Jacob's eyes scanned the room, he suddenly caught sight of a woman perfectly still amongst all the noise staring at him. He stared back for a few seconds and then looked over at where Tobias was dancing. When he looked back, the woman was no longer there. His eyes quickly tried to find her, and then, to the left of him, the woman tapped his shoulder. He turned to face her; she was pretty in the face, with blonde hair and green eyes.

"You gonna stare all night ... or you gonna buy a lady a drink?"

Without missing a beat, Jacob beckoned the barman over and said, "A drink for the lady."

The barman put two jugs in front of Jacob and took the coin from his hand. The woman picked up the jug and said, "And who is it that I be drinking with?"

Clinking her jug with his, he said, "Jacob. I am Jacob. And your name is …?"

"Pleased to meet you, Jacob. I'm Mary."

"A beautiful name for a beautiful woman. And the pleasure is all mine."

Tobias put his big arm between them and put his empty jug on the bar. "Ahh, and who do we have here then?" he asked.

"This is Mary, and might I ask you the same?"

Hanging off the side of Tobias with his arm around her was the woman he introduced as Sarah.

"Barman, some more drinks here," Jacob requested.

"Ahh, so we all know each other's names, so let's drink to that," Tobias said.

Jacob suggested they take a table and sit over in the far corner. All four sat and talked, laughed and drank. Suddenly the woman dancing on the table fell and landed in the lap of a man knocking him off his chair. As he fell back, his drink was thrown into the face of another. Angered by this, the man grabbed at him, picked him up off the floor and threw him backwards, slamming him into the flute player. The music stopped, along with the laughter. The barman shouted at the two men to stop, and the dog jumped up, snarling and barking!

Tobias stood up and bellowed over everyone, "TAKE IT OUTSIDE!!!!!!!!"

The room fell silent as everyone looked at Tobias' large frame standing there. He seemed even bigger now.

He pointed at the three musicians and said, "Play, play."

The men began to play, the flautist at first, then the other two joining in.

Tobias walked forward. clapping his hands together. "Dance, dance. Come, get up and dance!"

The music grew louder, and the flute player danced while he played. Within a few minutes, people were back to drinking and dancing. The man with ale over his face wiped it and held his hand out to help the other off the floor. Tobias, still clapping his hands, beckoned the barman to bring over a large jug of ale to his table. He turned and sat back down. Sarah wrapped her arms around him, swung a leg over to sit in his lap and kissed him hard.

Jacob sheepishly looked at Mary, picked up his ale and said, "Down the hatch."

Mary got hold of his face by the chin, turned it towards her, smiled and kissed him.

The barman put two large jugs of ale on the table. "Ahem," he coughed. "This is on the house."

Sarah threw her arms in the air and cheered, then she grabbed a jug and filled her smaller jug. As she drank, Tobias filled his. Jacob put a hand up in front of the barman and told him that would not be necessary and that they would pay for their drinks.

The barman shook his head, waved his finger and said, "No, please, sir, it's my pleasure. Your large friend stopped a fight happening tonight. And I don't need another fight in here like I had a few weeks ago."

Jacob leant forward and asked him what had happened. The barman told Jacob that a few weeks ago, four men had come in and were drinking and being aggressive. One of them had grabbed at Mary's arse, so she had slapped him and knocked his eyepatch out of place. In response, he had pushed her onto the floor. A couple of local men were in there that day who stood up for Mary, and a fight had broken out between the two local men against three of the four men. The barman had grabbed his musket from the bar, but before he could lift it, the fourth man had a pistol aimed at his head and had told him to put it down.

He took the rifle off the barman, then fired his pistol into the roof and shouted, "That's enough, lads. We've business to attend to." He then said that all four men left.

Jacob's eyes widened. "Did the man who spoke have a Scottish accent?"

"Yes," the barman answered. "Why do you ask? Do you know them?"

"No, but I'm looking for men that fit that description. Do you know where they went after leaving?"

The barman shook his head and said, "Ask Mary. She might know something."

Jacob turned towards Mary, who, having heard the barman, told him that she didn't know where they had gone. She said that she hadn't seen them before that night or since. She told Jacob the men came in that day, sat down in the corner and drank and ate.

"Sarah and I work here, and on that day, they just sat and talked. I had just brought over a large jug of ale to the table, and the man with the eyepatch grabbed at my arm ..."

Sarah, now filling up her drink again, said, "Yeah, that's right, and I saw her pull away from him. Then, as she turned, he got up and grabbed her. His hands were all over her arse and grabbing at her chest, so she smacked him one."

Jacob asked Mary if she could remember anything else.

"Well, I was thrown to the floor," she answered, "and then the fight happened. Sarah grabbed me and pulled me back towards the table over there."

After taking a mouthful of ale, Sarah said, "Yeah, an' before we knew it, one of 'em let off a shot into the roof, an' it all stopped."

Mary nodded and told Jacob that they then all left.

Tobias sat up. "Well, we can't do nothing about them right now," he said. Then he squeezed at Sarah's thigh, winked and added, "But there is something else we can do."

Sarah winked back, picked up one of the jugs off the table and said, "Well, you better both come home with us then ..."

Tobias put his hand into his coat pocket and pulled out his purse bag of money to pay the barman. As he did, a square piece of cloth fell out with it.

"What's that?" Jacob asked as he picked it up off the floor.

Tobias looked at Jacob's hand and said, "Oh, that. I took that from Jeremiah one time. It's called a handkerchief. Do you remember that time when that dog bit my hand right before we went to see him?"

Jacob thought for a moment ... " Yes, yes, I think I do."

"Well, I took it from a box he had on the desk and wrapped it around my hand."

Mary noticed something in the corner of the piece of cloth. It looked like stitching.

"Show me that, Jacob," she said.

Mary opened out the handkerchief and saw it was indeed stitching of a letter - the letter 'J'.

"This is what the Scottish man had on him," she said. "He gave it to the one with the eyepatch to wipe the blood from his nose."

"Are you sure?" asked Jacob.

"Yes, I'm sure. I'd never seen one before, and I could clearly see the letter on it".

Jacob stood up and gave it back to Tobias. "Was this the only one in the box, Tobias?"

Tobias took it from Jacob's hand and said, "No, he had a few in there."

Jacob clapped his hands together and said, "Tomorrow, we ride to see Jeremiah!"

Tobias paid the barman and followed the others outside. He put his arm around Sarah's shoulders and walked with her. They turned the corner and walked around the back of the alehouse to a door.

The two women lived in rented rooms at the back. Jacob stopped for a moment and said, "Wait. What about our horses?"

Mary pointed out that behind the alehouse was a small stable that could hold four horses. She and Jacob walked back to get them.

Tobias and Sarah opened the door and went to her room. As soon as she opened the door, Tobias spun her around and lifted her up to his waist, her legs wrapping around him. He kicked the door shut behind him. Tearing at each other's clothes and kissing each other, Tobias ripped open her dress, the buttons flying across the room. They fell onto the bed, pulling off their clothes and throwing them onto the floor ...

Jacob walked in front of Mary to get the horses; then, he felt his arm being pulled back, and he spun around. Mary pulled him back against the wooden wall of the alehouse and kissed him. Jacob held back for a second and then passionately kissed her, lifting her leg and loosening his trousers until they were both in the throes of passion ...

The next morning, Jacob awoke lying next to Mary. The sun was bursting through the window, lighting up her face and naked body. Her hair looked golden, and her skin was as if it were made of silk. She truly was beautiful, he thought to himself. She was sleeping soundly, so Jacob got dressed and quietly left the room, gently closing the door behind him. Mary's room was next to Sarah's, and Jacob had to walk past it. The door was open.

Tobias stood at the basin, washing his face. The bed was broken, and clothes were scattered over the floor. Sarah lay on the bed, naked and snoring deeply. Her huge breasts moved up and down with each breath she took. Tobias stood at the basin with no shirt on and long scratches on his back. He splashed his face and turned to see Jacob standing there.

Jacob shook his head. "My god, man ... You're an animal."

Tobias grabbed his shirt and coat and walked towards Jacob, saying, "Not so loud; my head hurts."

He walked straight past him and outside. As he did so, the sun hit his eyes. He squinted hard and shielded them with one arm.

"So I see you had a good night then," said Jacob as he stepped outside behind him.

Tobias stood next to his horse at the open stable and was sick all over the straw floor.

"Too good," Tobias replied, wiping his mouth.

Jacob took his horse by the reins and walked it out of the stable. "I think we should ride to Josephine and tell her we have information on her father's killers."

"Then let's get going."

Both men led their horses out to the road. It was quiet. A woman walked with a large woven basket full of bread, the smell of freshly baked loaves hitting the air. A small dog followed behind her, sniffing, its head twitching as its nose took in the smell.

"Good day to you," she said.

Both men acknowledged her as they mounted the horses. As the dog passed, it barked, causing Jacob's horse to snort and whinny and stamp erratically. Pulling on the reins and patting its neck, Jacob calmed the horse, and both men trotted down the road.

As they rode, they talked, and something sat uneasily with Tobias, which he shared with Jacob. It was obvious the four men worked for Jeremiah, as had they. But why rob George and Gabriel? It didn't make sense.

"I've been thinking the same thing, Tobias. Let's just get to Josephine and then ride on to Jeremiah."


A few miles down the road, they arrived at the tavern.

As they approached, Jacob said, "Listen, something just doesn't feel right. When we go inside, just tell Josephine and Gabriel that we could have found something out about the men. That we have to see a good friend of ours who could help us."

Tobias agreed. They hitched the horses and went to go inside. The door was locked. The door was never locked during the day.

Tobias banged on it hard, shouting out, "Josephine!"

Jacob stepped back from the door and looked at the windows. "JOSEPHINE …!!" he yelled.

They heard the door being unbolted, and Josephine opened it. "Oh, Tobias, Jacob. Come inside."

She was nursing a black eye and obviously shaken up.

"What the fuck has happened?" Tobias asked as he placed his hands on her arms.

Jacob stood next to her. "Who did this?" he questioned.

"It happened last night," she said. "I asked Gabriel to fetch a barrel of ale from the back room. I was cleaning the tables when two men came in and sat down. I told them I would be with them in a moment. I brought them over some ale, and when Gabriel came in, one of them grabbed me and covered my mouth …"

Jacob sat her down and fetched her a drink. "Please … continue," he said.

"Gabriel just froze. Two other men came from behind him and grabbed him. One had an eyepatch. I tried to struggle and break free. The man sitting down spoke and asked Gabriel where the money was. He had a Scottish accent."

Tobias and Jacob looked at each other, then back at Josephine.

"What else happened?" asked Jacob.

Josephine explained that Gabriel told the men he didn't have it. He said he needed more time and asked them to let her go. She said that the men took him with them and had hit her and knocked her unconscious. When she awoke, Gabriel was gone. Along with the men!

"FUCK …!" shouted Tobias. "FUCK!!"

Josephine sat with her head in her hands, bent forwards. She shook her head and said, "I don't understand. Why would Gabriel be in such trouble?"

Jacob stood up and paced the room. Tobias went behind the bar, looking for something stronger to drink than ale. He pulled out a bottle of rum, took out the cork with his teeth and drank from the bottle.

Jacob turned the chair and sat in front of Josephine. He told her that the four men worked for the same man they had worked for and how they had found out information about them. He explained they were going to their 'old employer' to find out who the men were.

"You know that we used to work getting money from people who owed it to someone else?" Jacob asked.

Josephine nodded and said, "Yes, of course."

"Well, Gabriel must owe money. We think that something went wrong, which caused your father's death," said Jacob.

Josephine scowled. "Are you saying that my father was killed because Gabriel owes money?"

Jacob sighed …

Tobias offered the bottle to Josephine and said in a low deep voice, "That's what it seems to be … If he didn't owe a debt, then no one would have been paid to get it back. Either something went wrong, or your father was killed to make a point."

Josephine shook her head. "No, no, no, no. It can't be true …"

Jacob put his arm around her. "I promise you we will find them. And find out the truth. And those men will pay with their lives."

Josephine looked at Jacob. "But why? Why would he owe money? Why would he need to borrow money? We are not rich by any means, but we are also far from poor. Why would he do this?"

Tobias swigged the brandy again and said, "They cannot be too far ahead of us. If we ride hard, then we should catch up with them, and we already know where they are headed."

Jacob stood up. "He's right, Josephine. They will take him back to Jeremiah. Will you be alright on your own?"

"NO!!" Josephine stood and wiped her eyes. "I'm coming with you."

Tobias held out his hands, the bottle still in one of them. "Whoa, whoa! You can't come along with us!"

Jacob joined in. "I'm sorry, Josephine, but it's going to be dangerous. You could get hurt."

Josephine went behind the bar and picked up her father's rifle. "Fuck that ... I'm going, and there's nothing you can do to stop me. They killed my father and now have my brother. I either ride with you, or on my own!"

Tobias looked at Jacob and then at Josephine. "Do you even know how to use that thing?"

Josephine pulled back the hammer and pointed it at Tobias. "You let me worry about that."

Tobias lifted his hands up and said, "Ok, little sister, ok."

# Chapter Nine



Dupree stood for a few seconds and said, "So, gentlemen. What do we do now?"

Tobias raised both eyebrows and looked at Jacob. "Yes, my skinny friend with a plan. What do we do now?"

"Ok, Dupree," said Jacob. "How much money do you have on you now?"

Dupree pointed at his purse that Tobias held in his hand. Jacob took the purse and looked inside. He closed it and gave it back to Dupree.

"We have at least a week to get the money back to Jeremiah, so here's what we will do," said Jacob. "We go to the docks, and you buy everything you were going to buy. We come with you and at the same time can learn what to buy. We are, as of this moment, three partners. Do you understand ...?"

Dupree nodded in agreement. "But may I ask you why you haven't just took all my money and a finger ...?"

Jacob smiled at Dupree. "That's simple - because I wish to be rich and not spend my life beating on men who owe debt just to make someone else rich ..."

Dupree smiled back. "Well, monsieur, I 'av never seen a trader or merchant that eez poor. And I 'av a feeling that with you two as partners, I vill never be robbed again. Sometimes gentlemen, beating on men has eets advantages ..."

Tobias tapped the head of his axe in the palm of his hand, "I'll drink to that ..."

Dupree got back in his cart, flicked the reins twice, and set off for Ipswich docks. Tobias and Jacob mounted their horses and followed behind.

Riding with the creaking of the carts wheels in front, Tobias asked Jacob, "So, you think this will bring us coin more than collecting debts?"

"Not only more coin, but frequent coin, Tobias."

"Well, I've done alright by myself these past years, Jacob. I think we can do both."

Jacob, silent for a moment, agreed and said, "Alright, Tobias. Alright, we can do both ... until we establish ourselves with Dupree."

"So we have an accord, Jacob?"

Both men looked at each other and laughed.

They travelled for a few miles, finally approaching the docks at Ipswich. Two large ships were anchored at the dockside. And various schooners scattered about of different nationalities. All about were traders with their goods. Spanish, French and also from Africa. Furs, silk, spices, fruits and vegetables, cotton of all sorts. A bustle of people bought and sold. Jacob hopped off his horse and tied the reins to the back of the cart. Tobias breathed in deeply, intoxicated by the various smells, mainly the spices but also teas and coffee beans.

Dupree climbed down from the cart and said, "Well, gentleman, welcome to zee rest of zee world."

Jacob's eyes flitted all over, taking in all the different colours. Cloth, spices and even the people.

"So, where to first, Dupree ?" Jacob said.

"Ah, first we go and see the Spaniards. Zey 'ave ze best furs, beaver, fox, rabbit, and sometimes black and brown bear."

Tobias clapped his hands together. "I have a good feeling, Jacob. I'm glad I listened to you."

Both men followed Dupree about all the goods for sale, taking in all the sights, sounds and smells, watching and listening, learning what to buy. What was worth money and what wasn't. Furs sold very well, and so did spices. But also materials such as silk and cotton, and leather hides. They filled the cart with the goods they had bought and made haste.

"Now we make our way to London road," said Dupree, "to zee large market on the outskirts of Colchester town."

Dupree whipped at the reins, and the cart trundled out of the docks and onto the road, followed closely by Jacob and Tobias.

After a while, Tobias could see a small tavern up ahead. Licking his lips and wiping his mouth, he said, "Ah, it's time the horses were fed and watered."

Jacob turned to him. "You mean time YOU were fed and watered!!!"

Tobias laughed. "Well, doing all this riding, we need to keep our strength up. Don't you agree?!"

Dupree pulled to the right on the reins turning his horse off the road towards the tavern. "Oui, monsieur, I do. I most definitely do!!"

An uneven dirt track led down to the tavern. Dupree pulled the cart outside and hitched his horse. He climbed off the cart, turned to the other two and said, "Come, gentleman, come. Ale and food await us."

Dupree walked inside and ordered three ales and a plate of beef. Jacob and Tobias hitched the horses and walked towards the door when something caught Jacob's eye. Pinned to a board was a large piece of paper with a drawing of two men squaring up to each other. Underneath the drawing was a notice that read 'FIGHT.' The notice was a fight between two local men that would be taking place in two weeks' time. The winner would be taking away ten pounds. Jacob called Tobias over to take a look at the notice.

"It says the winner takes ten pounds. I think we should come back this way and take a look."

Tobias looked and said, "Ten pounds is a handsome sum, Jacob. Maybe you should put yourself up, what with your father's past and him teaching you all he knew."

Jacob nodded; he was thinking the same thing. He had never lost a fight and had grown up with a fighter. It was in his blood.

"Exactly what I was thinking, Tobias. It would be another way to earn some coin. After seeing Jeremiah, we can return and watch the fight."

Tobias pulled off the paper, folded it and put it in his coat pocket and then walked through the tavern door.

"First things first, Jacob - I'm thirsty!!!"

Tobias walked in and sat down at the table where Dupree was. Three jugs of ale were already on the table. Tobias lifted a jug and said, "Cheers." He drank until it was empty.

Jacob pulled out a chair and said, "You was right; you was thirsty."

Dupree pushed a jug towards Jacob. "Drink up, drink up."

Jacob took a swig and then wiped his mouth free of froth. Dupree picked up the knife on the wooden board, cut a thick slice of beef and tore off a chunk of bread. He passed them to Tobias, who took a bite from both, chewed for a second and then, with a mouthful of food, ordered more ale.

Jacob sat back in the chair and asked Dupree, "So, how far is the market from here?"

Dupree cut another slice of beef, giving it to Jacob, "Oh, not very far at all, my friend. About an hour's ride."

Jacob took the meat. "And how much will we profit from the goods?"

Dupree took a gulp of ale. "Oh, we should make a handsome profit; at least three times more than what we paid."

The barman brought over three more jugs, and taking one, Tobias said, "Three times more? That is indeed a handsome profit!"

"Oui, oui."

Jacob banged his fist on the table. "I told you that we could make some good coin, Tobias."

Rocking back and laughing loudly, Tobias said, "Well, it sure beats getting punched or shot at to earn it, Jacob; I'll give you that."

Dupree cut another slice of beef and ripped at it with his teeth. He then explained to them both that after they had sold all the goods, they would split it three ways. Each would take half of his cut of the money and put the other half back in so that they could buy more goods to sell. This was how they would do business so that each of them had an equal stake. Both men agreed, and all three raised the jugs and took a swig to seal the arrangement. Dupree noticed the paper protruding from Tobias' coat pocket and could see a part of the drawing on it.

"What 'av you zer, Tobias?"

He took it from his pocket, opened it out, and placed it in front of Dupree.

"Ahh, a bare-knuckle contest. In two weeks from now, no less. I 'av seen a few in my time. Always a good way to make some more coin if you know who to bet on."

Tobias slapped Jacob on the shoulder. "Even better if you know the fighter, eh Jacob …?"

Dupree took a swig and wiped his mouth. "So, you know one of zee men zen?"

Tobias shook his head. "No, no, not one of them. No, but Jacob here comes from such stock; it's in his blood."

Dupree lifted his jug and placed a hand over his heart. "Zen, we should all go to ziss fight and maybe get a fight of our own with monsieur Jacob. At zee same time, watch zeez men and maybe 'av a small wager. What do you say to zat, gentlemen?"

Jacob took a swig of ale. "I think that would be a very worthy idea. I grew up with a father who would make extra coin as such. I myself have had a few fights and won."

Tobias explained the fight that had occurred in the tavern when they had met for the first time. He talked about how fast and hard Jacob could hit, the speed with which he moved and how impressed he was with him.

"Well, well, monsieur, eet seems we 'av another way to make money. Today 'as really turned out to be ze best day when it could 'av been zee worst …"

Jacob spun around the paper and picked it up. "Ten pounds prize money. That's a lot of money."

"It certainly is," said Tobias. "And you are right, Dupree; this day has turned out to be a really good day."

Turning and looking at Jacob, Tobias said, "We left yesterday to get a debt owed, and now we are business partners as merchants …"

Jacob put the paper into his coat pocket and said, "It is a very good day!"

With that, Dupree stood and said, "Well, gentlemen, it is time to be going."

He paid the barman, and all three men left the tavern. Dupree climbed up onto the cart, Jacob and Tobias mounted their horses, and all three set off down the road towards the market.

After riding for about an hour, they came to a fork in the road. Dupree pulled left on the reins and rode down the smaller road which led to the market. It was being held in a large field just on the outskirts of a small village. On the other side of the field stood a large house. The owner, a Mr Brendan Little, held the market every second Saturday as a way for the local villagers to be able to sell any goods they had. He had started this a few years ago, and over that time, the market had grown. More and more people would come to sell their goods. Originally there was no charge to set up a stall and sell one's goods, as he did it by way of the locals to earn extra money, but over time he realised this was a very profitable business and charged a penny on entry - the price of a loaf of bread. Brendan was a wealthy man and owned a lot of land, including the village. But he was also a very kind man and helped out the villagers by way of cheap rent and jobs and opportunities to make money, such as the market.

As Dupree approached, he rode through a large gate and stopped. Two men stood at the gate to take the payment of a penny to enter. Dupree pulled out three pennies and paid the men. As they pulled onto the field, Dupree pointed to a space next to another cart that sold vegetables and stopped. Jacob and Tobias tied their horses to the back of the cart and helped Dupree set up his stall. Jacob walked over to the cart selling vegetables, purchased a handful of carrots and gave them to the horses. Everywhere he looked, there were different kinds of goods for sale. People from all around shopped and haggled the prices. The smells of meat, bread, spices, and ale filled the air. Dupree laid out his goods on the cart. He removed one of the sides that was hinged, and as it was laid down, it showed a sign written on its side that said: 'Best Goods At The Best Prices.' Jacob and Tobias both looked at Dupree and smiled.

"That's very clever," said Jacob.

Dupree pulled a stool off the cart, placed it in front of the sign, stood on it and said, "Ah, well, we French do everything with a full heart, my friends."

He then took a deep breath, coughed and cleared his throat. "Ladeez and gentleman ... please, please. Come, gather around and see what the rest of the world has to offer you all ..."

Jacob and Tobias stood and looked at each other and then at Dupree.

"From ze other side of ze world, I bring you treasures," Dupree continued.

Tobias nudged Jacob. "What is he doing?" he asked.

People had turned their heads towards Dupree. And slowly began to gather around him, one, two, three, ten ...

"Come and see. Look at what I 'ave 'ere for you all."

Dupree grabbed a beaver fur, stretched it out over the length of his arm and showed it to the women in the crowd. "Zees is the finest fur, mademoiselle. You can take eet to a seamstress and make gloves or a 'at."

He then picked up a sheet of cotton material, grabbed a woman's hand and said, "Come, madame, feel it."

He took a pinch of spices with his fingers, rubbed them together and let the people smell them. The aroma and colour pulled the people in. He had exotic fruit, Indian silk and mesmerised the crowd with his banter. Different classes were in awe of him. Before Jacob and Tobias knew it, Dupree was handing out the different goods and taking people's money.

Within an hour, all but a few things remained.

Tobias clapped his hands and said, "Good Lord, Dupree. How did you do that?"

"Yes, that was amazing," Jacob said, tapping Dupree's shoulder.

"Well, my friends, as I said, we French 'av a certain way about us … and zeez things won't sell themselves."

While all this was going on, the owner of the house and indeed the field where the market took place had been watching Dupree's selling ability. He walked over to the three men and introduced himself.

"Gentlemen, I am Mr Little, the owner of this here land. I would very much like to make your acquaintance."

The three men shook his hand and introduced themselves.

"It's a pleasure to meet you, Mr Little," said Jacob.

"Ah, please call me Brendan. And the pleasure is all mine."

They talked for a while. Brendan complimented Dupree on his sales and invited them for drinks back at his house.

"I have many friends who are merchants, and I have made a lot of money from trade myself, but I can tell you that I have never seen someone with your flare for selling before. Maybe I can invest some money and put you onto some of my old contacts".

The men agreed and said they would meet him at the house after they had finished putting the rest of the goods away.

Brendan shook hands again and said, "Then I shall see you very soon."

"This truly has turned out to be a great day," said Tobias. "And to think that this morning I was just going to collect a debt and your finger, Dupree …"

Jacob pulled up the side of the cart and said, "See, I told you, Tobias. When an opportunity presents itself, you must grab it with both hands. Yesterday morning, this was to be my first job with you, and yet look how the events of the day have turned to our favour."

"Why yes, my skinny friend, I must admit this day has been a hell of a lot easier and indeed more profitable than just collecting debts. And now another opportunity presents itself with Mr Little."

Dupree climbed up onto the cart and took the reins in one hand. "Can I say that I myself am very pleased the day turned in all our favours … and that I still have all my fingers!"

Tobias let out a loud laugh, mounted his horse, looked at Dupree and said, "Well, the day is not over yet."

Then kicked his heels into the belly of his horse and trotted towards the big house.

Jacob mounted his horse and told Dupree that they would have to take some of the debt from him and take it to Jeremiah.

Dupree nodded and said, "Thank you for this, Jacob. Thank you."

Tobias had gone ahead, and Jacob caught up with him. "I have another proposition for you, big man."

"I'm all ears, Jacob."

Jacob told Tobias that when they take some of the debt back to Jeremiah that they should pay the rest. That way, Dupree would be free of the debt and be in their favour. He would be a solid partner to them both. Tobias agreed.

" Do you know something, Jacob?" he said. "If I hadn't of stopped off at Josephine's tavern to quench my thirst, and if those five men had not of followed me, and if you had not of had an argument with your father and gone to the tavern, we would never have met …!"

Jacob looked at Tobias and said, "Do you think it was by chance, or part of God's plan?

Tobias pulled on the reins to stop his horse outside of the large house and, looking at its grandeur, said, "I've no idea, my friend … but I'm glad of it."

Dupree pulled up in the cart and climbed down.

"C'est magnifique …!!! What a beautiful house!"

Jacob dismounted and nodded, looking at Dupree. "It most certainly is, my friend; it most certainly is."

Tobias approached the two large wooden doors and banged on the brass knocker, which made a loud noise that echoed through him. Within a minute, one of the doors opened. Brendan held out his hand and gestured to them all to come inside. They entered the house into a large open area with a beautiful staircase in front of them.

Brendan walked ahead of them and said, "Come, gentlemen, walk this way."

To the left, they walked through a door which led into a study. The walls were adorned with paintings, landscapes and men on horseback.

"Please sit, sit."

They all sat except Jacob, who stood looking at the paintings. Brendan took a bottle of brandy from the cabinet and four glasses and placed them on the small round table where the men sat.

"I take it you like brandy, gentleman?" he asked.

Dupree clasped his hands together. "Brandy eez always good, monsieur."

Brendan poured out four glasses and gave one to Tobias and Dupree. As he poured one for Jacob, he noticed that he was looking at a certain painting of a bare-knuckle fighter. He stepped over to Jacob and gave him the glass of brandy.

"Who is the painting of, Brendan?" Jacob asked as he took the glass.

"Ah, that was painted a long time ago, when I was a much younger and fitter man."

Jacob took a sip from the glass. "So you used to fight?"

"I had a few and then realised rather quickly that I preferred not to be hit," Brendan said, laughing.

"I myself have had a few, and I realised that I don't get hit," said Jacob. "My father was a decent man on the cobbles, so it's in my blood. And there is nothing more heart-pounding than two men standing toe to toe trying to beat the other".

"I agree, young man. I do like to watch a good fight," said Brendan as he took a seat next to Dupree.

"Well," said Jacob, "there is a fight in about three weeks just up the road a ways. About an hour's ride from here if you would be interested?"

"I may well be, but first, shall we talk of the matter at hand? As I told you earlier, I have many contacts in the trade business and know many merchants. And in all that time, I have never seen someone who can sell an item as well or indeed as quickly as you."

Dupree drank the brandy in one gulp and said, "Well, I am French, and as I told these two before, we 'av a certain flare."

The four men sat and talked and drank and discussed traders and merchants. Brendan told them how he had made his money from being a merchant and that the big money to be had was to sell in London. It had the biggest port, and ships from all over went there to bring in the goods that they had acquired from India, Europe and North America. He had worked for the East India Company and traded on their behalf to merchants from all over. He said if they wanted to make money, then the higher classes were the ones to sell to.

"They have all the money," he said.

Dupree settled uneasily in his chair. He looked at the other two men and then back at Brendan. "Monsieur, zat all sounds very, very good, but I think I must tell you zat today is ze first day zat we are partners. Certain circumstances have made zis so."

Brendan stood up, took the bottle of brandy and filled up the glasses. "That's a good thing, gentlemen; you see, it means you all have a great thing in common."

"And what would that be?" asked Jacob.

Brendan gulped down the brandy. "That you have nothing to lose …"

"How so?" asked Tobias

"Because you all have an equal interest. You have no choice but to trust each other, and the best part is that because you have just started in partnership together with little money invested, you have an even greater investment - yourselves!"

All three men looked at each other for a few seconds and understood the words Brendan had spoken.

Tobias placed his empty glass on the table. "And why would you be interested in helping us in trading goods, Mr Little?"

Brendan stood up and filled Tobias' glass. "It's quite simple. Watching Dupree have such a passion and skill for selling has quite literally stoked the fire within me. I once had such passion myself, and although I now have money and status within this small community here, I would like to help you to accomplish all you can in trading."

Tobias took the brandy and sat back in the chair.

Jacob looked around the room and said, "I think we all need to go away and think about your proposal Brendan. Today has been quite a day for sure."

Jacob, Tobias and Dupree all stood up, thanked Brendan for the drink and shook his hand. Brendan agreed that they should think about his offer and showed them to the door.

Leaving the house, Dupree climbed onto his cart and said farewell. As did Tobias, mounting his horse. Jacob shook Brendan's hand once more and told him that they would be back this way again in three weeks to attend the bare-knuckle contest taking place. All three men left the house and the grounds and headed for the road.

Once at the road, Jacob and Tobias stopped the horses and turned to Dupree.

"We must return to meet with Jeremiah and pay off your debt," said Jacob.

"Why, yes. Yes, of course," said Dupree pulling out the small lockbox from the cart. He split the money into three and handed both men their share of the profits made earlier. He then cut his share in half again and handed it to Jacob.

"Zis is all I can give you; otherwise, I will 'ave no money to put back into our partnership towards buying more goods."

Jacob split his share in half and gave it to Dupree. Tobias did the same.

"We are all partners now," said Jacob. "And so from now on, we must stay together. There is a tavern that you can stay at, which is along the way to Jeremiah's. You will be quite comfortable there."

"Oui, oui. Lead the way, Jacob. You both now 'ave my loyalty and friendship."

# Chapter Ten



Josephine put the hammer of the rifle back into place and laid it on the bar.

Tobias, still with both hands out in front of him, said, "Ok, I can see that you are serious and that you want to come along with us, but know that we are as serious when we say that it will be dangerous."

Jacob stepped towards Josephine. "And that means when we say something to you that you listen to us and not do anything that could get you or us killed. Do you understand?"

Josephine stood silent and then, switching her teary eyes between both of them, said, "This is my brother we are talking about - my kid brother - those men wanted money off him. A debt that he owes, and I don't know how or even why that is so. But I believe it is the same reason why my father was killed by these men, and I will stop at nothing to see them pay for that. Nothing!!!!"

Tobias put the bottle on the bar, picked up the rifle and held it out in front of her.

"Then you will be needing this, little sister …"

"We will find these men, and justice will be done," said Jacob. "But first, we need to see the man who employed them to retrieve the debt. That is where they will be headed with Gabriel. Now Josephine, let's saddle up your horse as we need to be on our way."

Jacob told Josephine to go upstairs to her room and grab a warm coat and hat for the ride. As she did so, he pulled on Tobias' arm and said, "Quick, let's go!"

Jacob ran outside, took the saddle from the stable for Josephine's horse, threw it behind a bale of hay and then covered it with loose hay.

Tobias, now behind him, said, "What are you doing?"

Jacob tapped him on the shoulder and said quietly, "Come on, man, let's get our horses and get out of here. We are not taking Josephine along with us, it's too dangerous for what we are about to do, and I, for one, want no harm to come to her."

Tobias grabbed the reins of his horse and the saddle and jumped up, swinging his right leg up and over. In one fell swoop, he was on the horse and galloping after Jacobs, away from the tavern.

Over the sound of both horses' hooves galloping up the dirt road towards the main road, both men could hear Josephine yelling at the top of her voice, "BASTARDS … BASTARDS!!!!!"

Both horses ran as fast as they could, thundering down the road. The noise of the hooves and snorting of the animals was loud, and both men had to almost shout in order to hear each other.

"Sly as a fox!!!!!" Tobias shouted. "I was thinking that it was a bad idea to let her come along."

"Exactly … I was just waiting for the right moment," said Jacob.

"She sounded very pissed off," Tobias said, holding onto his hat as his horse was in full flow.

Turning a bend in the road, Jacob pulled back on the reins to slow his horse and signalled to Tobias with his hand in the air to do the same. Both horses slowed to a comfortable pace.

Jacob turned and said, "She did, didn't she? But it had to be done, my friend. We cannot do this and be thinking of her safety at the same time."

"I agree," said Tobias.

"So, how are we going to do this, Jacob? What if Jeremiah has no idea of what has happened. Or indeed, what if he has?"

"I don't know, big man; let's just get to Jeremiah's house and then we will have to come up with a plan."

Both men rode along the main road that would eventually take them to the house. After a couple of hours, they were about half a mile from it. Jacob pulled his horse off the road and came to a stop. Tobias followed, and both men discussed what they were to do …

Jacob twisted around, opened a saddlebag and pulled out two apples from it. He threw one to Tobias and then split the other apple in half and reached down to feed his horse one half and sat back up and began to eat the other half.

With a mouthful of apple, he turned and said, "We will ride to the side of Jeremiah's house and hide amongst the trees. There will be a good vantage point for us to look through your spyglass; see if he has company."

"And if he has?" Tobias asked.

"Then we wait and see if they have Gabriel with them."

Tobias pulled his axe from his belt and lifted it, shaking it in front of Jacob. "This is all I need. I say we hide the horses, break the door down and get us some revenge!!!"

"All in good time, big man, all in good time. But first, we need to see …"

Both men set off again down the road. Dark clouds consumed the sun, and it started to rain within minutes. The air turned colder as they galloped towards the house. As they approached the small track that led there, they carried on past it and cut across, circling around through the land that lay to the side of the house. The rain had become heavier, and the clearing was thicker with trees. They made their way to a place where they would be well hidden. The ground was flooded, and the trees looked almost dead in appearance. From their position, they could see the front, side and back of the house.

Tobias reached into a bag on the saddle and took out his spyglass. He looked through it and could see four horses hitched to a post at the back of the house.

"Jacob. Here, look ... look." Tobias passed it to him and pointed to the back of the house. "Look there, four horses."

Jacob wiped the rain from the lens and saw the horses. "Right," he said. "They are here, so Gabriel must be inside with them."

Tobias tapped Jacob on his shoulder. "The window. Look through the window."

Jacob moved the sight along the house to the window and could see Jeremiah sitting at his desk and a man standing in front of him. It looked as though they were arguing.

Tobias put a hand on Jacob. "What do you see?"

Jacob handed the spyglass to him and said, "Have a look. I can see Jeremiah sitting at his desk, and there's another man. They seem to be arguing. Have a look."

"Yes ... Yes, I see ... And there's another man. He's pouring a drink. He has his back to me, though."


The men were indeed arguing. Earlier on, the four men had taken Gabriel to the house. Jeremiah had let them in but was confused as to why they had him with them. When he had opened the door and seen Hamish, or Hamish the Scot, as he was known, he was under the impression that the job was done and his money was in order. What he didn't expect was to see Gabriel with him and his men.

Hamish pushed his way into the house and said, "We need to talk and sort out the money you owe us."

Jeremiah stumbled backwards a few steps and was outraged by this intrusion. "How dare you push your way into my house? What is this all about?"

The rest of the men followed into the house, the man with the eyepatch firmly gripping Gabriel's arm.

The door was slammed behind them, and Hamish said, "Aye, well, it is what it is. Now, move yerself to yer study so we can sort this shite oot."

Jeremiah led the men to his study, and as they walked, he regretted the day he had hired Hamish and his men. He had been given a recommendation by a fellow money lender that Hamish's method always got results, but he wasn't at all impressed with the approach now.

Jeremiah opened the door to his study, where he always conducted his business and stood alongside his desk. "Now, what the hell is going on here, Hamish?"

The men entered the room and the one with the eyepatch, known only as Collins, shoved Gabriel down into a chair that was against the wall. Hamish told Jeremiah to sit down as he opened the drinks cabinet and took a bottle of brandy from it. He pulled the cork from its neck and took a swig straight from the bottle.

As he passed the bottle to Collins, he put a hand on top of Gabriel's head, turned to Jeremiah, and said, "Now, yer probably wondering why I'm here with this wee man."

Collins took a swig of brandy and gave the bottle back.

"Well, it's quite simple, yer see this fucking scroat has neh coin ter give yee. And so I've ney choice but to bring him to yer and get what's owed to me … off of you."

Jeremiah stood up and said, "Why this is preposterous! I pay you to retrieve a debt owed to me - to get the money owed, not just to bring the person to me and expect to get paid for it!"

Hamish threw the bottle to one of the other men and slammed both hands down on the desk hard. "SIT THE FUCK DOWN!!!!" he shouted.

Jeremiah sat, with fear spreading over his face.

Hamish then proceeded to explain what had happened when they had gone to see Gabriel. That he had no money and things had got a little wayward, and to make a point of how serious they were of reclaiming the debt, they had beaten up his father a bit too much …

Gabriel screamed at him. "You killed him … You fucking killed him!!!!"

Collins punched Gabriel straight in his mouth, splitting his lip and knocking his head back against the wall.

Jeremiah slumped back into his chair. "What does he mean, killed him?"

Hamish took the bottle of brandy back and said, "Things got a wee bit out of hand; it's no yer concern. We did what was needed to be done. His father owns a tavern, which I thought would now go to him. As it turns oot, this piss poor fuck has an older sister, so …"

Jeremiah sat up quickly. "So, what?"

Hamish took a swig of brandy, "So, we have him …. and she pays to get him back."

Jeremiah shook his head firmly. "No, no, no, no … My god, man, you have just kidnapped someone and are going to hold them for ransom! I am a lender of money - not a common criminal!"

Outside Tobias and Jacob had loaded their pistols and were planning to move up towards the house.

"Ok, let's make our way to the window to get a better view inside," said Jacob. "I think it would be best to come in from the back of the house as it's just one door to get through and then into the study."

Tobias agreed and put his pistol in his belt. With his axe in hand, they made their way towards the house. The light was fading outside, and the rain was heavy. This would be an ideal time to creep around the back of the house and break in. The noise of the rain against the window would mask them from those inside and also from the horses that stood out the back. Jacob had taken the large knife from his saddle and followed in Tobias' footsteps. They kept low and used the cover of the trees slowly towards the house.

As they got to the house, they could hear the shouts from inside where the men were arguing. They managed to get underneath the window. Jacob raised his finger to his lips for them to be quiet. He very slowly looked in through the window and could see Jeremiah, the four men and also … Gabriel. He crouched back down under the window and whispered to Tobias that Gabriel was in there. Tobias pointed behind Jacob to the corner of the house and signalled to go. They made their way to the back door. It was dark inside, but as they looked through the glass in the door, they could see the light coming from the open door of the study. The sky lit up as lightning streaked across it, and then a loud rumbling clap and bang of thunder echoed through the clouds. The back door had four panes of glass in it. Tobias took off his hat and placed it up against the bottom right corner one and held his axe up to it.

Jacob grabbed his arm and whispered, "Wait."

Tobias looked at him and said, "Wait? For what?"

Jacob pointed up towards the sky. "The thunder," he said.

The sky lit up again with forks of lightning that looked like a large branch of a tree, and then the thunder erupted again. Tobias struck at the window, smashing the glass. He put his hand through, turned the door handle and opened it.

As both men crept inside, they could hear Jeremiah saying, "I'm not a common criminal!"

Inside the study, Collins had stepped forward and said to Hamish, "Fuck this shit. This little prick is his problem now," he added, pointing at Jeremiah. "Let's just get our money and go."

Hamish looked at Collins and nodded, then looked back at Jeremiah. "Where's our money?"

Jeremiah looked at all the men in the room and said, "Listen, gentlemen. You get your money when I get my money. This situation isn't good for either of us. The deal is simple. If I could just go and get my debts myself, I wouldn't hire men like you now, would I …?"

Hamish scratched the top of his head. "I know that you keep a safe under your desk, and I also know you have the key to open it. So ... open it."

Jeremiah put both hands up and said, "Gentleman, gentlemen. This is not how business is conducted. I need my-"

Hamish suddenly pulled a pistol from under his coat, pointed it at Jeremiah's head and said, "Open it!"

Tobias and Jacob had crept along and were now a few feet from the door. Now both standing against the wall, Tobias turned to Jacob and, using his hands, signalled him to go to the other side of the door.

Jacob shook his head and pointed to Tobias and then the other side of the door and mouthed, 'You go.'

Tobias shook his fist at Jacob, and with his head right up to the open door, he slowly looked inside. All the men were standing and facing Jeremiah, and with that, Tobias quietly and quickly moved to the other side. As he did so, the floor creaked. One of the men turned his head around to look, saw nothing, and turned it back. Jacob put up a hand, gesturing for Tobias to ease up, and then smiled.

Jeremiah stood up with both hands in front of him and said, "Calm down, Hamish. Calm down. Please, I don't want to get shot. I have the key; it's in the drawer right here."

Hamish cocked back the hammer on the pistol. "Open it ... now!"

Fumbling for the drawer, Jeremiah opened it and put his hand inside. Instead of taking out a key, he took out his own pistol, which was already cocked. He aimed at Hamish and fired ...

The shot flew past his head, clipping his left ear. As it did so, Hamish also let off his shot which hit Jeremiah dead centre in his head, blowing his brains and back of his head onto the wall behind him. He fell backwards into his chair, his eyes and mouth wide open. Hamish grabbed the side of his head to cover the top of his ear that had been blown off. As the shot was fired, Collins jumped up and brought his hands up as if to defend himself, as did the other two men just to the side of Hamish. Gabriel let out a scream as he also jumped while sitting in the chair, bringing not just his arms but also his knees up as well.

At that second, Tobias burst into the room with his pistol out in front and shot straight at the first person he saw. As the shot hit him in the back of his head, one of the men standing next to Hamish fell forward, hitting the side of the desk and onto the floor. Directly behind, Jacob let off a shot from his pistol, catching Hamish in the back of his right shoulder and spinning him around. Gabriel's expression contorted and twisted as both hands came up to either side of his face. Still running, Tobias pulled the axe from his belt as the other man tried to remove his pistol from his coat and cock the trigger, spinning around to take aim. Tobias pulled the axe over his right shoulder and backwards, and then, with speed and power, he brought his arm forward. He launched the axe straight at the man, hitting him full in the face and sending him flying backwards. He crashed against the wall and landed on the man with his face blown off, lying on the floor. Gabriel let out a blood-curdling scream that echoed around the walls of the study.

Collins spun around, pulled his pistol and pointed it at Jacob, who was already closing in on him. He fired off a shot which went straight through Jacob's open coat, missing him by next to nothing. Jacob ploughed into him, knocking both of them into the drinks cabinet and smashing the glass and bottles onto the floor. As both men landed on the floor, the large knife Jacob had in his hand plunged deep into Collins' chest. Gabriel was still screaming …

As Tobias had let go of the axe and Jacob had smashed into Collins, Hamish did no more than make a run for it straight out of the door and into the back to where his horse was. Gabriel was still screaming …

Tobias went to grab at Hamish but missed him. His momentum in throwing the axe put him off balance, and he fell to the floor. Jacob, now on top of Collins, still with the knife in hand, and his chest, pushed the blade deeper, twisting at the same time. Tobias hit the floor and chair at the same time, banging his head as he did so. He got up as quickly as he could and made his way to the study door and then to the back door.

As he ran outside, Hamish's horse passed him, knocking him to the floor. Jacob came running out to see the back of Hamish and his horse and Tobias face down in the mud. Jacob helped Tobias to his feet, and they went back inside together to the study. Gabriel was still screaming!!!!

As both men walked through the door of the study, carnage was laid out in front of them. Gabriel sat there whimpering and mumbling to himself.

"It's ok; it's over now," Jacob said with his hand on Gabriel's shoulder. "Go and sit outside while we tend to all this mess."

Pointing to Collins, Gabriel said, "Tha ... That one's still alive; I can hear him breathing ..."

Jacob walked over to where Collins lay and knelt down beside him. The knife was still in his chest. He could hear him trying to breathe; a faint gurgling sound escaped his lips. Jacob put his hand over Collins' nose and mouth for a couple of minutes and watched as the little life he had remaining left him. He pulled out the knife and wiped the blood from the blade on Collins' shirt, and sheathed it away. He stood up and said, "He's dead now."

Jacob helped Gabriel up from the chair and walked with him to the study door. "Now, just wait outside for us; we won't be long."

Tobias was standing over the other two men. "Well, these two are definitely dead." He then turned to where Jeremiah sat in his chair. Seeing his head looking up, eyes gazing at the ceiling, and his brains splattered up the wall, Tobias said, "And so is Jeremiah."

Jacob walked over to the dead men and, seeing the man with the axe embedded in his face, he turned to Tobias and calmly said, "You might want that back!!!!"

"Well, of course I do. I ain't leaving it here," said Tobias as he bent down. He put one foot on the man's chest and, gripping the axe in one hand, pulled it from his face making a cracking sort of sound as he did.

Jacob pulled a face at the noise it made and said, "Nice …"

Tobias wiped the axe and put it back into his belt. "So, what are we gonna do about these bodies then?"

Jacob stood for a few seconds and looked around the room. "Nothing," he said. "Nothing at all."

Jacob turned towards the desk, stepped over the two men and went to the drawer that was open. Inside it was a key - a key that would open the safe under the desk.

Jacob picked it up and showed it to Tobias. "The key to the safe," he said.

"Ahhh, the safe," said Tobias. "Well, open it up. Let's see what's inside then."

Jacob knelt down, placed the key in the lock and turned it. The lock opened with a clacking sound. He grabbed the handle on the door and turned it, pulling it open. As the door opened, Jacob's eyes did so as well.

"Good Lord above," he said.

Inside the safe were three big bags full of coins. He grabbed the bags and put them on the desk. Tobias grabbed one of them, opened it and turned the coin out onto the desk. It was more money than he had ever seen.

"Fuck me!" he said. "That old scrote. Look at this, Jacob, look at this …"

Jacob's head was still below the desk, and when he stood up, he held his hand out to Tobias with a fistful of silver. "God is definitely looking down upon us, my friend."

Tobias ran both hands through his hair and rested them at the back of his head. "Fuck me; you can say that again!!!"

Both men stood for what seemed ages, just staring at the contents of the safe.

"Big man, listen to me," Jacob said, walking to the same side of the desk as Tobias. "We have to keep this from Gabriel. So while I go outside and walk with him, you grab a saddlebag from one of the horses out back and fill it up."

"Ok ... ok. But what about the bodies? What will we do about all of this shit?"

"I told you; nothing. This is not our concern. They are all dead, bar one. And if he has any sense about him, he will be long gone from here."

"Ok, Jacob, but wait a minute. What about Gabriel? I mean, he doesn't seem to be taking all this very well now, does he? Screaming and blubbering as he did ..."

Jacob put the silver into Tobias' hand and said, "We have just saved him from his kidnappers, my friend. Saved him from a debt that he still owes. And, more importantly, took revenge on his father's murderers. So, don't worry about Gabriel. Don't worry ..."

Jacob left the study and walked outside to where Gabriel was sitting with his back against the wall. "How you doing?" he asked.

Gabriel looked up. "I've never seen anything like that before, Jacob ... The wall ... covered in, in ..."

Jacob knelt beside him. "Listen to me. Those men killed your father. Kidnapped you and blackened your sister's eye. All to recover a debt that you owed. Now they are dead. Your debt is ... well, the fact is, there isn't anyone to pay it to now. So you're free of it. I don't know why you had a debt in the first place, but you ain't got it no more."

As they talked, Tobias went over to the horses out the back. He took a saddlebag from one of them, went back to the study and stuffed the coins and silver inside. He put it over his shoulder and went back outside to Jacob.

"Well, I think we should be going. Anyone could turn up, and we definitely don't want to be here right now," he said.

Jacob helped Gabriel up and went and got one of the men's horses and helped Gabriel get on it. Then Jacob and Tobias walked back to where they had left their horses among the trees, with Gabriel following them. Tobias threw the saddlebag over the horse and mounted it. Jacob did the same, and then all three rode through the trees and up onto the road and made their way back to Josephine.

The road was wet and muddy from the storm earlier. The sky was still overcast and the clouds dark grey. In the distance, the sky could still be seen with flecks of lightning, and the faint rumble of thunder could be heard. It was still raining, but light rain.

Gabriel was riding next to Jacob. "Cards ..." he said.

Jacob turned his head towards him. "What did you say?"

Gabriel shifted in the saddle and wrapped the reins around his hand. "Cards. A game of cards. That's why I needed the money, to play cards to win money."

As they rode, Gabriel explained that about a year ago, some men came into the tavern and introduced him one night to cards. He had fallen in love with the game they had played that night and would go to the next town to play for money. Some games he would make money, some he would lose. He had a high stakes game to play one night and didn't have the funds to cover the bets. He couldn't let or even ask his father for the stake due to his father's strong beliefs against such things.

During one particular night of playing, he had been introduced to a man who would lend money to people. The man's name was Jeremiah. Gabriel was so hooked on playing and gambling that he knew he was good enough to play and win, so he took a considerable loan from Jeremiah. The game did not go the way he wanted it to go, and he had lost all the money. He had accused two men of cheating, and a fracas had occurred, ending up with Gabriel not only in huge debt but also being beaten up by the men. When his father had seen the marks on his face the following morning, Gabriel had just told him that he was set upon by a couple of drunkards.

He had since tried to win some money back but had failed to do so. He couldn't go to his father because he was ashamed. He had gone to Jeremiah every week with small amounts to try and pay off the debt. On the last visit a few weeks ago, Jeremiah had told him to pay more or else.

Both Jacob and Tobias shook their heads.

"Why didn't you just ask for help from your father?" asked Tobias. "I'm sure he would of understood,"

"I know, I know," said Gabriel. "I was going to do that, but then those men came looking for me and then … Well, you know what happened."

"So you lied. You lied to your sister. You made her believe that those men had just, by chance, set upon you and your father to rob you. And had killed your father in doing so," said Tobias.

"Hold on a moment, Tobias," said Jacob. "There's more to it than that, isn't there, Gabriel?"

Jacob grabbed the reins off Gabriel and pulled on his reins to stop both horses.

"You never told the truth to cover up your gambling debt; I get that. But what about after your sister had sent a message to both of us? A message for our help. And you know what our kind of help would involve. Why didn't you tell her the truth? She would have helped you."

Gabriel sat uneasily in his saddle and couldn't look Jacob in the eye.

Tobias had stopped his horse and turned it to face both of theirs. "Yes, Gabriel. Why didn't you tell your sister?"

"It don't matter now, does it? She found out as soon as those men had come to the tavern. She will blame me for my father's death. I didn't know what to do. I made up the robbing part to save myself from blame. I thought that you two would find them and kill them before she, or even you, would know why."

Tobias rode up right next to him and said, "But we did find out why. By accident, with a handkerchief. We put two and two together, and when we went to tell your sister, you had been taken. And even though she knew the truth, she just wanted you, her little brother, back safe and sound."

Jacob, still holding the reins of Gabriel's horse, said, "But what about Jeremiah? If you hadn't been taken by Hamish and his men, and we would of caught up with them and killed them, what about Jeremiah?"

"What do you mean?" asked Gabriel.

"What I mean is this," said Jacob. "If you wasn't kidnapped, and they didn't take you to Jeremiah, then none of this today would have happened. And if we had killed those men, then Jeremiah wouldn't have got shot by Hamish. And your debt would still be owed. So what I'm asking is - What would you have done then?"

"I … I don't know."

Jacob and Tobias looked at each other and then at Gabriel.

Jacob let go of the reins and turned his horse. "Let's just get you back to your sister. We will discuss this later."

Jacob led the way, followed by Gabriel. Tobias pulled an apple out of his bag, fed it to his horse and then stayed behind both of them while they all rode down the road headed towards the tavern.

# Chapter Eleven



Jacob and Tobias rode along the road with Dupree behind them, the wheels of his cart trundling along the road. A while later, the tavern could be seen in the near distance.

"Just up the way, there is the tavern," Jacob said, pointing in front of him.

Dupree had been humming a tune. "Ah, yes, I see it, Jacob."

Tobias pulled gently on the reins to be level with Dupree. "Josephine is the woman's name," he said.

Dupree raised one arm in the air and said, "Ah ... a French name. A beautiful name for a woman, no? I zink I like her already."

"Yes, yes, indeed. A beautiful name for a beautiful woman," Tobias replied.

"Too beautiful for you, big man," Jacob quipped.

Tobias threw his head back and laughed. "Ha! You sound jealous there, Jacob. Have a liking for young Josephine, have we?"

Jacob turned towards Tobias with a smirk on his face.

Dupree looked up and laughed. "Eet would seem so zen. Ahh, ze language of love, all eet takes eez a look. We French know all about love."

Jacob stopped his horse and turned around in the saddle. "I haven't said nothing about love. Or, in fact, anything other than she is too beautiful for you. So, can we stop talking about it?"

Tobias and Dupree fell silent for a few seconds.

Then Tobias said, "It's ok, my skinny friend. She is very attractive. I, myself, when I first clapped eyes on her, I thought, now there's a woman who I would like to-"

"Tobias!!!!" Jacob turned, raising his voice.

Dupree slapped his leg and said, "Oh, yes, eets definitely love."

Tobias put both his hands in front of him, laughing, and said, "Whoa there, I'm just joking. She is too skinny for me. I like a good handful."

Jacob flicked his heels at the horse and said, "I don't even really know her. Now can we just get to the tavern…?"

The tavern was upon them and so rode up to the front. Jacob and Tobias sat on their horses as Dupree hitched his to the post.

"We will ride on to see Jeremiah and sort this debt out. You get a room and stay here and wait for us to return," said Jacob.

As Dupree got off the cart, Josephine opened the door with a small bucket of chicken feed in her hand.

"Jacob, Tobias, you're back . How did your trip go?"

"Hello there, little miss," said Tobias.

Jacob got off his horse and said, "Hello again, Josephine. This is Dupree, a … a good friend of ours, and he will be needing a room for the night."

Josephine held the bucket with both hands and said, "It's good to see you again, Jacob. My father is inside, so your friend can go and see him about a room. I have to go feed the chickens."

She excused herself and slowly passed Jacob by, rubbing her arm against his as she passed. After walking a few steps, she turned and said, "Well, I hope to see you again soon," then disappeared around the corner of the tavern.

Jacob stood perfectly still, watching her walk away. Dupree grabbed a bag from the cart, said goodbye, and went inside. Jacob just stood there, his eyes staring straight ahead, not looking at anything … just staring …

"Come on then," bellowed Tobias. "We best be going; it's a good hours ride from here."

Jacob blinked his eyes a couple of times and turned to Tobias. "Erm, yes … best we got going … yes …" He put his left foot into the stirrups, grabbed the reins and pulled himself up and into the saddle.

Tobias shook his head, and, as he kicked at his horse to move, he said, "You got it bad. Come on, let's ride."

As they rode alongside each other, Jacob had an idea. He turned to Tobias and began to explain that when they arrived at Jeremiah's, they should both make up the rest of the money owed and clear the debt. That way, all three could start their partnership with complete trust.

"How do you figure that?" Tobias asked.

Jacob explained that if they paid the debt, then Dupree would see it as a very kind act which in turn would give them his complete loyalty and, most importantly, his trust. And as far as he could see it, Jacob knew that those two things would be the greatest assets you could have in a business partnership.

"Think about it, big man," Jacob said. "Dupree was a man not only in debt but also low on funds to be able to trade."

Tobias nodded and said, "Yeah, yeah, I see that."

"So, think about the days to come. We save him from losing a finger, go into a partnership with him and now pay his debt. He will never do us wrong. It makes perfect sense, big man."

Tobias smiled and looked at Jacob. "I've said it before, and I'll say it again … I'm glad we met, my skinny friend."


An hour had passed by, and the two of them were approaching the house of Jeremiah. They rode up to it, hitched the horses and Tobias knocked on the door. Jeremiah opened the door, greeted them both and let them inside.

"Come, come. Tell me of any news you have. Let us sit in my study and talk."

All three men walked to the study and sat in the chairs.

Jeremiah sat at his desk, placing both hands on it and said, "So, what do you have for me, gentlemen?"

Tobias pulled the money out of his coat and threw it onto the desk. "That's the full amount," he said.

Jeremiah opened the bag of coins and tipped them out. He counted out the money and put it back in the bag. "Ah, good, good," he said. "And the finger?"

Tobias looked at Jacob and then back at Jeremiah. "Well," he said, "about that …"

Jeremiah took the bag of coins, opened the drawer of his desk and took a key that opened his safe that sat behind the desk.

"Yes, I'm listening," he said.

Tobias shuffled in the chair, looked at Jacob again, and then said, "Well, I didn't take it …"

Jeremiah placed the bag inside the safe, closed it and put the key back into the drawer. "I see, but my instructions were simple enough. Were they not?"

Jacob sat forward. "He paid in full - with no trouble."

Jeremiah stood up and walked to the front of the desk and sat on the edge of it. He held out his hand, holding a smaller bag, and dropped it into Tobias' hands. "That payment we discussed was for the debt owed, plus a finger. Now, seeing as I have received only one, your money will reflect that."

Tobias poured the coins out into his other hand and could see that it wasn't the full payment. This enraged him. He stood up, right in front of Jeremiah, and towered over him. His face contorted, and as he brought up his hand, he wagged his finger and said, "Now, you listen here-"

Jacob jumped up, pulled Tobias' arm down and said, "That's a fair deal, Jeremiah." Then he looked straight into Tobias' eyes and said, "Calm yourself, big man. Calm yourself."

Tobias, clearly vexed by this liberty of Jeremiah, looked into Jacob's eyes, stood for a split second and then stepped back. Jacob turned towards Jeremiah and explained that Dupree had told them that he had been robbed, which was why he hadn't paid off any of the debt prior. And that he had thought to take a finger might have made Dupree run. So instead, they had gotten Dupree to pay the debt in full, and that way, at least Jeremiah would get his money.

Jeremiah clapped his hands together. "You clearly have intelligence, young man. I can see why you did what you did, but the deal was for a finger as well. So I cannot pay you what was agreed."

Jacob took the bag from Tobias' hand and said, "And I can see not to waste your time any longer, and so if you would excuse us, we have other matters to attend to."

Jacob pulled on Tobias' arm and walked towards the door of the study.

Jeremiah stood and walked them to the front door. "I do hope that we have an understanding, gentleman. I will have more work for you in the near future, so I hope to see you again in a couple of weeks."

"Of course," said Jacob. "Work is work."

Jeremiah stood at the door of his house, pulled it halfway and said, "I bid you good day." He closed it shut behind them.

Jacob took the reins in his hand and mounted the horse.

Tobias stood next to his horse and said, "What the fuck did you do that for?"

Jacob turned the horse towards him, "Come on, big man. Get on your horse. We have to get back to the tavern."

Tobias mounted his horse and rode up towards the main road just behind Jacob. "Oi! Answer me. Why the fuck did you do that?"

"Look, we have business with Dupree, right? And we also have work with Jeremiah, so for now, we need to keep our interests open."

Tobias rode level with Jacob's horse. "He fucking held back on the coin. Now, in my world, where I come from, that is a direct insult, right?"

"As it is in mine, big man," said Jacob. "But does it not make more sense to use him as a means to make more coin so that we can invest more money into our business with Dupree?"

"It makes more sense to me to break a man's fucking jaw who insults me," said Tobias.

Jacob turned onto the main road, and as he did, the bright glare from the setting sun stung his eyes. He pulled his hat from the saddle, turned to Tobias and said, "Yes, I get that, but we all must choose our fights, my friend. If there is one thing I have learned from my father, it's that."

"But your father was a bare-knuckle fighter, wasn't he?"

"Yes, Tobias. But he knew when to fight, and sometimes, when not to."

Tobias rubbed his eyes from the sun's glare, kicked at his horse's underbelly to go faster and said, "And sometimes you just have to break a jaw. Now, come on; let's get back to the tavern."

As they approached the tavern a little while later, they could see Dupree's horse and cart.

"Well, that's a good sign right there, Jacob. Dupree is still here, so I guess you was right."

"How do you mean?" said Jacob.

"Trust ... he clearly trusts us. Trusts our partnership. He could have just ran."

Both men pulled their horses up to a slow trot and took them around the back to the small stables.

As they got off the horses, Jacob said, "He has more to gain than to lose, Tobias. As do we."

Tobias pulled his horse into the stable, removed the saddle and tossed a few apples on the ground. As he walked past Jacob, he slapped him on the shoulder and said, "Come on, partner; let's get inside."

"You go on ahead, big man. I'm just going to get fresh water from the well for the horses."

Tobias nodded and said, "I will have an ale waiting for you."

Jacob walked over to the small well and lowered the wooden bucket to fetch the water. As he pulled the bucket up, he heard a voice from behind him.

"You're back again then."

He turned to see it was Josephine. The sun had almost set, and in that light, he could see that she looked even more beautiful than earlier.

"Hello, again," he said with a pursed smile on his face. "We seem to keep, erm, bumping into each other."

Josephine walked up to the well and sat down on its edge. "That's probably because you keep coming here. To the tavern."

Jacob lifted the bucket out from the well and filled the second bucket that lay next to it.

"But you seem to leave as soon as you get here," said Josephine. "Anybody would think that you wanted to avoid me. That you thought me ugly …"

Jacob missed the other bucket spilling the water all over the ground and over himself.

"No … no! Not at all. I think you're the most beautiful woman I have ever seen. I am always staring at you – but not like that - not in that way! I mean, I'm always looking at you - but not in the way it sounds-"

As the words tumbled out of his mouth and the water splashed onto his clothes, he was, to say the least, very embarrassed. He placed the bucket on the floor and tried to wipe away the water on his clothes.

Josephine stood in front of him, undid the apron from her waist and handed it to him.

"It's ok, Jacob. I know what you mean to say. I find myself looking at you too."

The sun had shone its last light of the day, and night had emerged as if from nowhere. The light of the moon had now replaced it and, in that moment, standing close to each other, Josephine leant forward and kissed his cheek. They were now face to face and cheek to cheek.

Jacob kissed her lips and then pulled back. "I'm… I'm sorry, I didn't mean to-"

But before the rest of his words left his mouth, Josephine kissed him back.

They kissed each other for a few seconds, and then she stepped away, took back her apron and said, "I'm not sorry."

Josephine turned on her heels and headed back inside, leaving Jacob just standing there. He stood for a moment and watched her go inside. He stood for a moment more, smiled and then grabbed the bucket and walked over to the horses. Still smiling…..

Inside, Tobias had joined Dupree, who was eating a rather large plate of beef and bread, washing it down with an even larger jug of ale.

"So, where eez e?" Dupree asked, taking a mouthful of beef.

"He was just fetching water," said Tobias.

At that moment, Jacob walked through the door and into the tavern.

"Ah, Jacob," said Dupree, beckoning him over to the table. "Seet, seet. 'Ave sum food and ale."

Jacob sat down, still with a smile on his face. He poured himself a jug of ale and drank.

Tobias, noticing the smile on his face, asked him, "What's with the stupid smile?"

"Huh? What?" was the reply.

Tobias cut a slice of beef, put it on the plate in front of Jacob and said, "That smile you had on you as you walked in."

Dupree raised his hand in the air, signalling for another large jug of ale to George, who was behind the bar. George filled another jug, and as he was about to take it over, Josephine came from the back room.

"Ah, just the right timing, my girl," George said. "Could you take this over?" He pointed to Dupree's table.

Jacob drank from the jug again, emptying it and filling it up again. "Huh? What?" came the same reply.

Tobias cut another slice for himself and shook his head. "What's gotten into you, man?"

Josephine took the ale and put it down on the table. Jacob looked at her and smiled. Josephine went red in the face and turned back towards the bar.

Tobias noticed this, and when she had left, he said, "THAT stupid smile!!!!!"

Jacob took a drink, looked straight at Tobias and laughed. "Don't you worry yourself, big man."

Dupree sat back in the chair and patted his stomach. "Ah, good food and drink go well wiz good company. So, tell me, 'ow did eet go wiz Jeremiah?"

Tobias sat forward and put both arms on the table, grasping the jug with both hands. "It went well, Dupree, very well indeed."

"Ah, zat eez good, zen 'e believed your word," Dupree said as he put the jug back on the table.

"Not just that," said Tobias. "But we did something else as well. You see, we have paid off your debt to him completely."

Dupree sat forward, looked at them both and said, "What do you mean, paid eet off?"

"Exactly how he said it," Jacob said as he broke off a piece of bread. "We have paid what you owed him."

"But ... why?" Dupree asked.

Tobias and Jacob began to explain that now he was a partner with them; he was a partner in all matters. That he did not have to agree to be partners and could have chosen to have his finger taken, or indeed, have just run when they had gone to see Jeremiah. In order for their partnership to work, then trust must be at the core of it. And by paying the debt, they hoped this showed the trust that they had.

Dupree clasped his hands at the back of his head and said, "Mon Dieu ..."

He sat forward again and put a hand on each of their shoulders. "Partners, partners. I can promise you zees, my friends. I will never let you down. Ever ..." He stood up, pushed back the chair and said, "Now, eef you will excuse me, I must sleep. Today 'as been a 'ell of a day. Goodnight, gentlemen, goodnight."

As Dupree walked to his room, Tobias took a drink and, without looking at Jacob, said, "You know, Jacob, you're a good man ... A good man."

There was silence, so Tobias turned to look at Jacob, but Jacob was looking at Josephine. "Did you hear what I just said?"

Jacob spun his head back around. "What? What did you say?"

Tobias stood up and stretched his arms out, "Don't worry, I'm off to bed myself ... I shall see you in the morning."

With that, Tobias walked away a few steps, then turned and said, pointing towards Josephine, "Don't do anything I wouldn't do." He winked at Jacob and then left for his room.

Sitting there, Jacob looked around the room and realised that he was now the only one in the tavern at a table. Josephine was clearing away the other tables. He stood up and walked over to her.

"Do you need any help with that?" he said.

Josephine piled the plates and jugs together and said, "Ok, if you like."

Jacob went to grab the pile at the same time she did and touched her hand. He froze for a second, looking around to see if her father was about to come out into the room.

"Sorry," he said as he pulled his hand away.

Josephine smiled as she picked up the plates, took them to the bar and said, "You kissed me outside, but now you're sorry for touching my hand?"

Jacob picked up the other plates and took them to the bar. "Oh … I'm er, I'm sorry."

"Sorry for what?" she asked. "Touching my hand or kissing me?"

As she scraped food off the plates, Jacob was taken aback and said, "No, I'm not sorry for either of those. I meant I was sorry in case your father was here."

"Well, my father went up about half an hour ago and, knowing him, is already sound asleep."

She then handed Jacob a plate with small pieces of bread and crumbs on it and said, "Here, you can help me out and give this to your horses."

Jacob took the plate, and they both went out the back. Josephine opened the stable door and put her plate on the floor for the horse. As she did so, Jacob closed the stable door behind them. Josephine sat on a bale of hay, so Jacob put down his plate and then sat next to her. They both sat for a few minutes, neither saying a word.

Then Jacob turned towards her and said, "I'm not sorry for kissing you. Not at all. And …"

"And what?" she asked.

Jacob took her hand and said, "And I'd like to kiss you again."

He leaned forward and gently kissed her lips – softly, at first, and then with more passion. Then began to kiss her neck. Josephine groaned and ran her fingers through his hair. He kissed down her neck and onto her breasts. Josephine grabbed his head, pulled it up to hers and kissed him hard, opening her legs and wrapping them around his waist. She pulled at his shirt and his trousers. He lifted her up and back onto the hay, hoisting up her dress. They both caressed and touched each other, kissing and fondling. She let out a deep sigh as she felt him inside her, thrusting gently and with care. They made love for the first time. And this felt different from when he had done it with other women. It felt softer, gentler, like ... like it was meant to be.

After, they both lay there in the same position. Neither had moved nor wanted to. Panting and breathing, they both just stayed in that moment, together ... Holding each other.

After some time had passed, Josephine said, "I had better get back inside before my father wakes up."

Jacob sat himself up and sorted his clothes out, tucked back in his shirt, and she adjusted her dress.

She stood up and buttoned up her shirt, took his face in her hands and gently kissed him.

"I have to go, Jacob." She stepped back with him still holding onto her hand. "Goodnight," she said as she slowly opened the stable door, looked outside and then made her way back inside to her room.

Jacob sat there. He looked at the horse, which looked back at him, and he said, "Don't you tell a soul, boy ..."

The next morning, the sun started to rise. The chickens could be heard clucking, wings flapping as Josephine scattered their feed onto the ground. She was up early, her mind full of the night before. Happiness filled her heart. She found herself humming a tune as she threw the feed to the floor, completely lost in her own world. Unaware of anything around her – just the noise of the chickens and the soft hum that she was making. Suddenly, she was startled by Dupree, who was sitting behind where she stood.

"Morning, mademoiselle," was all he said, but because she thought she was alone in such a quiet moment, it made her spin around, turning towards him.

"Oh, my Lord!" she said. "I didn't see you there. You made me jump!"

Dupree tapped his clay smoking pipe on the side of his boot, emptying the burned contents and took a fresh pinch of tobacco from his pouch.

"I'm sorry, miss. I didn't mean to startle you."

Dupree stood up and walked over to the lantern hanging that was still lit, thumbing the tobacco into his pipe. "You're up early and 'umming a tune as well. What 'as made you wake so appee, zis fine morning?"

Josephine blushed and said, "Nothing; I just like the sun rising first thing and the sound of the bird's early morning chorus."

Dupree placed the pipe to the lit lantern and sucked on the end of the pipe, lighting the tobacco. "Ahh," he said. "Nothing to do with ze young Jacob, zen?"

Josephine blushed even more, her cheeks filling up red.

Dupree puffed a few times on the pipe, smoke blowing from his mouth. "Young love … eet eez a sight to behold, as beautiful as zee rising sun, no?"

Embarrassed and not knowing what to say, Josephine excused herself and hurried past. Dupree smiled to himself and watched her scurry back into the tavern.

Jacob had woken minutes before and just lay there in bed, staring at the ceiling, recounting the night before. He closed his eyes and relived it in his mind, smiling as he did so. He felt more alive than on any other day he had lived. He got up out of bed and went to the window to see the sun rising; it was a beautiful morning. He looked down and saw Dupree leaning on the gate of the chicken run, smoking. He turned and grabbed his shirt, put it on, opened the door and made his way outside.

"Morning, Dupree," he said as he walked towards him.

Dupree turned and greeted Jacob the same. "Ahh, monsieur Jacob," he said as he took the pipe from his mouth and held it in his hand and took a small bow. "Are you as 'appee as dear Josephine this morning?"

"She is happy?" asked Jacob.

"Oui, oui …very 'appee. So much so zat she was 'umming to 'erself feeding the chickens not ten minutes ago …"

A smile shot across Jacob's face as he raised his eyebrows in response.

Dupree pursed his lips and said, "I cannot think for one second what 'as made her so appee. Maybe the birds singing on such a beautiful morning ..."

Jacob leant his back on the gate and smiled again. The two stood for a while and talked about the last couple of days. They agreed that, after breakfast, they should start to make their way back to Chelmsford and to Brendan. The offer he had made was too good to turn down, and the opportunities to make some serious money for them. And, of course, the day of the fight was nearing. The piece of paper with the details was still folded in his jacket pocket.

"Ahh, eet vill be a good chance to make a wager, and a little bit of excitement as vell."

Jacob nodded in agreement and said, "Also, it's a chance to see how the two men fair and for me to size them up. I am going to challenge the winner."

Dupree put the pipe between his teeth and clapped his hands together. "Why, of course, zis eez what Tobias was talking about last night! I would very much like to see you in action," he said while throwing two jabs in front of him.

Jacob put up both hands in front of his face and leant back from side to side and, using his footwork, danced around Dupree, mimicking a fight.

Dupree, with the pipe still in his teeth, coughed and wheezed. He surrendered his hands in front and said, "Ok, ok, I give up. I give up ..."

After a few more coughs, Dupree sat back on the gate and asked Jacob where he had learned to move around so fast. Jacob stopped moving and, bringing his hands down by his side, said, "My father."

Jacob sat next to him and began to tell Dupree about growing up with his father ...

"He was a gentle man on the inside, my father. But as hard as you could be on the outside. Being a farmer, he was of a certain way. Weathered, you might say, so even his skin was tough, which came in very handy for being hit. But even more so was the natural talent that he had for hitting back. You could say that he could punch like a horse could kick. This, as you can imagine, was very useful when up against other men. It was easy for him to knock a man over with one or two blows, and more often than not, knock them out."

Dupree sucked on his pipe to try and get a puff from it. "Ee sounds like a man who you wouldn't want to upset," he said.

Jacob grabbed a long piece of straw from the floor, lit it from the lamp and held it out to Dupree's pipe.

"No, no, definitely not. But he wasn't at all like that. Well, not really. You see, my mother, God rest her soul, was very gentle and very loving. And my father knew that she hated any kind of violence, so he would never be hard or coarse around her. She knew that he fought but also knew he did it for extra coin. And so she turned a blind eye to it, and he never spoke of it to her. Ever.."

Dupree pulled out another pinch of tobacco, placed it in the pipe, pushed it firmly down and lit it again. "Oui, eet seems that the truest love of two people eez zat of zose who are different ... And so ee taught you 'ow to fight?"

Jacob nodded his head slowly. "Yes, he sure did. But as I trained with him, and as I got older, I always felt that if you could move and hit, circle and hit, move your feet and not just stand there, going toe to toe exchanging blows, then you would be better. My father could take a good punch as well as dish one out. But, I could never see the sense in that. He would take me to fights to watch and observe, and I noticed that they all had lumps and bumps over their faces: broken noses, scars over the eyes and such like. As I got older, I would get into scraps with local boys, and they would all just stand there, throwing wild punches. I would move, circle them, parry the punch, duck and come back with a punch ... And I have never lost - ever."

Dupree blew smoke up into the air. "Did your father ever lose?" he asked. "Ever get hurt?"

Jacob stood up, away from the gate. "No, he never lost a fight. And only one time did he ever get hurt…. The day my mother died … or so he says."

Dupree placed a hand on Jacob's shoulder. "The loss of a mother, a wife … eez the 'ardest thing to 'appen."

Jacob nodded for a moment and said, "Yeah, I guess. My mother died giving birth to me, so my father raised me alone. He would always tell me that she would be very proud of me …"

Jacob scratched his head for a second and then remembered a time when he was about twelve or thirteen years old. A fight that his father had that was quite brutal.

"Actually, I do remember him getting hurt … Well, a fight he had that went on for some time against a big brute of a man."

Dupree was excited by this and said, "Ah, tell me ze story of it, and try to remember all the details."

Jacob sat back on the gate and began to tell the story of the fight his father had with the man known as 'Bill The Brawler …'

# Chapter Twelve

===== March 1702, Henry and the fight of his life =====

The cockerel crowed loud and long. A sound that could wake the dead, or at least that's how Henry saw it. The sun had begun its morning climb from the earth towards the sky. Only the very top of it could be seen that early. Burning a bright orange and slowly casting its light over the land. Henry was already up out of his bed as he was every day. The same morning chores, feeding the chickens, then the sheep, then onto his beloved horse. It was but just a few days into the month of October, and the air was cold. A thin veil of frost lay on the ground. Henry had been ploughing his field for the last couple of days, turning in the horse manure in the hope of rich soil. His horse was strong and very durable – two traits that people often said about Henry himself.

As well as being a farmer, Henry earned some extra coin fighting. And today was such a day. Later on in the day, he would face a man who was known simply as 'Bill The Brawler.' This man had a reputation that walked ahead of him wherever he went. Tough, strong, and very durable. At the last fight that Henry had, Bill had been there watching it and, after, had challenged him for a fight to take place in a couple of months. That time was now upon him. Today was the day.

Henry's young son Jacob was also awake, up and excited. Since the death of his wife, while giving birth to their son, Henry had

101

raised the boy on his own. He had taught him how to fight since Jacob was old enough to walk and talk. It was hard to raise his son as both a father and a mother, but he had done a good job of it. Every now and again, Henry's sister had helped out when Jacob was very little, but she had a life of her own with her own children. He had raised him fairly but also hard. The way Henry saw things was that, in this world, the weak don't survive.

Jacob was excited and couldn't wait to see his father fight again. To Jacob, his father was the strongest, toughest man to have ever lived. He had watched him fight a few times before, and Henry had won every time. In fact, he had never lost. Jacob opened the door of the house and ran outside to where Henry was checking over the plough in the field.

He stopped as he reached him, put both hands up and stood in the stance of a fighter. "Today is the day, Father. Another man for you to knock down," he said.

Henry laughed, ruffled his son's hair and said, "We will see, my boy, we will see."

Jacob moved around him, throwing punches: three straight left jabs and a right. "Of course you will. You have never lost, have you?"

Jacob was twelve years old and tall for his age. And lean. Very lean. He loved fighting. He bounced around in front of Henry, shifting his weight from left to right.

"How many times do I have to tell you, Jacob?" said Henry. "Stop moving around so much. You have to stay in one place to be able to punch properly."

Jacob moved around his father, saying, "No, no, not me. I punch and move, so they can't land a punch back."

"You keep moving your feet fast like that, and you are more likely to trip over them and land flat on your arse without even getting hit!!!"

Jacob threw another combination of punches and said, "Well, that ain't what happened the other month when I beat up that big lad who lives up the road now, is it? He didn't land a single blow on me. But I gave him a black eye and a split lip."

"That is true, my boy, but I will stick to how I fight. I haven't lost a single fight myself …"

Henry lunged forward, grabbed Jacob and picked him up and over his shoulder. Roaring like a bear, he tickled his neck as he did, making Jacob squirm and laugh.

Henry put him down and told him to go and get the horse from the stable and bring it to him so that he could fasten the plough. Work still needed to be done, and the fight wasn't until later on that day.

As Jacob walked away towards the stable, Henry shouted after him. "Feed him some of those apples before you bring him, and give him some more water too …"

Jacob just raised an arm in the air as he walked. As Henry turned to the plough, he held his hands out as he would to fight and shifted his weight from side to side, just as Jacob did. He smiled … and shook his head.


Hours had passed by. Henry had ploughed enough for the day and was back inside the house, washing himself at the basin. The sun was at its highest in the sky; it was time to go and meet Bill.

Jacob was getting the small cart they had and was hooking the horse up to it. The fight was to be held at an inn a few miles back.

As he dried his face, Jacob called out. "The cart is ready, Father."

Henry walked out of the house to where the cart was. Jacob was already sitting on it with the reins in his hands.

"Can I drive it today?" he asked.

Henry adjusted his hat on his head and said, "Well, do you think we will get there in one piece?"

Jacob shook his head. "That was not my fault last time. That rock in the road made the cart jump and spill the milk."

"Well, who was driving it?" said Henry.

Jacob shook his head. "Not my fault."

Henry climbed up onto the cart. "Just make sure you look out for rocks this time …"

Jacob flicked the reins and clicked his mouth for the horse to move and set off up the path and out of the gate.

"Woah!" said his father. "The gate, boy. Close the gate."

Jacob jumped off the cart and rushed to shut the gate behind them, and then jumped back up and flicked the reins again.

"Slow down, boy, there's no rush. The man ain't going nowhere, not while there is money up for grabs."

Jacob said sorry, and Henry could see that he was excited and anxious to see him fight.

"Listen to me, son; there are two things you must always remember to do. Never hesitate, and always remain calm. A calm man can overcome anything. Remember this."

A couple of miles later, they were nearing the old inn. Henry knew that the man he was about to fight was very tough. The toughest he had ever faced. Jacob had only ever seen him in fights that didn't last that long – ones that were over within ten minutes or so. But this fight could go on for quite a while. He knew this.

As the cart got closer, Henry could see a large crowd gathered at the inn. Some were faces that he knew, but most, he didn't. They were here to see Bill The Brawler. He quickly searched the crowd but couldn't see Bill amongst them.

As they pulled the cart up to the inn, he turned towards Jacob and said, "Remember what I told you. Whatever happens here today, remain calm."

Jacob nodded his head. "Yes, Father. I will."

The cart stopped, and people surrounded it. A few of them cheered as Henry got off and walked towards the inn. Hands patted him on his back and shoulders, faces he knew wishing him luck. As he walked, the crowd parted to let him through and out the back.

When he entered the back of the inn, there was a large circle of people, and a gap opened to let him into it. On the other side stood an enormous man. Both in height and width. Broad shoulders and thick arms. His nose lay flat to his face, and his hands were the size of marrows. This was indeed 'Bill The Brawler.'

Henry was met by his good friend Finn O'mahaoney, or Finny, as he was usually called.

"Ah, bejesus, it's good ter see yer, Henry. You're looking strong, my friend. How do you feel?"

Henry pulled off his shirt and gave it to Jacob to hold onto. "I'm feeling fine, Finny, just fine."

Jacob took the shirt and just stared at Bill. "He … He's … huge …"

Finny took Henry by his shoulders, looked at Jacob and said, "Ah, well, the bigger they are, the harder they fall, boy."

Henry turned to Jacob and said, "Now, you get yourself up on that table there out of the way of this crowd." He helped him up onto it.

"Now then, Henry," said Finny. "How much are you going to wager for this one?"

"All of it," said Henry and handed over £20.

Finny standing at the side of Henry, looked over at Bill, took the money and said, "Ok, then."

The crowd was loud, cheering and clapping for the two men. Finny and Henry moved to the centre of the circle, as did Bill and his second. Wagers were made, and then Finny and the other man went back to the circle, leaving Henry and Bill in the centre.

A man came from the side with his hand raised and said, "Gentlemen … Away you go!!!!"

Bill came charging at Henry and threw a big right hand that just missed his head. No sooner had it missed when a big left came straight up through the middle and landed flush on Henry's jaw, making him jump back. Bill could punch!!!

Henry quickly circled him and threw two left jabs that caught Bill in his eye. Bill retaliated with a sweeping right hand, which Henry caught on his forearms. Bill then grabbed at Henry's arms in a bear hug and headbutted him full on his nose, splattering blood over both faces and making Henry stagger backwards. The crowd cheered, and the noise was deafening. Henry wiped the blood from his nose and snorted some onto the floor. Bill was smiling and gestured for him to come forward.

Jacob screamed from the table, "Move, Father … move …!!!"

Both men went straight at each other again. Bill threw a massive left hand, but Henry ducked under it and came back with a right, catching Bill under his chin and knocking his head up. As it did, he hit him with a huge left hook that sent Bill tumbling sideways into the crowd.

A big roar went up, and Jacob jumped up and down, cheering. Henry stood in the middle as Bill wiped his bloody mouth, pushing himself off the people in the crowd. He held up his huge fists and beckoned Henry again.

"Come on, then," he said, rolling his hands one over the other.

Henry held his hands high, covering his chin and walked towards Bill. He shifted his weight from side to side, as he had seen Jacob do many times, his fists bouncing in front of him. Bill came forward like a bull, but before he could let off his own punches, Henry hit him full in the face: one, two, three left jabs – fast and hard. Bill took all three punches and let go an enormous right uppercut which caught Henry just under the left cheek, producing a horrible cracking sound. His head went up and back, his legs went from under him, and he fell to the ground …

The crowd roared and bayed for blood. Finny put both hands up to his face and winced. Jacob's face was that of pure horror as he watched, in what seemed like slow motion, his father go down.

Bill threw his hands above his head and turned to the crowd screaming a victory cry.

Henry got up. Groggy, he shook his head. He could feel that his cheekbone was broken.

Bill had turned to the crowd with his back to Henry. He then heard a cry of, "Come on … Try that again."

Bill spun round to see Henry standing. He charged at him, breathing heavily and swinging wildly, missing every punch. Henry moved from side to side, leaning back, his hands high to catch any blows…

Bill grabbed at him and threw him into the crowd, but the circle of men didn't break, and Henry just bounced off them and straight back into the fight. He threw two jabs catching Bill's eye. A huge right missed Henry as he ducked under it. One, two more jabs caught Bill's eye again, splitting it open, blood spurting from the cut. A huge right again, and then a left, both punches missing Henry. With Bill's eye split, pouring blood down his face and into his eye, breathing heavy, he was tiring …

Henry sunk a left hand, followed by a straight right into Bill's mouth, knocking a tooth out. Enraged, Bill tried to grab at him again, but Henry hit him with an almighty uppercut sending him backwards. As Bill's head came back down, he was hit again and again. His hands came up to try and stop the blows, but Henry landed a four-punch combination that knocked Bill to the ground.

The crowd went crazy. Whooping and hollering, shouting and screaming. Bill got to his feet and, staggering, tried to land a massive blow. Henry blocked the punch and hit him fast and hard to the side of his head, knocking him over … and unconscious!!!!!!!!!

The crowd closed in on Henry. A few of the men lifted him up onto their shoulders, cheering.

Jacob jumped up and down, waving his hands in the air and screaming at the top of his voice. This was a day he would never forget …

Dupree puffed on the pipe, and the last remains of the tobacco glowed as he blew the smoke into the morning air.

"Wow," he said. "That sounded like one 'ell ov a fight, Jacob."

"Oh, it was. I can remember it like it was yesterday. It went on for a long time, or it seemed a long time to me. And Bill ... well, he was a giant of a man."

Tobias walked towards both men. His hair looked like a strong wind had caught hold of it; he was unshaven and with no shirt on.

"Talking of giants," Jacob said. "Morning, big man. You sleep well?"

"Who's Bill?" asked Tobias.

Jacob explained that he was just telling a story of a fight his father had years ago.

Tobias rubbed his chest hair and said, "Well, talking of fights, we should be leaving today to get back to Brendan to see that fight up that way."

"Oui, ve vere just talking about eet," Dupree said.

"We shall eat some breakfast and then be on our way."

Jacob looked at Tobias' hand. "What's with the basket?" he asked.

Tobias lifted his hand. "Oh, Josephine asked me to get some eggs to make breakfast with a nice ham she has cured."

Dupree clasped his hands together and said, "I vill 'elp you with zee eggs, my large friend."

Tobias carried the eggs into the kitchen and handed the basket to Josephine, who was cutting the ham into thick slices.

"Oh, thank you, Tobias. You can put them down over there."

Tobias did as she said and went back up to his room to put on a shirt and come down to sit with the other two for breakfast ... As he pulled back the chair and sat down, Josephine brought over the plates with eggs and ham and a loaf of bread.

"There you go, gentleman. Would you like some ale with your food?"

Jacob raised his hand and said, "Not for me, thank you."

Dupree did the same.

"I'll take a jug," said Tobias.

As she walked back to fetch the drink, Jacob's eyes followed her. As she turned to go behind the bar, her eyes looked back at him, and a huge smile stretched across her face. Jacob's head turned back to the table to see Tobias just looking at him, smiling and shaking his head.

"Why are you looking at me like that?" Jacob asked.

Tobias took a couple of slices of the ham and two eggs on his plate and said, "Well, my skinny friend, let's just say that the window to my room was open last night. And it is above the stables out the back …"

Jacob put his head in his hands and let out a quiet groan. "Please don't say anything in front of her. I don't want her to know what you heard."

Dupree took a piece of the bread and dipped it into his egg, took a bite and, without looking up, said, "I knew eet, I knew eet. Love can never be hidden. Eet's too beautiful to hide."

Jacob put his hands out in front of both men and said, "Please … Don't embarrass her, please."

Dupree shook his head in agreement, and Tobias, with a mouth full of eggs, bread and ham, said, "Our lips are sealed."

Josephine brought over the jug of ale and put it in front of Tobias. Tobias smiled, looked at Jacob, and then back at Josephine, and took a swig from the jug.

"AHH, that hits the spot," he said.

Josephine stood still, her eyes flitting between all three men and then she asked, "Is there anything else I can get you?"

From behind, George said, "Josephine, when you are finished here, can you set your brother his chores as I have to go into town?"

Josephine turned and said, "Yes, Father, I'll go and make sure he is awake and dressed."

She excused herself and left. George said good morning to the men and asked if they were to stay another night. Jacob told him that they would be leaving for Chelmsford as soon as they had collected their things from their rooms.

"Can we settle our bill with you now before you leave?" asked Jacob.

George took the money off him, then bid them fair well and left for the town.

Jacob told the other two that he would collect his things and meet them outside with the horses, and then he walked upstairs. As he reached the top and turned towards his room, he noticed Josephine coming from one of the rooms and closing the door behind her. He walked towards her and went to say something to her.

She placed a finger over his mouth, saying, "SHHHH," and then kissed him gently and slowly. She then placed her hand on his face and walked past him, smiling, and down the stairs.

At the stable, Jacob saddled his horse and fed some apples to it while waiting for the other men to come outside. Dupree came out first and hooked his horse up to his cart.

"Eet eez a beautiful day, Jacob, and ve should be back at Brendan's house in a few hours."

"Yes. We can discuss his contacts in London and then see about this fight."

Tobias came out with a saddlebag over his shoulder and went straight to his horse. "Well, the last few days have definitely been quite a journey, haven't they, lads?" he said as he put the saddle onto the horse's back.

Dupree nodded and said, "They certainly 'av, my large friend, and I zink the future holds great promise for us all."

Jacob took his horse out of the stables and got into the saddle. "The start of a long partnership and friendship awaits us," he said as he held the reins and trotted out with Dupree's cart just in front of him.

As they turned the corner of the tavern, Josephine stood in the doorway. "Have a safe journey, gentlemen."

Tobias came from around the corner and said, "Take care, little sister. We shall see you again soon." As he spoke, he blew her a kiss goodbye.

Dupree tipped his hat and said, "Au revoir, mademoiselle."

Jacob said, "Goodbye, Josephine."

Tobias turned in his saddle and said loudly, "Well, don't just say goodbye, you skinny runt. Get off your horse and give the woman a kiss."

Dupree joined in and said, "Yes, yes! Ve vill be waiting at ze top of ze road."

Jacob did not waste a second. He jumped off his horse and ran towards Josephine, picking her up off her feet, spinning her around and kissing her as he did. Tobias and Dupree let out a cheer and trotted off towards the road.


The sun was setting. It was still warm, and the sky burned a deep red. The sound of Dupree's cart echoed as it trundled along the road. They were about half a mile from Brendan's house.

"I hope he has still got that bottle of brandy," Tobias said, standing up from the saddle as he rode, stretching his back. "I feel as stiff as a corpse."

Jacob, stretching out his legs, said, "I'm with you on that one, big man. These saddles are rough on your arse, that's for sure."

Dupree, sitting on a rather large cushion in the cart, laughed. "I do not know vot you are talking about, gentlemen. My arse eez just fine …"

In a short while, they came across the entrance in the road that led down onto Brendan's property and to his large house. Dupree turned the cart into the lane, passed through the gates and drove down to the front of the house. Tobias and Jacob followed. Reaching the house, Tobias eased himself off his horse with a loud, deep groan. He walked to the post like he had been kicked in his arse and hitched his horse. Jacob did the same, then walked to the big doors and knocked on the large brass knocker. The noise it made was loud as it echoed through the house. He waited for a minute for the door to open, but no one came. Tobias grabbed the knocker and banged again. With no answer.

"Oh, don't tell me he isn't here," said Tobias. "I can taste that brandy in my mouth."

Dupree sat in the cart and looked up at the windows. "Maybe 'e eez around ze back."

"I'll go around and have a look," Jacob said.

Jacob took a few steps forward, and as he did, two dogs came racing from around the corner of the house. They stopped dead in their tracks when they saw the three men and started to bark.

"Woah there," Jacob said with his hands out in front of him.

The dogs barked louder and, with bared teeth, circled him and Tobias. Just then, a third dog came from around the corner with a pheasant in its mouth. It, too, barked but was muffled due to the dead bird in its mouth. Then, seconds later, Brendan appeared with a rifle in his hands.

"Down, boys. Down!" he yelled at his dogs.

The dogs stood still and were now growling.

"Gentlemen, you have returned. It's good to see you all." Brendan shook both Jacob's and Tobias' hands. "It's good to see you again," he said.

Dupree got off his cart and held his hand out to Brendan. "Monsieur, I 'ope you are vell?"

"Yes, yes ... as I hope are all of you. Please, come inside and take the weight off your feet."

They all went inside, and the three dogs ran past them.

"Please, gentlemen, take a seat in my study while I get this bird put away."

They all went into the study and sat down. Tobias fell into a chair and let out a long sigh; his legs stretched out in front of him.

Brendan came into the room and said, "You must be thirsty after your journey. Would you care for some brandy?"

Tobias' eyes lit up as he said, "Ah, you read my mind …"

Brendan poured them all a drink and then sat down. "So, I take it you have thought about my proposal then since you have been gone?"

Dupree downed the brandy in one go and said, "Oui, we 'ave … and zink eet would be a great opportunity to further our business."

Brendan put the bottle on the small table and said, "Help yourself."

Tobias didn't need to be told twice and leaned forward and filled his glass. Jacob sat forward and asked how they would go about working out the details.

"Ah, you mean money?" said Brendan. "Well, of course, I would take a cut of the profits, a small one, mind. As you can see, I have wealth already. For me, it's more about helping you than money."

Tobias downed the second glass of brandy and said, "You see, that's what I'm having trouble understanding. I don't see why you would want to – I mean, without favour …"

"Well, that's quite a simple question to answer. You see, when I was first starting out in trading goods, I really had no clue. Yes, I made some money, but I was only getting by. And then I met an old man who, like me now, had quite a bit of wealth himself. And he helped me to better understand the ins and outs of it all. What to buy, who to sell what to, and where to sell. He did this out of kindness. And if truth be told, young Tobias, I was as hesitant as you are now. You see, I believe in helping people find their way because I was helped in finding mine. This is the very reason I hold the markets here on my grounds. I charge next to nothing, and I do it simply because I can."

Dupree raised his glass, "Zat eez wonderful. Zee truest measure of a man ..."

Tobias raised his glass and said, "Yes, I can see why you're a respected man."

The four men sat and drank and discussed the best opportunities to buy and sell goods. London was a haven of a mixture of people from all walks of life, and that was THE place to sell at a higher price. Especially items such as silks and furs, spices and exotic foods. The upper classes had too much money and spent it on frivolous things. But also, it was where the most goods were brought in – at East London docks. A trade route that came directly from North America brought ships to the docks. And with them came goods straight from the New World. Larger furs: elk and black and brown bear; fish, tobacco and timber. There were great opportunities to be had, and Jacob, Tobias and Dupree wanted a piece of it.

Brendan went to his glass cabinet and took out another bottle of brandy. He sat back down, opened the bottle, filled his glass and placed the open bottle in the middle of the small table for the others to help themselves.

"Ok, gentlemen. I can see that this all seems overwhelming. The world is getting bigger and bigger day by day. New worlds, new lands and with them, new things. Different types and kinds of people, and with them, different ways of life. It all seems to be growing too big, too fast -enough to make your head spin. But I can assure you that there is enough to go around. Big companies have their hands in many things, but there is room for others. Room for smaller companies. Room for the likes of you. For us."

Jacob poured a glass and filled the other two. "It is overwhelming. And it does seem to be going too fast, but these last few weeks have as well. So I think I can say," Jacob pointed to both Tobias and Dupree, "not just for me, but for all three of us ... Exciting times are ahead of us." Jacob raised his glass high above his head and said, "To the future. To our future …"

Tobias, Dupree and Brendan each raised their glass and together said, "To the future …"

Jacob stood and walked over to the painting of Brendan. He stood to the side of it and in a fighting stance with his closed fists out in front of him. "Talking of opportunities, Brendan," he said. "That local fight is tomorrow up the road from here. It's being held in a barn behind the inn where we got the piece of paper from." Jacob pulled out the paper and placed it on the table.

Turning it around to read it, Brendan said, "Ah, yes. Yes, of course, a chance for a wager and, if I recall, a chance for you to study both fighters and to challenge the winner."

"That's exactly right," said Tobias.

"At every turn, there's always a chance to make some extra coin."

"Well, I don't know of any man zat doesn't enjoy watching a good fight. And wiz eet, good company food and drink," said Dupree. "Brendan, if you will excuse me for a moment, I 'av some food in zee cart zat we can all enjoy right now."

"Nonsense, my good man. I have a kitchen full of food. Give me a moment …"

Brendan went out of the study and into his kitchen, where he placed onto a large tray a big joint of beef, a loaf of bread, and a slab of cheddar cheese. He walked back into the study and placed the tray on the table. "There you are, gentlemen, help yourselves."

The four men ate, drank and talked. Before anyone had noticed, the sun had shone its last light, and night had crept in.

"Oh shit!!" Jacob said as he looked out the window. "Where has the time gone? We should have left while it was still light; it's going to be near impossible to find our way to that small inn down the road now."

"I have plenty of rooms, gentlemen. Please, feel free to take a bed each and rest here until morning."

"That's very kind of you, Brendan," said Jacob. "Are you sure it's no trouble?"

"None at all, dear boy," Brendan said as he got up from the chair. "It makes perfect sense seeing as we will all be attending the fight tomorrow anyway."

"Merci, Brendan, merci," Dupree said as he stood up, stretching his arms high above his head and yawning. "Vell, if you don't mind showing me vot room to take, I vill bid you all Bonne nuit …"

The three dogs were lying in front of the open fireplace in the living room, half asleep.

Walking towards the stairs, Brendan said, "Any one of them but mine, which is at the end of the hall." He then did a short sharp whistle which sprang the dogs up from the floor. They ran to the back door as he said, "Come, boys … outside you go for a piss."

He walked to the back door and opened it, the three dogs scrambling past each other to run outside, barking as they did.

Tobias outstretched his long legs laying back in the chair. He slowly brought his arms up straight above his head, clasping his large hands together, letting out a low to loud sort of roar.

"My word, you sound like a bear," Jacob said as he stood by the window looking up at the night sky, the stars twinkling, seeming to flicker and dance.

Tobias got up from the chair and said, "Well, now I'm going to sleep like one. If you hear any growling, it's just me snoring."

Brendan got the dogs back in from outside and walked to the study. "Well, gentlemen, I bid you goodnight. It's been a long day; I shall see you in the morning."

He turned and went to bed, and the dogs returned to their spot in front of the fireplace. Tobias went upstairs, fell onto the bed and was asleep in seconds. Jacob sat back in a chair, his mind thinking of everything that had happened in the last few weeks and what would happen in the future. His life had gone from nothing to everything in such a short time. It made his head spin. But he was also excited and curious about it all. One of the dogs came and sat in front of him, nudging his leg with its nose. He tapped on his legs, and the dog jumped up and nestled onto his lap, letting out a small groan and licking its lips as it did. Jacob rubbed the dog's ears and patted its head. Within minutes both had fallen asleep.

The sun had started to rise, an orange glow above the treetops. Jacob was still asleep, his eyes twitching. The dog was now on the floor in front of him, pawing at his leg and woofing at him. He stirred in his sleep, half opening his eyes and turned onto his side. The dog woofed again, wagging its tail and staring straight at him. Jacob opened his eyes and lifted his head, looking around the room. The dog pawed at his leg again and now barked.

Jacob sat up and rubbed his eyes. "What is it, boy?" he asked.

The dog ran to the door, turned and barked again, wagging its tail faster. The other two dogs were now at the back door, also barking. Jacob got up and let the dogs outside. The sun lit up the sky with a beautiful bright orange. He rubbed the back of his head and went outside. The dogs ran off together, sniffing the ground, stopping for a second, cocking their legs and then running to another spot, doing the same. The air was crisp with a slight chill to it. The sun had no heat as yet, but Jacob could tell it was going to be a beautiful day. He walked out and sat on a fallen small tree, watching the dogs run around. It was quiet – the kind of silence where every noise could be heard. Jacob loved these mornings. On his father's farm, he would often be up early enough to enjoy such mornings. The birds were singing their morning chorus, and he could see two squirrels chasing each other along the branches of a tree.

Dupree had got up at the same time, dressed and grabbed his pipe, filling it with tobacco while he walked downstairs. As he got to the bottom, he noticed that the back door was open and could see Jacob sitting. He walked to the fireplace, where the fire still burned ever so slightly. He lit the pipe and walked outside to where Jacob sat.

"Good morning," he said.

Jacob turned around to see Dupree standing there, puffing on the pipe. "Morning," he said.

One of the dogs ran up to Jacob and dropped a stick to the ground, and then backed itself up, barking. He picked up the stick and threw it. The dog took off after it.

Dupree sat next to Jacob, and they talked about the day to come. About the fight. And what the future could bring. The stick kept getting thrown, and the dog kept bringing it back. Soon Tobias and Brendan had woken and joined them outside. As they talked, the sun rose higher until Brendan mentioned making breakfast. The men talked, and the dogs ran around chasing sticks and each other.

After they had eaten, they started to get themselves and the horses ready for the ride that would take them to the small inn an hour or so up the road to watch the fight.

# Chapter Thirteen



It was a little while after midday, and the small inn was bursting at the rafters with people. They had come from all over to see the fight between the two men. Sean O'Reily was a large man originally from Ireland who was to be fighting a local man, Bartholomew 'Barny' Brown. They had met twice before, with a win awarded to each of them. In their last fight, though, Bartholomew, or Barny, as he was known, had won by a knockout. So this fight would be somewhat of a grudge match with Sean looking to avenge the loss. He had never been knocked out before, and it had sat very uneasily with him ever since.

The inn was bustling, and the ale flowed, with the atmosphere high in anticipation of the fight to come. Sean had arrived early and took a seat in the corner of the inn. He sat with an ale in his hand, watching all the people arrive and take place out the back. He had always done this before his fights, taking in the atmosphere, the looks of excitement on people's faces, the banter and chat that would be spoken about who would win – which fighter was the best. Sean absolutely loved the atmosphere at fights. He was a huge fan of fighting, not just himself, but any fighter. He had a passion for watching fights and an even bigger one for participating. As he sat in the corner, with people out the back and in the bar, a roar went up, and fists raised to the roof. Barny had just walked in …

Sean was over six feet tall and heavy-looking, with a thick moustache that had a bald line through it on the right-hand side – a scar resulting from a split lip. He had been hit so hard in a fight that his tooth had cut clean through it. To Sean, it was a battle scar, and he was proud of it.

Barny wasn't a tall man, standing at five feet and nine inches, but was extremely stocky with wide shoulders and muscular arms. They were short but powerful. Barny packed a punch.

As Barny walked through the bar, he noticed Sean in the corner and nodded as he went out the back. Sean stood up, his head above the people in the bar and made his way out the back as well. The inn was packed with people. A circle had already been formed, and as the bar emptied, it grew in depth with men hungry to watch a good fight.

Jacob, Tobias, Dupree and Brendan had pulled up outside. With Brendan sitting next to him, Dupree pulled his cart up to the front and tied off the reins to a post. The other two men did the same, and all four walked into the bar as it was emptying out the back.

"We have got here just in time, it would seem," Brendan said as the people took their places out the back.

As they walked to where the crowd gathered, Tobias gestured to the barman who was just about to come from behind the bar, held four fingers up and said, "Jugs, please."

The barman rolled his eyes and sighed. He quickly poured out the ale, took the money and made his way outside. Tobias handed two jugs to Jacob and took the other two.

On the way out, Tobias noticed Sean's head above the crowd. Through the noise of it all, he said, "Let's hope he ain't the winner, Jacob," and then grinned.

Dupree and Brendan had joined the circle of men and beckoned the other two towards them. They squeezed to the front with Tobias' large frame making some room around them.

"Ah, thank you, my boy," Brendan said as he took a jug from Jacob. "He is some size, isn't he, Jacob?"

Nodding, Jacob said, "Well, as my father always told me, the bigger they are-"

Tobias interrupted, "The harder they hit!"

Brendan laughed at Tobias' remark and said, "Exactly what I was thinking."

Jacob took a swig from his jug. "We will see … we will see."

The crowd was restless and excited for the bout to start.

"COME ON, BARNY!" a man yelled at the top of his voice.

"YOU CAN DO IT," yelled another.

The two fighters were on opposite sides of the circle, both with the seconds they had brought with them. Sean took off his shirt to reveal his large frame and long hairy arms. He weighed considerably more, which could be seen by his round stomach. Barny was clearly more muscular, with hardly any fat on his body. Both men stood and threw punches, limbering themselves up. A man came from the side of them both to the centre of the circle, and he looked familiar to Jacob. It was Finny, the Irishman who used to be his father's second.

Finny raised his right arm and said, "Gentlemen, step forward and come out fighting." Then he dropped his arm and stepped back and to the side.

Sean walked forward. Barny came out straight at him, and as he did so, Sean threw an almighty right hook, landing clean on his jaw and putting him down to the ground, onto his hands and knees.

The crowd, which was mainly made up of local men, fell silent … A few cheers went up as Barny fell over to his side and onto his back. He lay there for a few seconds, breathing heavily and with both hands up by his head. Sean stood over him with his hands high in the air above his head, then turned to the crowd behind him and let out an enormous roar.

All around were open mouths … seconds went by, which seemed like minutes … Barny got to one knee and then stood up and shook out the pain from his head. Sean, with his back to him and still with his hands in the air, didn't notice.

Then his second screamed at him, "HE'S UP! HE'S UP …!!!!!"

Sean turned and saw Barny up but still groggy. He launched at him and hit him with another right, sending him rocking back, and then landed a left uppercut which caught flush under his chin, lifting his head up and knocking him back and onto his arse.

Sean raised his arms again and roared again. Barny shook his head and held his jaw. It was broken. He bit down as hard as he could to try and hold it together and not show that it was, in fact, broken.

Sean turned to the crowd and bellowed, "IT'S OVER … I'VE WON!"

Again he turned to face Barny only to see him on his feet. As Sean rushed towards him again and threw another big swinging punch, Barny ducked, sidestepped and came up with three crushing blows to Sean's face. Another huge swinging punch came up towards Barny's head, missing him as he shuffled backwards out of the way. He circled Sean, ducking under another punch and catching Sean with another fast flurry: left, right, left, right. Sean's head bounced backwards as Barny circled and threw them. Sean grabbed Barny's arm and shoved him sideways into the crowd, knocking over a few of the men watching. He tried to catch Barny with a left and then a right, but Barny dodged them both and countered with a massive left hook which sent Sean to one knee.

The crowd was now going mad. Cheers and clapping rang around the courtyard of the inn. Sean wiped the blood from his mouth, turned to look at Barny and, with a smile, he got up. Barny came forward and landed two more blows. Sean countered but missed, then took two more, followed by another two fast and hard right hands. He brought his hands up to cover his face and jaw and got hit on his hands and forearms as Barny wailed away at him. The pain was unbearable in Barny's jaw, but the fighter in him carried on. Sean sent another huge left hook which caught Barny on his eye, cutting it and sending blood spurting down his face and chest. Barny tried to circle him again, but Sean hit him in his ribs, winding him as it landed.

Both men came together in the centre and grappled each other, spinning around as they did. Barny leapt back as Sean threw another punch and then launched himself forward, hitting Sean with a powerful straight right hand full on his nose, putting him down once more. Sean, now on both knees and his bloody hands in the dirt, snorted and sneezed. Thick blood splattered onto the floor and over his left arm as he cocked his head to the side. Both men were battered and bruised. Lumps and bumps were appearing over their faces and hands. Sean rose up from the floor, but Barny was too quick and rushed across to him and hit him with a big uppercut which put Sean on his back. Snorting and panting hard, blood and spit coming from his nose and mouth, Sean rolled onto his front, then to his knees. His head bowed down … Barny just stood there, his jaw throbbing with the pain, breathing heavy, blood trickling from his ears … Then, Sean got up, groggy and tired. Barny, seeing this, let out a big sigh, lifting his chest up and then back down. He walked forward, hands held up, fists closed. Both men circled each other, breathing heavily; both tired, both sore. The crowd bayed them on.

"DO HIM …"

"KILL HIM …."

"KNOCK HIM OUT …"

Both men had fought with everything they had. They now stood in front of one another. Arms heavy. Tired and in pain …

A man shouted from the back, "A DRAW … A DRAW …"

Barny looked around the crowd with just his eyes flitting from face to face. He wasn't about to let a draw happen. No matter how much pain he was in or how tired he was. He had won the last fight by knocking Sean out. It wasn't going to end like –his - in a draw.

Barny leapt forward with a right hook, putting all he had into the punch. Sean leant backwards, the punch whooshing past him just in front of his chin, and then caught Barny on the top of his head with an overhand right, knocking him down … Barny hit the floor hard, knocking up dust and dirt as he did. He was out cold.

Sean stood with his legs wide apart, holding himself up. That was it. The fight was over… The hardest he had ever–had - the hardest either man had ever had. For a moment, there was total silence … and then a huge roar went up. Hats were thrown high in the air, and arms were held high as the crowd acknowledged a fight truly worthy of one of the best their eyes had ever seen.

Tobias slapped Jacob on his back. "Well, we did see, didn't we?"

Jacob raised both his eyebrows, nodded and downed the rest of the ale. With complete confidence in his face and voice, he said, "Well, he will …"

He made his way over to where Sean and his second stood, surrounded by a group of well-wishers.

"Where eez 'e going?" Dupree asked.

Tobias called after Jacob, but he did not turn around and kept walking towards the group. Sean, covered in blood, was wiping away most of it. His second poured a wooden bucket of water over his head to see if blood was still flowing from any cuts or nicks.

Jacob calmly walked through the men and straight up to Sean. "That was a good fight you had there."

Sean held a piece of cloth over a cut on his eyebrow to stop the blood that was trickling down his cheek. "Cheers, it was a tough one. That Barny is a hard man."

Finny had come over to congratulate Sean on his win.

Jacob held out his hand and shook Sean's. "Yes, it looked a tough one."

As Jacob talked, there was still a hum of noise around the fighter from the small crowd surrounding him. Finny patted Sean on his shoulder, and his second dipped the cloth into the bucket of water, rinsing the blood from it.

"I would like to challenge you myself," Jacob said.

Sean took the cloth from his second and held it up to his eye. "What did you just say?" he said, leaning forward to hear better.

"I said I would like to challenge you …"

Sean laughed and turned towards his second. "Did you just hear that? This young lad wants to fight me … Me!"

The crowd around them laughed along with Sean and his second. Except for Finny. He looked Jacob up and down. Jacob just stood there in front of the bigger man Sean.

"Come now, lad, move along before you vex me," Sean said, still laughing.

"I ain't going anywhere. Do you accept my challenge? Or do you only fight those that you think you can beat?"

Sean leant forward and put his face up to Jacob's. "Boy, I could beat you with one hand tied behind my back. Now fuck off before I do give you a beating."

Jacob pushed his face forward and snarled, "You couldn't do it with four fucking hands …"

Sean, enraged by this, went to shove Jacob backwards, but Jacob quickly sidestepped and parried both arms away from him. The crowd opened up around both men. Sean's second grabbed at him, and Finny stepped in front with his arms out wide.

"Woah, woah! Hold up there, big man," he said.

By this time, Tobias had grabbed Jacob from behind. "Ease up, Jacob. Calm yourself."

Jacob shook off his grip on him and said, "I am fucking calm!!!!"

The people who had left the back courtyard and gone into the inn for ale had heard the commotion and began to pile back outside. And with that, they formed a large ring around the men. Sean was being held back, and Jacob stood there with Tobias behind him, plus Dupree and Brendan now.

Barny had come around again and was also standing next to Jacob with his second next to him.

On the other side, Sean was now being held back by at least five or six men, all of them struggling to keep him at bay. He was livid, trying to get over to where Jacob stood.

"I'll fucking snap you in half, you little prick … I'll tear your fucking arms off!!!!!" he screamed at Jacob, trying to get over to him.

The crowd stood in anticipation, watching this spectacle, not knowing what was really happening.

Barny turned to Jacob and said through gritted teeth, trying to keep his jaw closed, "I think you should go home, boy. Before you get seriously hurt."

Jacob looked straight into Barny's eyes and smiled. Then he winked and turned back to where Sean was.

"Let the big bastard go," he said. "Come and rip my fucking arms off then."

Sean let out an almighty scream and threw off the men holding him, and ran across the yard like a bull, still screaming as he did. He charged at Jacob and threw a hard right hand … Jacob ducked under it and moved to the side as Sean missed him. A left hand followed, and Jacob ducked under and moved to the back of him, slapping Sean's head as he did. Sean spun around and went to grab at Jacob. As before, he moved to the side and parried Sean's hands away, but this time Sean tripped up on his own feet and fell to the ground. He banged his fists on the dirt and scrambled to his feet. Jacob stood there, his fists bouncing in front and his whole body moving quickly from side to side.

Sean rose from the ground, angry and maddened and flew with an enormous rage at Jacob again. He wailed away at Jacob, throwing huge swinging punches at him from every direction. Jacob just slipped and moved and parried every single punch that was put his way. Sean was breathing heavily but was so angered that this did not deter him from trying to take Jacob's head off his shoulders. Every time he threw a punch, Jacob ducked, slipped, moved and parried his way out of the way. Sean launched forward again, threw a right, missed, then a left, missed, another right, then left … Jacob just slipped them all. Not a single punch landed.

Tobias, Dupree and Brendan all stood watching, not really believing what their eyes were seeing. The crowd watched in silence. Barny and Finny watched side by side, not really knowing what was happening. This young, skinny man was making an absolute fool out of this huge, experienced fighter. Who but half an hour ago had beaten Barny and knocked him out.

Sean, completely out of breath and tired, not just from this moment but from the tough fight he had just had, was literally fighting on pure anger. Jacob was a few feet away from him, swaying and bouncing on the spot. His hands were still held in front of him. Sean, snorting and panting, stood and took a deep breath. He held it for a second and then took three steps forward. He pulled back with his left arm and threw a big, fast left hook straight at Jacob's jaw. Jacob blocked it with his right hand, leaned his body slightly to the left and threw a straight left hand through the middle and flush onto the centre of Sean's jaw with a punch that was half jab, half uppercut. Sean hit the floor with a crash. Flat on his back, his arms and legs splayed out on the dirt floor … out cold!!!!

Jacob stood for a moment, looking down at the big man laid out in front of him. The crowd was silent. Then muttering began amongst them. Barny walked towards Jacob, grabbed his arm and raised it high above his head. The crowd reacted, and cheers and whistles echoed all around. Barny had just seen and witnessed a remarkable sight. In all the years he had been fighting, he had never seen a man win against such an opponent with ease.

"Who are you, lad?" Barny said under the noise of the crowd.

"Jacob," came the reply.

And still with gritted teeth, Barny said, "Great fucking fight, lad ... Great fight!!!"

Tobias ran to Jacob, grabbed him around his waist and lifted him in the air, bouncing him up and down, cheering and whooping. Jacob took it all in and raised both hands up while being held up.

As his feet touched the ground, Finny came over and shook Jacob's hand. With a huge grin, he said, "My god, lad, that was something else! I've been in this game for many years, and I can honestly say that was truly unbelievable. It's a pleasure to meet you, lad; my name is Finn O'mahaoney."

Jacob, shaking his hand, smiled and said, "I know, Finny, you know my father ... Henry."

Finny didn't hear what Jacob had said over the cheers and clapping. "Who?" he said.

Jacob leant into Finny and repeated himself. "My father, Henry. Henry Hammond."

Finny took a step back. "You're Henry's son? The fighter, Henry Hammond? Works a farm just outside of Hadleigh."

Jacob nodded and said, "I am, indeed."

A wide smile spread across Finny's face. "Well, now that makes sense. The apple definitely hasn't fallen far from the tree."

Dupree placed both hands on Jacob's face and gently shook it. "Très bon ... très bon ... you vere great; a great fight. Come, come, ve must celebrate!"

Finny agreed and said, "Yes, lad, you have earned a drink. Let's get you to the bar and fill you with ale." He patted Jacob's back and said, "Bejesus, that was a good fight. We must talk about your future. I can get you matches where you can earn some good coin. A man of your talent should be paid to fight. But first, let's get you that drink."

As they all went back into the inn, Jacob turned around to see Sean still out cold on the floor. He then looked at Tobias, winked, and said, "I told you we would see ..."

# Chapter Fourteen



Jacob, Gabriel and Tobias were about half a mile from the tavern. The dark storm clouds had gone. It was still overcast, but the sun could be seen between them. The rain had almost stopped, and it was now only spitting lightly. The road was wet and muddy, and there was silence as they rode, albeit for the noise of the horses breathing and snorting and the sound of their hooves trotting through the wet mud. Jacob and Tobias were riding side by side with Gabriel behind them, sitting slumped in the saddle, his head bowed.

Tobias looked behind at him. "Wonder what he's thinking right now," he said.

With his eyes fixed ahead, Jacob said, "Well, I would imagine he is relieved of his troubles of debt, and scared shitless what his sister will do to him."

Tobias half laughed to himself. "Yeah, that woman has a temper that I wouldn't want to be on the end of, that's for sure."

Jacob nodded in agreement and said, "Yeah, but she is a sweet woman all the same."

Tobias smiled at Jacob. "Well, you would say that. Every time you see each other, you're at it like rabbits. Oh, and that reminds me. When we stay there later tonight, can you go a bit easy?"

Jacob turned his head towards Tobias. "What d'you mean?" he said with a smirk.

"Well, all I can bloody hear is Bang, Bang, Bang from the bed. I don't know if you're fucking or fighting her!"

Jacob laughed loud and was clearly embarrassed. "You can talk!" he said. "I remember a certain man who completely broke a bed not so long ago ... A woman by the name of-"

Tobias suddenly sat bolt upright. "LOOK!!!!!" he said, pointing. "Up ahead. Smoke!!!"

Jacob looked to where he was pointing. Smoke billowed up to the sky, the wind whipping it about.

"God above. That looks like it's coming from the tavern, Tobias!!!!!!"

Tobias stood up in his saddle. "It must be. Quick, Jacob, ride ... RIDE!!!"

The two men snapped at the reins of their horses, whipping the necks and kicking at the underbellies.

"FUCK ...! FUCK!" shouted Jacob. "COME ON, COME ON!"

Gabriel looked up to see both men suddenly ride off fast and then noticed the smoke.

He, too, slapped the reins and took off after them, holding on for dear life, shouting ahead at both men. "WHAT IS IT???"

Jacob thundered down the muddy road. In front of him were trees that covered where the smoke was coming from. The road ahead had a long bend in it which went up a hill. Just beyond that, around another bend, lay the tavern. His horse ran at full speed, snorting and panting as it rode around the first bend in the road and up the hill.

Tobias was right behind him. "GO ...! GO!!!" he screamed at Jacob.

The horse sped up the hill and round the second bend and onto the straight.

Just beyond the trees, Jacob could see the tavern. Thick black smoke came from the roof. As he got closer, he could see flames within it, flicking and dancing. He raced closer and closer, his mind racing just as fast. Fear was etched across his face.

"No, I, no ..." he mumbled to himself.

The horse galloped as fast as it could, and as it cleared the clump of trees, Jacob could see ... It wasn't the tavern; it was the old barn that sat back behind it, where George had kept his cart and stored bales of hay.

Jacob rode the horse straight around the back towards the burning barn, hoping to see Josephine out there. But she wasn't.

He jumped off his horse and shouted as loud as he could. "Josephine ...! Josephine!!!!"

Tobias pulled hard on his reins, and the horse came to a skidding halt. He, too, jumped down. "Where is she?" he asked as he reached the barn scouting the place for any signs of her.

"I can't see her," Jacob shouted over the noise of the roaring fire which had engulfed the wooden barn. He turned and ran towards the tavern, kicking at the door as he entered. "JOSEPHINE!!!"

Tobias ran around the back of the barn to search for her. Gabriel turned into the small dirt road leading to the tavern. He could see the flames flicking and dancing all over his father's barn and Tobias running around to the back, calling out his sister's name. He jumped off the horse and ran to the tavern and inside. As he entered, he could hear also hear Jacob calling her from the back of the kitchen.

Gabriel ran upstairs, calling out for his sister. He looked in all the rooms, calling her name.

He looked in the final room at the end of the hall, her room, but she wasn't there. As he came out, Jacob had run to the top of the stairs.

"IS SHE HERE??" he shouted.

Gabriel, with a desperate look on his face, said, "No ... no. She's not up here!!!"

Jacob grabbed at his hair on either side of his head and screamed out, "FUCK ...! FUCK!!!!"

He turned and ran back downstairs, then outside to where Tobias had come around from the other side of the barn.

"She's not in there," he said to Tobias.

Tobias walked over and grabbed him by his shoulders. "Maybe she is in the next village, getting supplies. Food. She isn't here, but maybe she is somewhere else ..."

Jacob looked straight at his face, listening to his words.

Tobias tapped reassuringly on both of Jacob's shoulders. "Maybe she's safe ..."

Jacob swiped Tobias' hands away and turned around. "No ... no ... There's something wrong. I can feel it ..."

Tobias placed his hand on Jacob's shoulder and turned him back to face him. "You don't know that. WE don't know that. Maybe she's at the village down the road."

Jacob paced up and down, his shadow lit by the fire flicking about on the ground.

"We don't know," said Tobias again. "All we can do is wait. She isn't here. Her body isn't here. Which means she hasn't been burnt, which means she is ok. Maybe she went to get help."

Gabriel came running out in a panic. "Quick. Come, look ... quick!"

Both men ran inside the tavern. Gabriel was at the big fireplace. He pointed to the top of it. There, stuck in the wood, was a knife stabbed through a piece of paper - a note. Upon it were scribbled the words: JEREMIAH'S TOMORROW.

Jacob ripped the paper from under the blade and stared at it. He walked towards Tobias and slammed it into his chest. "Safe, is she ...??!!"

Tobias took the paper and looked at it.

Jacob stood next to the fireplace with his elbow on the shelf. "Hamish ..." he said. "FUCKING HAMISH!!!!!!!"

Tobias scrunched the paper into his fist and threw it into the fireplace. "We will get her back, Jacob. He won't get away with this."

Jacob stood with both elbows on the shelf and his head hanging between them. In a low voice, he said, "It's all your fault." Then he turned and screamed at Gabriel. "IT'S YOUR FUCKING FAULT, YOU LITTLE PRICK!"

He launched himself at Gabriel, but Tobias got a hold of him and held him in place.

"Calm down, Jacob," he said. "This won't get her back. We got back him, didn't we? And we will get Josephine back."

Jacob pushed himself away from Tobias and went to the bar. He pulled out a bottle from behind it, took out the cork and gulped it down. He slammed the bottle on the counter and, without turning around, said, "You did this ... You caused this ... Your father, Jeremiah, those men, Hamish ... and now your sister ... He has your sister ..."

He turned with the bottle in his hand, took another gulp and threw the bottle at Gabriel, missing his head and smashing against the wall.

Tobias stood in front of Gabriel. "ENOUGH!!!!!!" he shouted. "The boy's been through enough. Now go outside and calm down."

Jacob stepped forward, pointing at Gabriel. "Enough ...??? Enough ...? That little-"

Tobias leaned forward. His frame swelled up. As he leant towards Jacob, he said, "YES ... Enough. Now go and cool off. This ain't gonna get poor Josephine back. You tell me to be calm all the fucking time. Well, now it's your turn ... So fuck off and be calm."

Tobias turned to Gabriel, who, by this time, was quivering and shaking with both fear and anger.

Quietly, Gabriel said, "She's my sister."

Jacob looked at him. "What did you say?"

Looking at the floor, Gabriel lifted his head, stared straight at Jacob and screamed at the top of his voice, "SHE'S MY FUCKING SISTER!"

Both men just stood and looked at him. No words – just looked. Through gritted teeth and with a softer voice, Gabriel said the words again ...

Jacob sank himself into a chair.

Tobias put his hand on Gabriel and said, "We will get her back, I swear on it ..."

# Chapter Fifteen



With his ear bleeding heavily, Hamish jumped onto his horse, dug hard with his boot into its underbelly and turned the horse to make his escape from Jeremiah's house. As the horse ran out of the backyard, it clipped Tobias coming out of the house, knocking him over, and he fell flat into the mud. Hamish, using the reins, whipped at the horse's rear and rode fast up the muddy track, out of the gate and onto the road. He rode hard and fast, his mind racing. What was left of his ear was bleeding, the blood running hot down his neck, soaking the shirt he wore under his coat.

He rode for about ten minutes, looking behind as he did to see if they were following. His mind was running through what had just happened. The shot that hit his shoulder had only gone in about half an inch due to the thickness of his coat. It hurt and stung, but it wasn't enough to stop him from making a run for it. He rode around a bend in the road and stopped just past it, pulling the horse into some trees. His ear was bleeding too much, and Hamish knew that he had to stop it before he bled to death.

The storm had passed overhead, and the sun could just be seen through the still overcast sky. He ripped a piece of material from his shirt and sprinkled gunpowder onto it. Then, using the flint he had in his saddlebag, he struck at it, causing the sparks to ignite the powder. He knew the only way to stop the bleeding was to burn the wound. He held the lit piece of cloth against his ear. It sizzled as it burned the flesh, stemming the bleeding. He screamed out as the pain shot through his head. Dropping to his knees and cocking his head, biting down hard and wincing so much that his face contorted was all he could do to try and control the pain. It surged through him like a cold wind would bite through a man's body. He slumped to the ground in agony ...

After about five minutes had passed, he pushed himself up from the wet ground and gathered himself together. No one was following him. He grabbed the reins that hung from the horse's neck and slowly mounted it. The sky was grey, but the light had improved. The rain had eased off, and it was now spitting lightly. He kicked at the horse and moved it back into the road. This day had not gone to plan. As he rode, he thought about what had just occurred. It all happened so quickly. One minute he and his gang were in a controlled situation, about to get the money from Jeremiah, the next ... chaos!!!!!

He had taken Gabriel as insurance to get his money. As he rode, his mind replayed that day he and his gang had gone to retrieve the debt from Gabriel.

———◆———

The day before, they had stayed at a small inn a couple of miles down the road from his father's tavern. Hamish knew that Gabriel would be along that road with his father going to the town. It would be a perfect place to stop them and threaten them both to get the debt for Jeremiah. What he didn't plan on happening was George's bravery. When they stopped the cart, it was supposed to be a simple thing. Threaten and scare them both, and take the coin they had on them that they were to use to buy and stock up on supplies for the tavern. Collins had taken his place at the side of Gabriel, Hamish on the side of George and the other two men blocked the road. Collins pulled out his pistol and pointed it at Gabriel's head.

Hamish pulled out his pistol and held it by his lap. "Morning te yer, Gabriel. You have something for me????"

Gabriel looked at his father. "I'm sorry, Father," he said.

George, astounded and confused by what was happening, asked, "What in God's name is going on here?"

Hamish, slumped in his saddle, the gun resting in his lap, said, "Your boy there owes a considerable debt ..."

George turned to his son. "Who are these men, Gabriel, and what are they talking about?"

Gabriel looked into his father's eyes. "I'm sorry, Father," he said again. "There really is no other way."

Gabriel stepped down from the cart. "You see, these gentlemen are here to kill you. And I had to have a reason for your death. I am in debt. Too much. With you gone, I will take ownership of your precious tavern, pay off the debt and will never need to borrow again. These men set upon us to rob us, and you got shot. Your wounds caused your death. Well, that's the story I will be telling anyway."

Startled by his words, George demanded to know what was going on. "What are you talking about, boy? Who are these men?"

Gabriel turned to Collins and said, "Do it. Do it now."

Collins raised back his arm and struck Gabriel across the head with his gun, cutting his head open. Gabriel winced in pain, clutching at his head. George stood up in the cart but was swiftly pushed back down by Hamish.

Gabriel stood by the side of the cart. "You have never loved me, Father. You always treated me like a dog. Fetch this, carry that."

George, frightened and confused, said, "Why are you saying these things? You are my son; I have raised you on my own and have always tried-"

Gabriel snapped at him. "QUIET! This is the only way. With you gone, Josephine and me will take over the tavern. No one will ever find out the truth. Hamish and me have it all worked out ..."

George clasped his Ids together and begged his son. "Please, Gabriel. I don't understand ... Please don't do this. You're my son ..."

Gabriel turned away and walked back behind the cart.

BANG ... BANG!!!!

Two shots were fired. He carried on walking up to the bend in the road.

After a few minutes, Hamish came up behind him. "It's done," he said.

"Now stick to the plan, Hamish, and you will soon have all that is Jeremiah's," Gabriel said.

———◆———

Hamish's ear had stopped bleeding, but the pain from it and his shoulder were intense. He was angry and couldn't get his head around what had just happened. This was not the plan that he and Gabriel had hatched together. There was only one thing left for him to do: ride to the tavern and take Josephine.

As he rode towards the tavern, he thought about how he could turn this around. He was injured, and he hadn't gotten a single coin for any of his troubles. All sorts of thoughts went through his mind. How did this all happen? How did Jacob know that he would be at Jeremiah's house? Was this all Gabriel's doing?

He thought back to the time he had first met Gabriel. He and his gang had gone to see Gabriel to collect part of the debt he owed Jeremiah. And Gabriel had told Hamish about a plan that they could both benefit from. Gabriel wanted his father out of the way. He had always thought and felt that his father was hard on him. That he never showed him any love as a father should his son. He believed his sister had all of his father's love and attention. He had felt this way even as a small child - ever since his mother had died. It had weighed heavily on him his whole life. So much so that he wanted his father dead.

Gabriel loved his sister and didn't want her to think her father's death would have had anything to do with him. So, he hatched a plan that would get rid of his father. To do this, he needed the help of Hamish. All he needed was for Hamish to realise that he could have all of Jeremiah's money and that he and his gang could take over Jeremiah's business. The one thing that never entered Gabriel's head was that Josephine would enlist the help of Jacob and Tobias. Or that they also worked for the same man that Hamish worked for.

Gabriel was a very clever young man. He knew that he couldn't just hire someone to kill his father. He couldn't do it himself, either. He had to make up a plan that would free him from any connection. He knew that if he borrowed money and made up a story of needing it for a stake in a card game and never paid it back, men would be hired to come and look for him. He knew that hired thugs were indeed hired to rough people up, scare and intimidate them. That they also must be of low intelligence. If not, then surely it would be them who had a money lending business and not the men who hired them. By that thinking, they could be manipulated, and the easiest way is by greed. Gabriel's entire plan was based on this. And if it didn't turn out the way he planned, if Hamish did not agree, he would pay the debt back and would have to devise another plan.

Hamish rode up the hill and around the bend; he could see the tavern up ahead of him. He pulled the horse into the trees just a way before, off the road. He could see clearly through to the front of the tavern. He sat and waited for a little while, scouting the place. From where he was, he couldn't see any horses or carts. Maybe there were no visitors to worry about.

Josephine stepped outside and walked around the side to the well, just along from the chicken run. She lowered the bucket into it, drawing water from the well. As she pulled it up and emptied it into the other bucket to take inside, she turned around. Hamish stood behind her. Startled, she dropped the bucket spilling its contents over the floor and vanishing into the dirt.

In front of her stood the man who had taken Gabriel. The man who had killed I father. The one who had been in the tavern with his gang earlier that day ... She froze for a few seconds, staring right into his face.

Covered in blood and with immense pain clearly showing on his face, Hamish moved forward to grab at her, saying as he did, "You're coming with me."

As he grabbed at her dress, Josephine brought up her knee as hard as she could, catching Hamish between his legs. As her knee connected with his balls, he let out a cry and a lungful of air, bending over and falling to both knees. Josephine pushed Hamish to one side and ran as fast as she could inside to grab the already loaded rifle that sat behind the bar. Hamish let out another groan as he clambered to his feet, clutching at his balls. He turned and ran towards the tavern door as best he could. The door sprang open, and Josephine, with the rifle in hand, aimed and fired. The shot whistled past Hamish's head. His hands came up to his face as he continued forward. Within a few feet of Josephine, he rushed upon her with his arms stretched out to grab at her. Josephine brought up the butt of the rifle and smashed into Hamish's face, hitting him straight on the nose. His head knocked back, but the momentum of him running and his weight smashed into her, and they both fell on the floor, with Hamish landing on top. Josephine screamed, grabbing at his face and his hair, clawing, pulling and slapping for her life. Hamish tried desperately to grab her hands while she fought him off and struggled with him on the floor.

As he battled to stop her, grasping both her hands, Hamish attempted to stand up and pull her to her feet. As he did, she brought up her knee and kicked at him again, once more catching him in his balls. But this time, Hamish let go of one hand and punched her full in the face, knocking her unconscious. She stopped struggling and lay on the ground, lifeless. With one hand holding his crotch, Hamish slumped into the nearest chair to catch his breath and take a moment to recover himself …

After a few minutes, Hamish got up from the chair, took a few deep breaths and focused on what he had to do next. Josephine was still unconscious on the floor. Hamish looked around for something to tie her up with. He needed to be able to move her. He decided that he would take her to Jeremiah's house, knowing that Jacob, Tobias and Gabriel would be coming back to the tavern.

After searching around, he found a bedsheet in the back room and ripped it into strips. He used it to tie Josephine's hands and feet. As he did so, she groaned and softly moaned, still unconscious. He left her on the floor and walked to the barn outside. Inside was her father's cart. Knowing that time was against him, he hooked the cart up to his horse and brought it out the front. He went back inside the tavern, picked up Josephine and carried her outside. He placed her in the back of the cart and covered her over with a sheet. He returned inside, found a piece of paper and wrote a note for Jacob to find. He pinned it to the fireplace with a knife from behind the bar.

Hanging up around the room were lamps. He took one, lit it from the fireplace and left the building to attach it to the cart. The day was drawing in. It was still light but overcast. As he secured the lamp, he looked over at the barn door, which was wide open. Inside, he could see the bales of hay. He stood for a moment, then went back inside the tavern. A minute later, he came back out with another lit lamp. Hamish walked over to the barn and threw it inside onto the hay. The oil in the lamp spilt across the hay, lighting it and spreading fire across the bales. He stood and watched as the fire quickly spread up the walls and across the roof. Within seconds, it became out of control. He smiled to himself, turning and getting onto the cart.

Hamish whipped at the horse and trundled out of the small road at the tavern. He made his way over the field, through the trees and then along the back of them so as not to come across Jacob and the other two. His shoulder hurt, and his ear throbbed. He would have to wait until he got to Jeremiah's house before he could tend to his wound properly. As he rode, the cart bumped and shook over the rough ground, which woke Josephine. She opened her eyes and was aware straight away of being tied and under a thick heavy sheet.

She shouted out, "Help me! Stop … stop! Untie me, you bastard!" She kicked with both feet at the side of the cart, banging and shouting.

Hamish stopped the cart, went around to the back and took the sheet off her. "Shut yer noise, missy, or another smack to the head you'll be getting."

Josephine, in total defiance, spat at Hamish and screamed, "You won't get away with this. You will pay for what you have done …"

Hamish grabbed at her dress, ripped a piece from it, then grabbed her face on either side and squeezed it hard, opening her mouth. He shoved the cloth into her mouth and then threw the heavy sheet back over her.

"Make another sound, and I'll kill yer. Make no mistake about it, I'll kill yer …" he said as he got back in the seat and drove the cart back to the house.

# Chapter Sixteen



Tobias grabbed a bottle from behind the bar and took a swig. Jacob sat forward in the chair with his elbows on his knees and his head just hanging down. There was silence in the room. Then Gabriel stood up quickly.

"The barn. The fucking barn!" he said as he ran outside towards it.

Tobias stepped away from the bar and walked towards the door. As he passed by, he tapped Jacob's shoulder. "Come on, my skinny friend, we all need each other's strength right now."

Jacob lifted his head. "That barn's lost to the fire; ain't no saving it now."

Tobias carried on walking to the door. "I know, I know, but as I said, we need each other."

As Tobias walked outside, Gabriel was on his knees, sitting on his legs. He sat still, just watching the flames consume the barn. Tobias stood behind him, a few feet back.

Jacob came outside and went up to where Gabriel sat. He knelt down beside him and said, "Come on, Gabriel, we need to get Josephine back ... And I'm ... I'm sorry for what I said ... Let's get ready and go kill that bastard."

Jacob helped him to his feet and turned to Tobias. "Hamish must of taken her to Jeremiah's already. We missed him on the way back, which means he double backed and took cover in the trees on the other side. We ride now before it gets dark. He already has the advantage, and I ain't leaving her with him the whole night ... Now, get your horses."

===== February 1711, Back to the fight with Sean =====

As Jacob made his way towards the bar, the crowd cheered and patted him on his back as he passed. Not only had they witnessed a truly epic fight between the two men that they had come to watch, but they had also just witnessed an even better one.

Finny sat down with Jacob and put a bottle of brandy on the table. "I remember you now as a wee kid," he said. "You was at the fight with your father when he fought 'Bill The Brawler ...'"

Jacob poured a glass of brandy and nodded. "Yeah, that's right, and what a fight it was"

Finny clapped his hands together. "Ahh, indeed, indeed. Your father was a hard man. One of the hardest to be sure. He could hit like a horse could kick. Knock a man's head off ... He is well, I hope?"

Jacob explained how his father works on the small farm now, keeping himself to himself and working just as hard as he used to fight. Finny listened and waved at the barman for ale to be brought over.

He drank the glass of brandy, wiped his mouth and said, "Oh, bejesus, a pity he gave up when he did. It wasn't his fault, you know."

"What wasn't his fault??" Jacob asked with a confused look.

"The fight. The last fight he had," Finny said.

Jacob just sat there, with no clue what he was talking about and shrugged his shoulders ... The bar was filled with men drinking and talking. Tobias grabbed at the large jug of ale and filled his glass.

"What happened in this fight then???" he said as he swigged the ale.

Finny looked at both men. "He never told you ..." he said. "Well, I'm sorry, lad, but I think I may have said something out of turn here. Perhaps it's best that your father tells you ..."

Jacob sat up in his chair and leaned forwards. "No, I think it's best you continue. You can't leave a story half-told, now, can you?"

Tobias shook his head slowly, drank the ale and said, "Can't be doing that, old man. You have our interest now."

"Well, I guess it's common knowledge to those who were there," said Finny. "You see, his last fight ended badly. Not for him, but for the other man. Brutal, it was …"

Jacob hung on his every word. "Yeah … and????"

"Well, he hit the other man so hard - I forget his name now … Anyhow, he went down and stayed down …"

Jacob, still a bit confused with what Finny was saying, said, "Right … How long for??"

Finny replied, "Well, for good. As in never getting up again …"

Jacob sat back in his chair. "You mean … dead??"

Finny nodded. "Well, I hope he was dead; they fucking buried him …"

Tobias laughed out loud at what he had just said, and so did Finny. Jacob just sat there.

"Ah, come now, lad, it happens sometimes," Finny said. "Part of the game. Nobody's fault. It's a fight, not a game of cards …"

Jacob didn't much care that a fighter was killed; it was that his father hadn't told him. He sat and thought how much that must have weighed upon Henry. He hated fighting and only did it to earn extra coin. The fact that Henry had killed a man in a fight must have sat terribly within him. It made sense now why Henry had never fought again. There were only a few fights that Jacob had not seen of his father's, and this one was one of them.

Another jug of ale was put on the table.

"This is from that gentleman over there," the barman said and pointed to the bar.

Standing at the bar with his glass raised was a smartly dressed man.

Finny looked over at the man and then raised a glass back. He turned to Jacob and said, "Well, my lad, that there is Mr Wells. A wealthy man who has a few of the best fighters around in his pocket. And it's safe to say that he has noticed you …"

Jacob acknowledged Mr Wells and then turned to discuss matters with Finny. He told Finny that he had other interests that would make him coin but that he would definitely be interested in making some more whenever the time arose with any fights that he could match up for him. He told Finny that whenever he was in the area, he would drop in to see if any matches could be made. Finny agreed.

"I shall look forward to seeing you again, young Jacob. And if any come up, I will leave a message at the tavern you spoke of."

With that, Jacob stood up, shook Finny's hand and left the inn. On his way out, Barny extended his hand.

"That was something else to see, young man," he said.

Jacob shook his hand and said, "Thank you, you fought well yourself. If your jaw hadn't of broken so early on, I think you would have beaten him as well. It was a pleasure watching you fight."

Barny nodded. "Likewise."

Dupree and Brendan got back in the cart and made their way onto the road, with Jacob and Tobias behind them.

"You sure can fight, my skinny friend," Tobias said as both horses trotted along the road.

"Well, I told you we would see, didn't I, big man?"

Tobias, with a big grin on his face, said, "You certainly did. But tell me … would you have won against a fresher man? A man who hadn't just had a fight before??"

"Well, he seemed fresh enough to throw as many punches as he did now, didn't he?" Jacob answered. "And correct me if I'm wrong, big man, but not a single blow landed on me."

Tobias laughed and said, "I'm not surprised … a man as old as that. And anyway, next time, don't fight for free. I thought the idea was to make money from it."

Jacob shook his head. "Well, I didn't expect him to launch at me like he did. I thought that he would accept my challenge and arrange a date to fight."

"Oh, he accepted it, alright," said Tobias. "Accepted it and acted on it."

"Yeah, well, so did I," Jacob said. "Anyway, I proved something more valuable to myself. I can fight and fight well. And soon enough, word will get around, and I should have all sorts stepping up to try and beat me. That's where the money will start to roll in."

All four men made their way back to Brendan's big house. It was now late in the afternoon. When they reached the house, they were met by the three dogs, barking and running alongside, weaving in and out of the cart and horses.

"You are more than welcome to stay here again, gentlemen, if you have nowhere else to be," Brendan said as they all dismounted.

Tobias tethered his horse and said, "Well, I could definitely do that. Best bed I've ever slept in. Slept like a baby."

Jacob and Dupree agreed, and so all three stayed the night.

In the morning, Brendan gave them the address of a man in London who would help them and introduce them to the right merchants to help build up their business. 'John Crawford' was his name, and he had the right connections to be able to sell to the right people in the right places. Brendan had known John for many years and made many deals with him. He handed Jacob a letter to give to John that explained his wishes to help them.

"Just give him this letter, and he will help you all in every way he can," Brendan explained. "John is a very good and old friend of mine. He can get you the best prices and also the best places to sell. Plus, the best people to meet."

Jacob took the letter and then handed it to Dupree.

"You best hold onto this; after all, you're the one with all the experience and that French flair for selling."

All three men said their goodbyes to Brendan, shook his hand, left the big house and made their way up the track and onto the road. Brendan's three dogs ran alongside them until they heard a long whistle from Brendan. They then turned and ran back.

Tobias and Jacob rode either side of the cart. As the wheels trundled along, they all spoke of what the future may hold. It would take a couple of days to reach London, and they would have to stop along the way.

As the hours passed and the light began to fade, Dupree suggested that they set up camp in a clump of trees that lay up ahead. Night would be upon them very shortly, and they needed to rest the horses for the long journey to London.

# Chapter Seventeen



London was a bustling city full of tall buildings and cobbled streets. It had houses that stood next to each other, with rooms stacked on top of each other. A vibrant and alive place to be, people were cramped together. They were thrown in with each other from all walks of life, from the very poor to the rich. At the heart of it was where they were to find John Crawford - in the East end.

As the three men approached the East end of London, two things were made apparent to them: the noise and the smell … The crowds were huge – there were people everywhere, on every street. Houses were three stories high, with rooms for rent in each of them. People were selling anything they could get their hands on. There were drunks pissing wherever they liked and women selling themselves for the pleasure of men. Children, dogs, pickpockets, and women selling flowers, bread, meat: whatever they could sell, they did.

Jacob, Tobias and Dupree had never seen anything like it before. The rich and the poor were mixed in together. All around, new buildings were being built. London was indeed a hub of new and exciting things.

As they made their way through the muddy, dirty streets and through the crowds of people bustling and jostling their way along, Tobias stopped and asked for directions to the address of where John Crawford lived in Spitalfields. They continued on until they reached a tall house along a row of near-identical tall houses. Jacob knocked on the door of the address, and a woman answered.

"Yes, may I help you?" she said.

Holding the letter in his hand, Jacob said, "We are looking for a Mr Crawford. John Crawford."

"And who shall I say is calling?" the woman answered.

Jacob looked around at the other two men and said, "Well, we are here on behalf of Mr Brendan Little. We have this here letter for him to read."

The woman asked them to wait at the door and then closed it as she went inside.

A few minutes later, a man opened the door, a smartly-dressed, elderly-looking gentleman, and said, "My housekeeper mentioned the name Brendan Little; I have not heard that name for a long time. You have a letter from him?"

Jacob handed the letter to John and said, "Yes, sir. Brendan has asked us to give this to you for you to read in the hope that you can be of assistance to us."

John took the letter, opened it pulled a pair of spectacles out of his breast pocket, and began to read it. After reading the letter, he folded it and looked at all three men standing at his door.

"Well, I haven't seen or heard from Brendan in many years, but the letter says that you are good friends of his, so you had better come inside so that we can talk."

They went inside, and John led them to his sitting room.

"Please, sit. Can I offer you gentlemen a drop of the good stuff?"

Everyone agreed, and as they took their glasses, John sat down and said, "Well, you seem to know my name, but I do not know yours."

Jacob introduced himself and the other two and said, "It's a pleasure to meet you, John."

They all clinked each other's glasses, and John sat back in his chair.

"Well, now, gentlemen, Brendan mentions in the letter that you are all in business with each other and that you require my help. Or, to put it another way - that I point you all in the right direction."

Dupree sat forward, "Oui, monsieur, we are recently partners. I myself 'av been trading for a number of years, but not in London. Only in ze other side of Chelmsford, mainly local markets."

"That's right," said Jacob. "But we would like to get a taste of a better life. And Brendan has assured us that you could help."

"Well, I can certainly introduce you to certain merchants and traders to get you better prices. Then it would be down to your good selves to make a go of it. And there is no reason you can't. The world is a huge place, and trade is even bigger. Here at the port of London, we have ships from all over, bringing goods of all sorts. Tea from China, textiles from India, sugar from Jamaica, spices, fruit, tobacco, lumber, rum, coffee … the list goes on and on."

Tobias rubbed his hands together. "So, when do we start?"

"Not tonight," John said. "But if you come back in the morning, we can start to make you some new friends to help you."

John stood up and held out his hand. "Well, it's a pleasure to meet you, gentlemen, but if you excuse me, I have other matters that concern me."

Jacob and the other two men shook his hand, thanked him for his time and walked to the front door.

"So, gentlemen, if you require somewhere to stay, down the road, along from Spitalfields market, there you will find lodgings. Until the morning, then."

Jacob, Tobias and Dupree said goodbye and stood by the horses.

"Vell, zat went rather vell, no?" said Dupree as he climbed up into the cart.

Tobias leant on the side of the cart, looking down the road towards the market. "Well, we should find some lodgings for the night and then see what London has to offer. We passed an inn back there, and I'm gasping."

Jacob put his foot in the stirrup, swung his leg over and sat in the saddle. "Sounds good to me, big man. Just past the market, John said. So let's go have a look."

All three men rode down towards the market. They stopped outside a sign that read, 'Rooms for Rent – half a crown a week.'

Dupree pointed at the sign. "Ere, zis looks promising. All we need eez a bed to rest our eddz."

Jacob nodded. "Yes, that will do. It's going to take us a week or two to find our feet in London."

Tobias jumped off his horse and hitched it to Dupree's cart. "Well, let's get inside and get a room each. Then we will head straight over to that inn up the road."


Later that evening, they walked to the inn up the road. Outside, a man stood pissing against the wall. Tobias walked straight past him and into the inn. There were about a dozen people sitting and drinking. A man sat with a woman on his lap, kissing her while fondling a second woman in the chair next to him. It was loud with laughter and people talking and drinking.

Tobias went up to the bar and told the barmaid, "A bottle of brandy and three glasses."

The barmaid, a large woman with a full bosom, said, "We ain't got none, my dear, fresh out. But we 'av rum and beer an' cider. We also 'av wine, but you don't look the type to be sipping on that."

Tobias stood tall, placed both hands on the bar a shoulders width apart and said, "Right, my dear, then I guess it's a round of all three."

"All three?" the barmaid replied.

Tobias leaned forward. "That's right; we will start with the beer. Three tankards of your finest."

"It certainly ain't fine, but it does the job," she said.

Tobias smiled. "Sorry I didn't get your name …"

The barmaid bent down, produced three tankards and began to fill them with beer. "That's probably coz I never gave it. Wot's your name?"

Tobias leant on the bar with his elbows, his face inches from hers. "Tobias," he said.

"Nice to meet yer, Tobias. The name's Maggie."

As she filled the second tankard, Tobias grabbed the first and drank all the contents, tipping back his head and then placing the empty vessel back onto the bar.

Without looking and now filling the third, Maggie said, "Thirsty was yer?" Then she looked up and winked at him.

Tobias wiped the froth from his mouth, winked at her and said, "Always, my dear, always."

Jacob came beside Tobias. "We have grabbed a table in the corner," he said and pointed to where Dupree sat.

Tobias put an arm around Jacob's shoulder and pulled him into his chest. "Jacob, this is Maggie … Maggie, this is my good friend Jacob."

Maggie nodded and said, "It's a pleasure," as she put the third tankard onto the bar.

Jacob, in turn, grabbed the two beers, nodded back and said, "The pleasure's all mine, Maggie."

Maggie smiled as Jacob walked over to the table and then asked Tobias, "So, what's next?"

With a big grin, Tobias took her hand, kissed it and then said, "Well, who knows …? A dance?"

Maggie pulled back her hand from his. "I meant to drink …"

Tobias stood straight up again, picked up the tankard and said, "Fill it with cider."

Dupree took the beer, drank a mouthful and then gestured towards the bar with his head. "Eet doesn't take eem long, does eet?"

Jacob turned his head to see Tobias laughing and joking and flirting for all his worth with the barmaid. "No, not at all. The man is an animal. He has the sexual appetite of an army of men."

"Oui, oui," said Dupree. "More zan any Frenchman I 'av ever known, and we are famous for eet."

As the two of them sat and talked and Tobias flirted with Maggie, the tavern got fuller and louder. Music started to play, and people began to sing and dance and drink ... and sing and dance and drink.

Tobias had given Maggie a bag of coins and had told her to let him know when it had run out. By this time, he had joined the other two at the table. The atmosphere was joyous with all around having a good time.

The door to the tavern opened, and in walked a large black man. His frame was as big as Tobias'. Across his chest, he wore two gun belts that crossed each other, and placed within them were four pistols. Upon his head, he wore a red bandana. He walked straight to the bar; his eyes fixed only upon it. Some of the people noticed him enter, and their eyes follow–d him. But undeterred from their drinking, no real attention was paid to him by anyone - except for Tobias. He couldn't take his eyes off the man. There was something about the man that caught Tobias' attention.

While cleaning out some of the tankards with a cloth, Maggie asked him, "What can I get yer?"

The man answered in a soft, quiet voice. "Rum ... A bottle, if you be so kind."

Maggie placed a glass in front of him and a bottle of rum. She filled the glass and then left the bottle next to it. The music was loud, and the people even louder. They danced and drank. Any toils or troubles they may have had were lost for the evening. A good time was being had by all.

Suddenly, the door swung open, and four men barged their way in.

"OI! YOU!" one of the men said, with his hand pointing towards the large black man. "Ain't no pirates allowed round 'ere ..."

The black man just stood dead still at the bar. Without turning around, he took the glass, drank its contents, and then filled it again.

"OI! I'm talking to you, negro. Are you deaf ...? I said, ain't no pirates allowed round 'ere."

The four men were watchmen hired by local rich merchants who owned warehouses along the waterfront at the docks. Whilst patrolling, one of the men had gotten his hands on a crate of rum, and all four men had been drinking instead of performing their duties. They had seen the large black man and had followed him into the tavern where he now sat. Combined with a misplaced air of authority and the consumed intoxicating rum, they had all got a drunken idea of hounding a 'pirate.'

The black man drank the glass of rum and, with his back to the four drunk watchmen, said, "Do yourselves a favour. Go about your duties, and leave me well alone ..."

The men turned and looked at each other, smiling.

A second man stepped forward. "Listen 'ere, don't you-"

The black man spun around, stepping away from the bar. "Don't what???" he said aggressively.

As he did, the watchmen could see the four pistols hanging from his chest. And now, up close, they could see the actual size of him.

Tobias stood up from the table, walked to the bar and stood next to the black man. He filled his glass with the man's bottle of rum, leant on the bar to one side and drank it down in one swig. Then, turning the glass in his hand, Tobias said to the watchmen, "I think you should do as he says, gentlemen. Four against one isn't a fair fight. But now, there's two. So be good little men, walk out that door and keep on walking ..."

The large black man looked at Tobias and said, "I don't need anybody's help. Especially with these fools."

Dupree sat uneasily in his chair and whispered to Jacob, "Should we do something?"

Jacob, picking dirt out from under his fingernail, looked around the room and said, "I think they can deal with it..."

The first watchman who spoke pulled a knife from under his coat and held it out. "I don't scare that easy," he said, waving the knife as he spoke.

As soon as he did so, Jacob, with fast reflexes, bolted out of his chair, grabbed the man's arm, pulled it back behind him and landed a clean blow to his chin, knocking him to the floor. In that split second, the other three watchmen froze. Tobias and the large black man did not and rushed over to them. Tobias hit one of the men, sending him flying into a table and chairs, knocking the bottles and glasses up into the air and onto the floor.

The black man hit one with such force that he was knocked out before he hit the floor. And then, as that one hit the floor, he punched the third watchman, knocking him out through the door and onto the street. He then grabbed the man that Jacob had hit. He lifted him clean off the floor, headbutted him full in the face, and then threw him out of the door. Tobias then picked up the man he had hit and threw him out onto the street. Jacob grabbed the fourth man by his feet and dragged him outside.

Tobias held out his hand to the black man and said, "I'm Tobias."

Shaking his hand, the man said, "They call me Solomon."

Jacob introduced himself, shook Solomon's hand and said, "Don't think I've ever met a pirate before."

Solomon rolled his eyes. "Well, you have now."

Tobias held out a glass of rum and gave it to Solomon. "So, how do you become a pirate then?"

Solomon swigged the rum and began to explain …

# Chapter Eighteen



Solomon was born in Whitechapel. The son of a servant woman whose own parents had worked on an English plantation and had been given their freedom. Solomon's mother had become pregnant and ran away to the East end of London to have her child. When Solomon was a small child, his mother had taken work wherever she could. Mostly this was as a servant but also as a washerwoman, weaver and dyer – anything she could do to feed her and her son.

As Solomon grew older, he grew bigger – much bigger than most boys his own age. At fourteen, he stood six feet tall. This gave him the look of being much older. Like most boys his age, he had his fair share of fights and getting into mischief, but nothing could have prepared him for what was about to happen …

England was at war with Spain and France. A war at sea. Trade to and from the New World was a most profitable business. The Royal Navy was not only fighting for trade routes across the oceans with Spain and France but also struggling with the constant high sea robberies by pirates.

The Royal Navy was vast in men. Many had simply volunteered for King and country, while others had been 'press ganged' into joining. The high seas of trading goods from all over was indeed a very lucrative business. Spain, who had an alliance with France, had taken over the waters and, with that, trade. So, England was at war.

That very fateful day had come to Solomon in the form of Soldiers of the Royal Navy. He was walking along the muddy streets of London, along with many others, when he suddenly found himself being ushered, quite violently, along with other men, to join the Royal Navy. Before he even knew what was happening to him, he was bundled along, taken down to the docks and forced to board a large 'sloop' ship. Here, he would be introduced to a life at sea, fighting for the King's Navy.

Three years had passed by, and Solomon, after many battles with the Spanish and French, had found himself in a sinking ship. After quite a lengthy battle, he found himself in the sunken ship's 'jolly boat' along with six other men. The only survivors from the combat, they found themselves drifting on the Atlantic ocean. One of the men was badly injured from a long, deep gash. Solomon had ripped part of his shirt and wrapped the wound tight to try and stop the bleeding.

As they drifted, the ship that had been their home for the six months that they were at sea was but a wreck, ablaze and defenceless against the power of the sea, sinking as it slowly took on water. In the distance, they could see the Spanish galleon that had set upon them hours before. Now he and the other men were set adrift and at the mercy of the ocean.

After a while had passed, the sea had taken them and the jolly boat far from their ship. The smoke could still be seen high into the sky, but the voluminous waves obscured the line of sight of the burning ship. All the men were wounded in some way or another with cuts and bruises. Some were worse than others, but none as bad as the young lad, James, with the deep gash on his thigh. The blood was now soaking the ripped piece of shirt that Solomon had wrapped it in. The sea had become rough, and the small boat was taking quite a battering. This made the poor lad even more uncomfortable than the rest.

The pain was becoming unbearable, and his moans and groans showed this to the rest of the men. Solomon took off his shirt and ripped more strips of cloth from it. Every now and again, he would redress James' wound. But he knew from experience that the cut was too deep and that no matter how tightly he wrapped it, the young lad was losing too much blood. Among the men was a very experienced sailor.

Solomon turned to him and said, "Where do you think we are?"

The older man looked towards the horizon and answered, "Where we are is not of concern. Where we will be is … and right now, it's looking like we are heading towards the bottom of the ocean."

Solomon tied the cloth off around James' thigh and then said, "Why do you say that? There must be a hundred ships out there. One must come upon us."

The older man, William, known as Will, pointed out to sea. "Aye, laddie. Do yer see any? We are in a jolly boat. Small. Your average size ship in these waters won't even see us, even if we see them."

Solomon looked out to the vast emptiness of the sea and then back at the men who were all looking near done - battered and bruised. The situation they found themselves in did not look good at all. But Solomon had faith in God. And that was all he had. A belief that he would not die. Not this day. Not here, at sea.

"You can think what you want, old man; God will save us."

Will slowly turned his head and looked at Solomon. "God has nothing to do with it, boy. The sea is her own mistress … that you can be sure of."


They had drifted by the hands of the sea all night. When the morning came, Solomon was shaken awake by Will.

"Wake up, boy … Wake up."

Solomon blinked heavy and rubbed at his tired eyes to open them. "What is it?" he asked.

Will shook his arm with his right arm while pointing out to sea with his left. "There, look …"

Solomon sat up and looked out to where Will pointed. His eyes blurred from the sleep and the burning sun. He rubbed his eyes again. "Where??? Where am I looking??"

Will grabbed Solomon's hand and pointed it out. "There …"

Solomon furrowed his eyebrows and brought his hand up to his eyes to block out the bright sun.

Blinking and squinting, he looked to where Will pointed … There he could see … land!!!

In the far distance was land. Solomon stood up and placed both hands over his eyebrows to get a better look. "It's land; it's bloody land!"

The small boat bobbed up and down, and as it did, the sight of land disappeared and then appeared again. Will shook at the other men who woke to look at the distant sight of land. Solomon went to James and shook his arm. There was no response. He shook him again.

"James … James," he said as he shook him. Solomon grabbed at the young lad's face and turned it towards himself. And felt the coldness of his skin.

James was dead. He had lost too much blood during the night and had died. Solomon bowed his head, placed one hand on the boy's chest, and then covered his face with the half of his shirt that he had not ripped into strips.

As the rest of the small crew whooped and hollered at the sight of land, Will turned to see Solomon knelt down next to James' dead body.

He moved next to him, placed a hand on Solomon's shoulder and said, "I'm sorry, lad, I truly am. He gave his life for the King. He fought bravely and died from his wounds. He deserves a sailor's send-off, so we must let the sea have him."

Solomon nodded in agreement. He bound together James' hands and feet and then tied the covering over his face, tight to his head. He gently lifted his body up to the side of the boat and said, "May God take your hand and lead you to paradise." Then he let him go overboard.

The body went into the water, and within minutes, the sea had taken him down into the depths below …

The current of the sea steered the small boat in the general direction of the land. For a few moments, all were quiet. The thought of what had just happened weighed heavily in their minds.

Solomon sat at the front of the boat, looking towards the land, which seemed to be getting nearer by the minute.

"So, where do you think it could be?" asked Solomon.

Will scratched his head and then his chin. "If I were to take a guess … I'd say more likely to be an island of the West Indies … The Caribbean."

One of the men suddenly spoke out. "Is that a …?"

Solomon turned to where the man pointed, and the man said it again. "It is … It's a ship … Look!!!!"

As the sea swelled and rose, Solomon could see in the distance that there was a ship. He couldn't tell how big it was but could just make out it had many sails, so it was of considerable size. Maybe a small sloop. As the sea swelled again, the ship went from his sight and then appeared again. This time closer. A lot closer.

Will stood up and grabbed onto Solomon's arm. "She be going some speed, laddie."

Will cupped his hands over his eyes for a better look. The ship got closer and closer until Will could make out the sails and two masts. "She be a schooner, lad."

The men clapped and cheered.

"Thank the Lord above," one of them said.

"We are saved," said another.

Solomon clapped his hands together. "I told you so, old man," he said. "I told you that we would not be dying out here."

Will, still with his hands cupped, mumbled to himself. "No, no, no," he said under his breath. "Is that-? I can't quite make it out … Is that flag …?"

Solomon was smiling along with the rest of the crew. "What are you saying, Will?? Speak up, man!"

Will shuffled along the length of the small boat. The swell of the sea was rising up and down.

"No, it can't be …" he said again.

The ship now came into full view. Its size could now be determined. The sails were catching the wind, and the sun's rays caught something from the ship - a flash of light glinting at them.

Will knew what that glint was. A spyglass, looking at them. And now he could see properly.

"By Christ! It is … it's a, a …"

Solomon grabbed at Will's shoulder. "What is it, man? Wha-?"

It was then that they could all see the flag flapping high atop the mast. Their blood ran cold…

It was a skull and crossbones!!!!!!!!!!!!!!

# Chapter Nineteen

===== February 1711, London =====

Tobias sat for a few seconds as Solomon poured out a glass of brandy and slowly lifted it to his lips, staring through the bottom of the glass before putting it to his lips and gulping down the contents.

"So …?"

Solomon rolled the small glass around in his fingers, looking into it, lost in his thoughts.

"So what?" he said.

Tobias looked at Jacob and Dupree with his hands out, palms turned up, then back to Solomon.

"So, what happened next?" Tobias asked.

Solomon stood back from the bar, pulled out some coins from his purse and dropped them onto the bar. "That's for the drinks, Maggie, and sorry for the trouble."

He then turned to the three men who had been hanging on his every word for the last ten minutes and said, "Well, that's a story for another time."

He held out his hand and shook Tobias'.

"I thank you for stepping in to help against those fools; most would not. But I have a few things to be getting on with and so must bid you all a farewell for now. If there is anything that I can help you with, just ask. I will be in London for a few days."

Jacob shook his hand and said, "No need to thank us, but there is something you can do for us. We are in London on business as merchants, and maybe you could steer us in the right direction."

Solomon smiled and leaned forward towards Jacob's face. "I'm a pirate. Stolen booty is my living. If you have the coin, then I can get you the goods. Meet me down at the docks in the morning, and we can talk about making money."

Jacob agreed, and Solomon left the inn. Tobias laughed at him.

"Why the laughing?" asked Jacob.

"Because you don't miss a trick, do you?"

Jacob sat back down at the table with Dupree. "Opportunities, big man ... opportunities. Grab 'em when you can."

Tobias grabbed the bottle and sat at the table. "Oh, I agree, my skinny friend," he said as he sat, looking back to where Maggie was busy behind the bar. "Which is why I'm gonna be in her bed by the end of the night."

Jacob shook his head, as did Dupree. "And what makes you so sure of that, then, big man?"

Tobias smiled at Maggie as he caught her eye, and she smiled back. "It's me charm, ain't it? Women love me, and I love them ... Well, for a night anyways." Tobias banged his fist on the table and let out a loud laugh.

Jacob stood up, drank the brandy, and said, "Well, you enjoy yourself, big man. I'm going to go feed the horses."

Dupree and Jacob left together, and Tobias sat at the table staring at Maggie and smiling as she smiled back ...

The next morning, Jacob woke and just lay there in bed. From the second he opened his eyes, his mind was already thinking things over. Here, in this moment, he lay in a room in London. So much had happened in such a short time. His mind went over everything. From the row with his father to the chance meeting of Tobias and

Josephine. He lay there, alone in the bed, staring at the ceiling of the room. The stench from the River Thames filled his nose.

How quickly his life had turned around. He thought of where he would be right at this moment had he not sat there in the tavern that day. He knew he wouldn't be in the room at this moment. The thoughts swirled around in his head. From Tobias to Jeremiah to Dupree. Meeting Brendan and John Crawford. Leading him here, to London, to this room. And now, on this very morning, in this busy, bustling city, he was to go and meet Solomon - a pirate … As Jacob lay there, thinking of it all, it seemed a million miles away from the morning with his father, but also like it had only just happened.

He sat up in bed, his back against the wooden wall. He could already hear the sounds of the street down below. People were bustling about. London was alive all day and all night. It didn't stop. His head spun for a few seconds. His mind raced. He brought his hands up to his face and just sat there covering it. His ears were picking up on all sorts of sounds from beyond the window. In the distance, he could hear the shriek of seagulls. The docks brought the ships and, in turn, brought seagulls - hundreds of them.

As he sat in bed, he could hear the fast pace of life going by. Tobias was always astounded by the fact that he took opportunities as soon as they presented themselves to him. But Jacob knew he had to. Life went by fast. The row that he had with his father, Henry, was for this very reason. Henry's life was the same as it had been from when Jacob remembered as a small boy to now. Nothing had changed. The same life, the same daily routines. Day in, day out. Jacob had watched this his whole life. That was not the life for him. Meeting Tobias had presented an opportunity, and he had taken it. And now, here in this room in London, was where it had taken him.

He moved his hands from his face, rubbed the sleep from his eyes and got up and dressed. He filled the basin on the small table by the window with water from the jug and splashed his face.

At that moment, there was a knock at his door. As he dried his face with the sleeve of his shirt, he said, "It's open."

The door opened, and Dupree's head came from behind it. "Morning, Jacob. Zee sun is shining, and I have a good feeling today."

Jacob patted his face dry with his arm. "You do? Well, let's hope so. Today we meet with Solomon. Do you realise, Dupree, that we have gone from meeting Brendan to John to Solomon? All within a few weeks."

Dupree pushed the door wide open and stepped inside the room. "Oui, oui …. eet eez good, no …? Zee start of something great. I can feel eet in my bones. You must feel eet too??"

Jacob nodded his head, tapped Dupree's arm, smiled and said, "I do, I really do …"

"Zen zat eez good. Now let us get out of 'ere and find zat brute, Tobias."

"Well," said Jacob, "if he did what he intended to do, then it won't be hard. Let's go over to Maggie's inn."


Tobias was asleep. As he slept, he stirred and had a feeling of being touched. Lying flat on his back, he turned to be on his side. He felt it again. He opened both eyes, blinked a few times and then closed them again. He felt it again, on his back and neck. He opened his eyes again, this time fully and turned his head to look around. There he saw Maggie, naked and kissing him on his neck and down his back. The effects of the brandy and ale had worn off, leaving him with little memory and a sore head. He turned over onto his back, opening and shutting his eyes fast, trying to wake himself up. His chest was being kissed as Maggie kissed up into his neck and onto his lips. Now he was awake …

He grabbed Maggie's hips and lifted her body up, so she sat straddled onto him. She let out a gasp and threw her head back as she felt him deep inside her. She moved her hips backwards and forwards and began to ride him, getting faster and harder until she shrieked with pleasure …

BANG, BANG, BANG.

Jacob and Dupree were at the door of the inn.

"Zey are probably still asleep," said Dupree.

BANG, BANG.

Jacob knocked on the door again. "If I know him, he ain't sleeping, Dupree …"

Maggie, while still riding Tobias, put her hands on his chest and said, "Stop! There's someone at the door."

Tobias grabbed her by her hips and thrust deep and hard. "Fuck the door; they can wait," he said.

Maggie dug her fingers into his thick-haired chest and moaned and groaned until …


BANG, BANG!!!!

Tobias eventually leaned out of the window to see Jacob knocking on the door.

"Oi…!" he shouted. "I'm up! I'm up. Give me a second."

Tobias came away from the window and walked towards the door, passing the bed where Maggie lay face down, her hair strewn across her face. He slapped her arse as he passed and said, "You stay there; I'll get the door."

Jacob and Dupree stood outside. The door opened, and Tobias stood there naked.

"Fuck me, Tobias! I didn't need to see that," said Jacob.

Tobias stood there scratching the back of his head, then turned and waved the two men to come inside, saying, "You might not, but she did …"

Dupree shook his head and mumbled to Jacob, "Ee eez truly a beast …"

Tobias walked towards the stairs, pointed to the bar and said, "Help yourself; I'm gonna put some clothes on." He then walked upstairs.

A few minutes later, Tobias returned with his trousers on and his boots and shirt held in his hands. He pulled out a chair and sat down, pulling on his boots.

"Fuck me … I've a mouth as dry as a summer field."

Jacob stood at the bar, grabbed a bottle and placed it in front of Tobias. "Well, take a swig from that, and hurry up and get dressed. We have got to find Solomon this morning."

Tobias took a long swig from the bottle and then wiped his mouth with his bare arm. "Ahhhh, that's better," he said.

He stood up from the chair, put on his shirt and said, "Right, I'm ready. So, where are we looking then??"

Jacob and Dupree made their way to the door of the inn, and Jacob said, "Well, he told us last night to meet him at the docks. So, I guess that's where."

Tobias, still looking worse for wear, shuffled behind him as they walked out onto the street. "Right then, the docks it is."

The three men walked along the street, passing people everywhere. The noise was loud as people went about their day. Street sellers, market traders, small children running and playing, dogs running and shitting everywhere. They walked down past the market and onto the road that led down towards the docks. The smell of the sea was in the air, along with the smell of shit. London was indeed a dirty place. They made their way to the River Thames and down onto the docks. Ships of all sizes were stretched out across the river. The docks were laden with goods of all proportions: food, textiles, spices, cloth, animals, barrels of rum, brandy, wine, furs, tea, coffee, sugar and all sorts.

As Jacob looked around at everything, he could see the seagulls. Long before you saw them, you could hear them and that sound they made. Whenever you heard it, the sea was close by.

As they wandered along the side of the docks, taking in all its glory, smells and colours, looking out for Solomon, a loud voice echoed out.

"Ahoy there."

From a small sloop ship anchored just off from the docks, they saw Solomon at the bow holding a rope from the rigging, standing on the side of the rail.

"Ahoy there, lads," he sounded out again.

Tobias stopped and turned to see him and stopped the other two to look.

Solomon jumped down from the rail with the rope in his hands and slid down the rope onto the wooden floor of the dockside. "So you have found me then," he said.

All four men shook hands, and Solomon turned towards his ship with a hand outstretched and said, "Welcome to my home …"

Tobias looked at the sloop and, recalling stories he had heard of pirates, said, "I thought it would be bigger …"

Solomon laughed out loud. "It's big enough for me and my crew, and she is fast … And I can be upon large ships quickly. Quick enough to board them and get my fill of booty."

Jacob stepped forward, slapped Tobias on his back and said, "And that's what matters now, don't it, Tobias?"

Tobias felt awkward that he had said something out of turn. "I didn't mean no disrespect, Solomon. I just had a bigger picture in my head, is all," he said.

Solomon smiled, placed a hand on Tobias' shoulder and said, "None taken, big man … None taken."

Solomon invited them to come aboard so that they could talk. They spoke about taking all the stolen goods that Solomon could find for a fair price. The three men had left the house of Brendan the week before with a letter to give to the contact, John Crawford. However, like everything that had happened since they had all met, things changed. Who could have known that they would meet a real-life pirate? This had now changed the path that they had come to London for.

Dupree knew that they couldn't just rely on Solomon for the goods that they needed to build up their partnership. But meeting him had certainly added another avenue for them. Jacob was the one out of them all that grabbed at every and any opportunity that would come their way. He truly believed that life was a journey but that most people just carried on with their daily work and chores. Because of that, they missed or didn't even look to see those opportunities. Jacob would never be one of those people. And now, within a day of coming to London to meet a man who could introduce them to other contacts in the merchant world, they had come across a pirate ... They could have gone to any one of the many inns and taverns that people in London frequented, but the one they walked into was the introduction to Solomon.

Jacob and Tobias had spoken before about how this path they walked kept changing. Was it meant to be? Was it in God's hands? Life was going fast for them. And Jacob knew in his heart and his soul that as long as he kept moving forward and met any and everything head-on, he would have the life that he had always dreamed of. He would have success and wealth and be the man that his father wasn't.

Solomon spoke of the trade ships that he stole from. He explained that the goods on them were different most of the time and that the oceans were full of these ships. They all knew of the peril of encountering a pirate ship, as this was just a part of the trade routes, as were pirate hunters. There were also huge galleon gunships that protected the vessels that carried the most expensive goods. Pirates with large gunships and crews were more than capable of entering a fight with these galleons to retrieve such a prize, and a lot of them would be blown to bits and end up at the bottom of the ocean. Solomon, even though still known as a pirate, wasn't of the magnitude as legendary pirate captains such as Henry Jennings,

Benjamin Hornigold, or the infamous Edward Teach, better known as 'Black Beard.'

He used this as an advantage by going after smaller ships. His ship was fast and needed to be. The larger pirate ships never entertained the smaller trade ships, so that is where Solomon plied his trade and plundered the booty. He could earn a very handsome wage by keeping himself and his crew busy with the smaller ships.

Solomon told Jacob, Tobias and Dupree that he would be at sea for about two weeks at a time and that he would be leaving in a few hours. They had all agreed to meet again at the docks, and the difference in time could be a couple of days on either side of two weeks. All four men agreed, shook hands and parted ways …

# Chapter Twenty



===== October 1713, Back to Jeremiah's house and
Josephine's kidnapping =====

Hamish turned the cart into the dirt track that led down to Jeremiah's house; the muffled sounds of Josephine's gagged mouth could just be heard over the trundling of the wheels. He pulled up halfway down the track, the horse snorting and chewing at the bit as it stopped. Hamish stood up on the cart, reins in his hand, and scouted the front of the house for any signs of Jacob, Tobias and Gabriel. He couldn't see anyone. It was quiet, and there seemed to be no one around. Even Josephine's muffled sounds had ceased. This was due to the cart stopping as Josephine was also listening for any voices or sounds.

Hamish jumped off the cart and stood, patting the horse, calming it to be quiet. He walked towards the house, scanning the front and sides as he did. Josephine lay perfectly still as she heard Hamish walking away. As her eyes flickered and blinked, she tried to control her breathing and bring her heartbeat down so that she could listen and hear any sounds. Hamish walked to the front of the house and stopped. He looked through the windows for any signs. After a second or two, he made his way down the side of the house towards the back door.

Josephine lay still, bound, gagged and scared out of her mind, not knowing what was happening. But she controlled her breath until her heartbeat was slower, and she was calmer. Her eyes blinked fast as the discomfort of the gag in her mouth made them water. Her mind raced as she concentrated hard, listening out for Hamish. She thought for a moment - could this be a chance for her to escape?

She tried to loosen the bindings on her hands and feet, twisting and pulling at them. They were too tight; she couldn't free herself ...

Hamish was now at the back door, which remained open. The horses of two of his dead men were still tethered. They snorted and whinnied as he approached the door. He stopped at the entrance, his eyes wide open, listening. Hamish drew his pistol and softly walked into the kitchen. He could see the study door open. As he walked towards it, the floor creaked underneath his foot. He stopped dead in his tracks and held his breath for a second. There was no sound ... He carried on forward towards the study door and walked through it. As he did, his eyes were met with the carnage that lay before him. There, slumped with his head back over the chair, looking up to the ceiling, was Jeremiah. The wall behind where his body sat was covered in blood and pieces of brain.

Hamish's face contorted, and he squinted at the sight. On the floor to his right lay Collins, a pool of blood around his body and his clothes soaked with it ... Hamish walked and knelt down beside his dead friend. Collins' eyes were still open, and a deathly stare met Hamish's eyes as he leant over the lifeless body.

"I'm sorry, laddie," Hamish said as he placed his hand over Collins' eyes and closed them.

Over by the desk lay his other two men - a bloody mess: one with no face and the other a deep bloody wound caused by the axe that Tobias had thrown. Hamish frowned, and upon remembering the incident, he suddenly felt the pain in his shoulder from the shot lodged in it. He fingered at the shallow hole, wincing as he did. Hamish then remembered the safe behind the desk. He quickly went behind the desk and immediately saw that it was open ... And empty!!!

Meanwhile, Josephine sat up in the cart and kicked off the heavy blanket that covered her. The setting sun just above the tree lines was the first thing her eyes saw. She turned her head around until she could see the house, and there was no sign of Hamish. She knew, in that split second, that he must be inside. She also knew that this was her chance to escape. Josephine shuffled on her bottom to the edge of the back of the cart and jumped off. She tried to hop along the track, but this proved too difficult. She tumbled to the ground due to her hands tied behind her back and her feet bound. As she hit the ground, she quickly turned back towards the house - still no sign of Hamish.

Breathing heavily and scared, she again tried to loosen the strips of cloth that bound her hands and feet. This again, to no avail. She sat pulling and squirming at the bindings, desperate to be free of them. And then she stopped ... The gag made her breathing heavy and difficult. Her wrists and ankles were now also hurting and sore. She sat still for a moment, frantic and afraid ...

And then, she suddenly knew what to do ...

Josephine lay on her side and wriggled her hands to her bottom, arching her back as forward as she possibly could. Bringing her knees up and her head towards them, she wriggled and struggled until her hands popped underneath her bottom. She then sat up and rolled onto her back, bringing her knees up to her chest as high as she could and tucking her feet in, touching her bottom. Breathing heavily and now crying in a desperate attempt, she pulled her hands down to her feet as low as possible and wriggled and struggled to get her hands over her feet ...

"NNNGGGG," came a muffled sound as her hands came free of her feet. Panting and crying, Josephine pulled at the binding on her feet, loosening it and kicking her feet free. She scrambled to her feet, and as she pulled out the gag and took the first steps into a run, she felt an almighty crash into her back, knocking her hard onto the dirt floor ...

Hamish was on top of her.

"Not so fast there, missy," he said as he grabbed her arms from behind her and dragged her up from the floor.

Josephine kicked and screamed as she lifted her legs off the floor, trying to knock Hamish backwards so that she could get free from his hold on her.

"Arrrrgggghhh ... Get off me, you bastard! Get off me!" she screamed at the top of her voice. "Let me go! AARRRGGGHHHH! HELP ...! HELP!!!"

Hamish spun her around and hit her straight on her jaw, knocking her out.

Still holding onto her, he threw her over his shoulder and went back into the house ...

Josephine was sitting tied to a chair, with her head slumped forward. She slowly opened her eyes; blood from the cut at the corner of her mouth was dripping onto her legs. She slowly blinked her eyes open and shut. A deep moan came from within her. Her hair had fallen forward, covering her face. She moved her head from side to side as she slowly regained consciousness.

Suddenly, she shot her head up, her eyes blinking profusely. She went to move but was aware straight away of being tied to a chair. She went to call out, but the gag was back in her mouth.

She tried to break free and scream, but it was futile. She was again bound and gagged, but this time to a chair.

Sitting in front of her was Hamish. With a crooked smile, he said, "Try to get away again ..."

Josephine slumped her head down, her chin touching her neck. Tears trickled down her cheeks as she realised that she couldn't ...

She sniffled and twisted her head to her left shoulder and then her right, trying to wipe away the tears. "Mmmffff ... Mmmfff, mmmfff ..." she mumbled.

Hamish stood up, his shoulder wrapped with a bandage. While Josephine had been unconscious, Hamish had managed to dig out the shot that was lodged in his shoulder with a heated knife and wrapped the wound in a brandy-soaked bandage.

"What was that, missy???" he said. "Och, ye will have to speak up. I cannae hear what ye are saying …"

Josephine, her eyes still slightly wet and her head slightly bowed, looked straight into Hamish's eyes and tried to make her muffled sounds heard once again. "Hummfff, hnnnggg, hunngg humffff …"

Hamish walked behind her, and as he did, he gently pushed her hair back on one side and placed it over the back of her ear.

Josephine cocked her head back and stared straight at him, his image upside down to her. Raising both her eyebrows, she said again, "Hmmfff, hnngg, hnnngg hummmfff …"

Hamish smiled as he pushed back her hair on the other side of her face and walked around her to the front. "I told ye; I cannae understand a word ye'r saying, missy."

He then grabbed her around her throat, gently squeezed, and pushed her head up and back just under her chin. She didn't take her gaze from his face for a second. Hamish then held the cloth gag with the other hand and pulled it from her mouth. As he did, his grip on her throat tightened until he felt her gulp, and then he let go and stood back.

Josephine coughed and spluttered. She took a deep breath and then quietly said, "I said, I'm going to enjoy killing you …"

Hamish sat back down on the chair directly in front of her and laughed. "Oh, ye will now, will ye? Well, I'll look forward to ye trying, lassie …"

Josephine gulped again, slowly blinked and just smiled.

Hamish took out the large knife from his belt and picked at the dirt under his fingernails. Without looking up, he said, "Ye'll nor be doing a fucking thing till I get what I'm owed, missy."

Josephine sat upright in the chair, her hands tied behind her and her feet tied to the legs of the chair. "And what is it that you are owed?"

Hamish stood up and walked towards her. He stood with his legs on either side of hers. With the knife held out, he placed the tip of the blade onto her face.

"Oh, you have nae idea," he said. He then slowly moved the knife down her cheek, onto her neck and down to the first button of her shirt.

"But ye'r gonna know. That ye can count on, wee missy ..."

Josephine shuddered as the blade was placed under the button, and Hamish cut it off. He then moved the knife down to the second button and did the same again. Josephine tilted her head back as Hamish, using the blade, opened up her shirt, pushing it past her breast.

Josephine spat right in his face and said, "Do what you will, but know that you will be dead soon enough."

Hamish did not move an inch. As the spit dribbled down his face, he simply wiped it off and then licked his fingers. He then moved the blade across her nipple and said, "Och, have neh fear; ye'r nor ma type, missy ... But you will know what I'm owed."

And as soon as he said that, Hamish grabbed the chair and spun it around to show Josephine the full carnage of the study they were sitting in.

Josephine gasped out loud as she was shown the bloody mess of the four dead men.

Hamish grabbed both sides of her head and leant towards her left ear, shouting, "THIS ... THIS IS YOUR BROTHER'S DOING!!!!!!!"

Josephine tried to turn her head away, but Hamish's grip was too strong.

"LOOK!" he said. "Three of them were ma men, one of them like a brother. All your wee bastard brother's doing."

Hamish let go of her head and stepped back from the chair.

Josephine turned her head to one side. "What do you mean?" she asked. "What has my brother got to do with this?"

Hamish sat back in the chair behind her. On the floor was the bottle of brandy that he used to soak the bandage on his shoulder. He pulled the cork and took a swig from the bottle. "Ahh, of course," he said. "Ye have nae idea, do ye …?"

Josephine turned her head from left to right. "No idea of what?" she questioned.

"Your brother, and your father …"

Josephine tried to turn her head all the way around to face Hamish. Now she was angry and flustered. "What the fuck are you saying …?? Tell me what you mean."

Hamish took another swig from the bottle. He then walked past her towards the desk where Jeremiah's dead body sat and pointed to it.

"HIM …" he said. "It all started with him …"

Josephine's mind was all over the place. She was bound to a chair in a study with dead bodies covered in blood. As she looked around, frantic and scared, not knowing why she was there, she could see that the back of Jeremiah's head was blown off. The two men lying on the floor to the left of him both had severe head wounds, and Collins was lying in a pool of blood. There was blood everywhere. And now, after all that she had been put through, here she was, with Hamish, confused and frightened.

"Please … I … I don't understand what you are saying. What has all this got to do with my brother and my father?"

Hamish turned to face her and sat on the edge of the desk. He began to tell Josephine the story of what had happened and what events had led to this moment. He explained how and why her brother had thought up an elaborate plan to kill her father - hiring Hamish and his gang to kill him. How Gabriel, her dear little brother, had played along with a fantasy of being weak and fearful, making her and everyone who knew him believe that her father had been robbed and killed by chance. But that it was his plan all along. Hamish then explained how her brother had betrayed him, and now, this was the reason that he and Josephine were both in Jeremiah's study.

"And so ye see, missy, ye are ma way of getting what I'm owed … YE will get me ma money, and ma revenge …"

Josephine just sat, tears falling down her face. "NO … No, you're lying … It isn't true … He wouldn't … My father was-"

Hamish banged the bottle hard onto the desk. "YES … YES, HE FUCKING WOULD … AND HE FUCKING DID!!!!!"

Josephine dropped her head and cried. She shook it from side to side, crying. "NO! No … My father … my father…"

Josephine lifted her head and struggled to break free from her binds and screamed out loud, "MY FATHERRRRRRRR …!"

Suddenly a voice shouted from outside. "HAMISH!!!!!!!"

Josephine recognised the voice. It was Jacob.

"HAMISH!!!!!!! IT'S ME … JACOB."

Hamish grabbed the chair and spun it around to face the door of the study. He held his pistol to Josephine's head and the knife at her throat. Her tears trickled down her face. Her eyes were red, and the pain of the truth showed on her face.

"HAMISH, WE ARE COMING IN … ALL WE WANT IS JOSEPHINE."

Hamish pulled the chair back to the desk. "AYE … THEN COME AND GET HER …"

Josephine struggled in the chair and called out to Jacob. "JACOB … JACOB …"

The tears rolled down her face as she struggled and shouted. Hamish, with the cloth still in his hand that held the knife, covered her mouth with it and forced the cloth back into her mouth.

"Shut it, lassie," he said.

Josephine turned her head from side to side to stop him, trying to move her whole body, struggling to break free, knowing that Jacob and Tobias were seconds from her.

Hamish put his arm around her neck and pushed the barrel of the gun into the side of her cheek. "Hush now, lassie; it will all be over soon enough …"

At that moment, Jacob ran through the door of the study and, upon seeing Hamish and Josephine stopped dead in his tracks and threw his hands out in front of himself.

"STOP …! STOP …!" he said. "Please! Please, don't hurt her!!!!!"

Tobias came into the room, his axe in his hand and held high above his head. "YOU FUCKING HURT HER, AND YOU WILL BE DEAD A SECOND LATER …"

Jacob instantly turned towards Tobias, grabbed his arm holding the axe and pulled it down to his side. "Stop, Tobias, stop!"

Hamish tightened his grip around her neck, pushing the pistol harder into her cheek. "Aye, laddie … Do as yer friend says, or she dies right now …"

Tobias, his face red with anger and scared for Josephine's life, pushed against Jacob's blocking arm, making Jacob push back harder.

"TOBIAS!!!!" Jacob shouted at him to stop, looking straight into his eyes, urging him to see that they were at a disadvantage right now.

Angry, scared and breathing heavily, Tobias saw it in Jacob's eyes and stopped pushing towards Hamish.

Gabriel came from behind the two of them and stood in front of them. Seeing her brother's face standing in front of her, Josephine tried to scream at him. Her muffled sounds were now louder as she struggled in the chair that bound her, tears rolling down her face …

Hamish released his arm from around her neck, put the knife against it, and then pointed the pistol at Gabriel. "WHERES MY MONEY?" he shouted.

Gabriel held his hands up in front of him, waving them down to Hamish. "Calm down … calm down. You will have your money; it's outside."

Josephine pushed her head as far forward as she could with the knife held against her neck. Her face contorted with rage as she tried again to make her words heard. "HMMMFFF…. HNNNGGG … HMMMFFF… HNNNGGG …"

Jacob and Tobias were confused at what had just been said within those few seconds. Why did Gabriel just say he could have his money????

Jacob grabbed Gabriel's left shoulder and spun him around to face them both. "What the fuck are you saying????" he asked.

As Gabriel spun around to see both men's faces scowling back at his, and as the words came from Jacob's mouth, his eyes fixed upon the pistols in the belts of both men.

Tobias grabbed at Gabriel's coat and said, "What the fuck is-?"

As the words left Tobias' mouth, Gabriel grabbed at both pistols, pulling them from their belts and jumped back from the two men. As he did, he cocked both pistols and held them up to their heads.

"GET BACK, THE BOTH OF YOU …!" he screamed.

Tobias moved forward towards Gabriel with his finger pointing at his face. "What do you think you're doing…???" he asked.

Gabriel thrust his hands out with the pistols and said, "I said get back … Move … Over there …"

Jacob grabbed Tobias by the arm and walked over to the chairs with him. "Why are you doing this, Gabriel …???" he asked.

Gabriel moved around towards Hamish, pointing the pistols at the two men as he did.

Josephine did not take her eyes off of her brother for a second, following him, her gaze solely fixed upon his face.

"HEY!" shouted Hamish, still pointing his pistol at Gabriel. "Where's ma fucking money, ye wee bastard??"

Gabriel kept the pistols pointed at the two men and turned his head to Hamish. "Everything is fine, Hamish. The money is out the back in saddlebags on their horses."

Josephine, her eyes fixed on her brother, tried to speak again, shaking her head and crying.

Gabriel turned towards the two men. He signalled to Tobias with his head looking at the axe still in his hand. "Throw it on the floor," he said.

Tobias stared at Gabriel and tightened the grip on his axe.

"I said throw it on the floor, big man …"

Tobias gritted his teeth and curled his lips. "Why are you doing this? That's your fucking sister …"

Gabriel walked towards him, pointed the pistol at his face and said in a quiet voice, "Put it on the floor, now … Or your head will look like Jeremiah's …"

Scowling at Gabriel, Tobias slowly bent down to the side and placed his axe on the floor. Gabriel swiftly swiped at it with his foot, kicking and spinning it across the floor, where it stopped a few feet from the wall. Still pointing the pistols at Tobias and Jacob, he slowly walked back to where Jeremiah's drinks cabinet was and put his back against it.

"Hnnnggg … Hmmmfff … Hnnnggg …" Josephine said once more.

Gabriel looked straight at her and said, "Dearest, Sister. I never meant for this to happen. Not this way … You was never meant to know …"

Hamish pushed her chin up with the knife and, with his forearm holding the pistol, pulled back the top of her head. "Listen to me, ye little wretch of a man. Ye talked me into yer little plan, told me I could have all that Jeremiah had, and here we all are. Jeremiah, dead, my men, dead, and no fucking money. Ye betrayed me, and for all I know, ye sent these fucking two to kill my whole gang, me included."

Gabriel looked at Hamish and shook his head. "NO …! No! They was nothing to do with me." Then, pushing himself off from the cabinet, Gabriel stepped forward, looked at Jacob and Tobias and said, "They were her idea ... she called for them. I tried to talk her out of it - said that it was a robbery that had gone wrong. That whoever the men that killed our father was would be long gone, a bunch of bandits, but she wouldn't listen ..." Gabriel turned to Hamish and pointed a pistol at him. "Your men should have dealt with them. You should have dealt with them. Then we wouldn't be in this mess now."

Out of the corner of his eye, Hamish saw Jacob move and swung his arm towards him, his pistol pointing at his head. "Ye just sit still there, laddie. Don't ye be getting any ideas now ..."

Jacob flitted his eyes between Hamish and Gabriel and then looked at Josephine, her eyes still fixed on her brother.

Gabriel pointed both pistols back at the two men and moved to the side of his sister. he then placed one of the pistols against her head.

Hamish pointed his pistol back at Gabriel and said, "Whoa there. What are ye doing, man?"

Gabriel turned his head, looked at Hamish and said, "This ends here. The money is outside in two saddlebags, one on each horse. That's your payment, as agreed."

Josephine moved back and forth, side to side, struggling to get free. "HNNGG ... HNNGG ... HNNGGG ..."

"Shhhh, Sister. It will all be over soon ..."

Jacob stood up. "You won't get away with this; you will have to kill us all. If you don't, then I will spend the rest of my life hunting you down, and I will kill you."

Gabriel laughed at Jacob and waved the pistol at him. "Sit down ... Sit down and be quiet." He turned to Hamish again. "Go on then. Go and see. Your money is all there. I have not betrayed you, Hamish. We had a deal; what has happened here was not part of that deal. I hired you and your men to kill my father, and that you did. Now your payment is waiting for you outside. These two were not part of that plan ..."

Hamish looked at Gabriel and then at the two men. "What are you going to do about them?" he asked.

"I'm not going to do anything - you are!!!!"

Hamish looked back at Gabriel and saw him pointing to the axe that lay on the floor.

"I thought that seeing as it was those two who killed your men," Gabriel said, "and that axe was used, you could seek revenge on your men, and kill them in the same way ..."

Hamish stared at the axe and then at Jacob and Tobias.

"Go on, pick it up," said Gabriel. "If they try and fight, then I will shoot both of them."

Hamish looked around the room at his men lying dead and then back at the two men sitting in the chairs. He rubbed at his unshaven chin and then turned to Gabriel. "What about her???" he asked.

"She is my concern, not yours," said Gabriel. "Now, pick up the axe and avenge your gang."

Hamish looked at the axe on the floor, its blade glinting orange from the last rays of the setting sun through the window of the study. He looked back at Jacob and Tobias.

"If I'm going to die here today, then I will die fighting," Tobias said.

Hamish lifted up his arm, pistol in his hand and pulled the trigger. The shot hit Tobias in his right arm, knocking him backwards off the chair and onto the floor.

"Then that will even the odds," said Hamish.

Jacob jumped up off the chair, and Gabriel screamed at him. "SIT!! SIT DOWN ... NOW!!"

Tobias lay on the floor, clutching at his arm and let out a loud cry. "ARRRGGHHHHH ... FUCK YOU!" he screamed out.

Hamish moved quickly to where the axe lay on the floor. Tobias stood up and threw himself at the axe. Both men grabbed the handle at the same time and struggled to get it. Tobias, on the floor, had a hand on the axe, and Hamish, standing over him, had his hands on the handle as well. They both pulled at it to free it from the other, pulling left and right. Gabriel pointed a pistol at them both and one at Jacob.

Josephine moved from left to right on the chair she was tied to, lifting it from side to side from the floor. She lifted it, moved the legs to the right and crunched one of the legs straight onto Gabriel's foot. Gabriel let out a scream, and as he did so, he squeezed the trigger of the pistol pointing at Tobias and Hamish. The shot from the gun fired, and Tobias let go of the handle of the axe. With the force of Hamish struggling for the axe, he suddenly stood bolt upright and was hit in the back of his head from the shot. It went through his head and out of his left eye, killing him instantly, his body falling to the floor on top of Tobias.

Jacob moved as fast as he could towards Gabriel and Josephine. Gabriel hit the back of the chair, getting his foot clear, causing the chair and Josephine to topple over onto the floor, leaving her on her side. As the chair fell, Gabriel swung his arm towards Jacob and pulled the trigger. The shot from the pistol hit the top of Jacob's thigh, sending him to the floor and crashing into the desk.

With both pistols fired and now empty, Jacob on the floor, Josephine lying on her side still tied to the chair, and Tobias trying to drag Hamish's dead body off himself, Gabriel made a run for it. He ran out of the study door, through the kitchen, out the back and towards the horses. When he reached the backyard, the horses were nowhere to be seen. The shots that were fired had startled them, and they had run from the house. Gabriel did no more and ran through the backyard and onto the field to make his escape …


Josephine struggled and tried to loosen the bindings that tied her to the chair. She breathed hard through her nose as the cloth that gagged her made it difficult to breathe. Jacob held his thigh where the shot had hit him and, with his other hand on the desk, pulled himself up and went towards Josephine. Tobias grabbed at Hamish and managed to push him off, the weight of his dead body making it difficult. Tobias' arm was throbbing and bleeding quite badly. He held his hand over the open wound to try and stop the flow of blood.

Jacob picked up the knife that Hamish had left on the desk and began to cut at the binds on Josephine's hands and feet. As he cut through the strips of cloth on her hands, setting them free, Josephine pulled the gag from her mouth and breathed deep and hard, coughing as she gulped in the air. Jacob put the knife to her feet and began to cut at the binding, releasing her ankles. Josephine pulled her legs free and scrambled to her knees, embracing Jacob and kissing him.

The tears had dried, leaving streaks on her face. She asked Jacob, "Are you alright? Your leg, how is your leg …??"

As she embraced him, she could see the blood coming from the hole that the shot had made. She quickly grabbed the cuttings of cloth off the floor and placed them over the wound. She grabbed Jacob's hand and placed it on the cloth, holding it to the wound.

"Keep that on it," she said. "It will stop you from losing too much blood."

Jacob sank back against the desk to catch his breath for a moment. Josephine went over to where Tobias was now standing, holding his arm.

"Oh, Tobias, are you ok?" she said as she held his arm, seeing how bad the wound was.

"I'm fine, little missy, but we don't have any time for this. Your brother is getting away …"

Tobias grabbed his axe and made his way as fast as he could to the backyard. He could see Gabriel trying to run across the muddy field, which was proving difficult for him. Gabriel's feet were sinking into the boggy, muddy field, and as he tried to run, he couldn't get very far, very fast. He was out of breath, scared and getting more and more tired by the minute. Tobias ran straight across the backyard and onto the muddy field. He lifted his legs high as he ran to try and catch up with Gabriel. The strength in his legs seemed to cut through the thick mud with much more ease than Gabriel could, but there was a fair distance between them.

"I'M GOING TO KILL YOU …!!!" Tobias screamed at the top of his voice as he ran as fast as he could to try and catch him.

Josephine, meanwhile, didn't run to the backyard. Instead, she ran to the front of the house where the cart was. She knew her rifle was in the front of the cart, which Hamish had taken from her and placed there when he took her from the tavern. Josephine grabbed the rifle and checked that it was still loaded. It was … She then ran as fast as she could down the side of the house and into the trees that lay along the field. She ran through the clump of trees. The ground was waterlogged, but she could faster through the water than through thick mud. As she ran through the trees, she could make out to her right the field … and her brother …

The light had faded fast from the sun setting, but it was not yet dark. The overcast clouds made it seem darker. As she ran through the trees alongside the muddy field, she could hear Tobias' screams at Gabriel. By now, she was level with her brother, but the distance was still quite far as she looked across to her right at where he was in the field. The trees opened up, and she was now in a small clearing between them. Josephine stopped running and turned towards the field. There, tired and now nearly walking, was her brother. Tobias had made up quite a lot of ground behind him. The mud was thick, and Gabriel was struggling to make it across to the other side. He was panting and breathing hard. She could just make out the breath snorting from his nose and mouth as he tired …

Josephine was also panting hard herself. In the cold air, her breath swarmed around her head and just as quickly disappeared. She tried hard to control her breathing, slowing down her heartbeat and calming herself. Gabriel was snorting and panting like a bull that was about to charge. His legs were heavy; his muscles hurt with every step. The thick mud smothered his boots, adding weight to them …

Jacob had pulled himself up from the floor and was now sitting half on the edge of the desk. His leg was hurting, burning. He held the cloth against it, picked up another piece, wrapped it around the cloth over the wound, then around his entire thigh and tied it off tight. He made his way to the backyard. Every step was agony. He used the tables and chairs to hold onto as he limped through the kitchen and out to the back.

As he looked out across the field, he could see Tobias and, in front of him, Gabriel. He couldn't see Josephine; she was nowhere in sight. He desperately scanned around to try and find her, but he couldn't see her anywhere. As he looked around, he saw one of the horses just at the start of the field, on the other side of the yard. He had one thought: his rifle …

Jacob slowly made his way to where the horse stood. As he limped across the yard, the pain from his leg was too much. He winced and groaned and fell to the floor from the agony he felt. He looked up at where the horse stood. He tried to lift himself up, but as soon as he got halfway up, he fell to the ground again. He began to crawl along the ground, trying to make it to a tree so that he could pull himself up. The horse stood there, snorting, and then turned its head and looked straight at Jacob. It started to walk towards him. As Jacob pulled himself along the ground, he looked up and could see the horse.

"Come on, boy," he said. He clicked a sound with his mouth to beckon the horse over. Slowly, it made its way to where Jacob was. He grabbed at the reins that hung down and pulled himself up to the saddle. There was his rifle. Jacob grabbed the top of the saddle and managed, with great effort and pain, to get himself up and into it. The horse turned around in a circle, snorting and whinnying. With the reins in his hands, Jacob managed to settle the horse down and pointed it towards the field.

Josephine was still and calm … Her heartbeat was slow. She could see across the field to where her brother was. She knelt down on one knee, brought the rifle up and nestled the butt into her shoulder. She looked down the barrel of the rifle and took aim at where her brother now stood, his hands on his knees, his head bowed, the steam from his breath surrounding his head.

She took aim with him clear in her sight. She cocked back the hammer and steadied herself. Then she shouted out, "GABRIEL … GABRIEL … GABRIELLLLLLL!!"

Jacob positioned the horse and took the rifle out. He took the gunpowder from the pouch and the shot and loaded the rifle. He packed the gunpowder and then cocked the hammer. The horse jostled and moved, so he patted its neck and whispered into its ear, calming the animal. He raised the rifle and took aim …

Gabriel heard his sister call out his name the first time. Panting hard, he looked around to see where the sound came from … Then he heard it again. He turned his head around, trying to see her, and then came the third cry out of his name, louder and longer. As he turned towards the trees, he could make out the white shirt just in the clearing. He squinted his eyes to see better … As the image became clearer to him, he could see it was his sister.

Gabriel brought his hand up to his eyes and said to himself, "Josephine …"
BANG!!!!!!!!!!!!

The sound echoed throughout the field. Gabriel stood still … Then collapsed to the ground.

Jacob was still looking down the sight of his rifle. He stopped, lifted his head and placed the rifle across his legs.

Across from where Gabriel lay on the ground in the mud, where the trees cleared, a plume of smoke could be seen.

Josephine stood up, the rifle by her side in her right hand. She took a deep sigh, let out the air in her lungs and said, "That's for Father …"

When the shot was fired, Tobias ducked his head as he ran towards Gabriel, closing the gap between them. He stopped running as he saw Gabriel fall to the ground. He, too, could see the plume of smoke coming from the clearing in the trees, rising up and disappearing into the night that now blanketed the land around him. He stood for a few seconds, the air from his lungs blowing hard from his nose and mouth. He looked around and back towards the house. There, behind him, he could see Jacob riding across the field towards where he now stood. Tobias turned back to where the plume of smoke came from and could now see Josephine walk out from the clearing and onto the field, towards where her brother lay still on the ground. Tobias began to run again, slower this time, breathing heavily, towards Gabriel …

Josephine made her way to where her brother lay still. The light had now gone from the sun and was replaced with the moon's blue light. As she walked towards her brother, she could see Tobias running, and Jacob was riding a way behind him. As she got closer and was nearly upon where her brother lay, she could hear coughing and spluttering. Gabriel lay still with no movement, but Josephine could see that he was gasping for air, barely clinging to life. She walked right up to him and slumped to the ground onto her knees, the rifle still in her hand.

Gabriel was coughing and trying to breathe. Blood gurgled in his throat as he did so. Splatters of blood hit his face as he lay there, taking his last breaths. His eyes were wide open. Josephine sat there, looking him straight into his eyes, watching the final moments of his life. Gabriel's eyes blinked fast as his chest rose and fell, with very short breaths, until … the last breath left his lips.

Tobias stopped running about ten feet from where Josephine sat next to Gabriel's now dead body. He walked towards her and stood at Gabriel's feet. Breathing heavily he asked, "Is he dead????"

Josephine sat with her head bowed. Her hair fell forward, covering her face. Without looking, she said in a soft low voice, "He is … He is …"

Tobias didn't say a word. He stood for a moment staring at Gabriel, laying there, lifeless, his eyes open and staring up into the night sky.

Josephine began to cry and then sobbed, shaking her head, "Why … why … why …?" she cried out.

Tobias stood next to her, bent down and put his arms around her. He stood her up and cradled her head in his chest. Her cries were muffled, both arms just hanging as Tobias tightened his grip with his arms around her. He turned away from Gabriel's body and walked Josephine away back towards the house. Jacob was now upon them and pulled back on the reins of the horse a few feet from them. Tobias held out his hand and grabbed at the reins …

Jacob stayed on the horse, his leg bleeding and hurting. "Josephine … Are you alright?" he asked softly.

Tobias took hold of her and lifted her up and onto the horse, into the arms of Jacob.

Sobbing, she nestled into Jacob's chest and held her arms around him. He stroked her hair and kissed the top of her head. "It's all over. You're safe now …" he said.

With the reins in his hands, Tobias turned the horse and walked it back to the house and, without looking back to Jacob, said, "He's dead. He can't hurt her anymore … not anymore."

# Chapter Twenty-One



Solomon boarded his ship, and his small crew set sail for the Atlantic ocean. As the ship slowly sailed away from the docks and into open waters, Solomon shouted from the stern to the three men standing at the quayside. "TWO WEEKS' TIME, GENTLEMEN … TWO WEEKS' TIME."

Jacob, Tobias and Dupree all stood waving as Solomon's ship sailed away from the docks.

Dupree clasped his hands together and rubbed them over one another. He took in a deep breath and let out a long sigh … "Well, my friends, eet eez a beautiful morning. What say we go and see Mr Crawford and then stock up on our merchandise?"

Tobias stretched out his arms to the side of him, lifted his heels off the ground and said, "Yes, Dupree. That sounds like a good idea." Then, as he passed by Jacob, he slapped him on the shoulder and said, "Let's go."

Watching as Solomon's ship sailed out onto the open sea, Jacob turned and followed both men. They walked through the various stalls scattered along the length of the docks and up onto the street, heading for the house of John Crawford.

As the three men walked along the street, passing where their rooms were just down from the Spitalfields market, Tobias turned to Jacob and said, "What about Jeremiah?"

Jacob, walking with his head down, wishing to himself that he couldn't smell the horrendous odour of shit that just hung in the air of London town, looked up at Tobias. "What about him?" he asked.

Tobias crossed the road with Dupree a few steps in front and said, "Well, I thought that the idea was for us to be able to-"

Suddenly a horse and cart sped past them as Tobias grabbed at Dupree's arm, pulling him backwards, narrowly missing him ...

"Sacré bleu!" said Dupree. "Zat was close, no ...? Thank you, Tobias."

Jacob shouted out after the driver of the cart, waving his fist high in the air, but the cart was already far away, thundering down the street.

"That was indeed a close one, Dupree," replied Tobias.

They crossed to the other side of the street, and Jacob, still behind Tobias, said, "What was you saying, big man?"

"Well," Tobias said, as they walked past the window of Maggie's little inn, peering through it to catch a glimpse. "I thought the idea was to make as much coin as we can."

"That's right," said Jacob.

"Well, I have been thinking that Dupree, seeing as he has many years of experience in buying and selling goods, well, he could stay in London. You know, getting to know his way around as it were."

Jacob, tired of how long Tobias was taking, hurried him up with a wave of his hand.

"And we," Tobias continued, "We could ride out to Jeremiah's and see if we could pick up another job or two."

Dupree turned around. "Zat eez a good idea, Tobias. I can find my way around, talk to Mr Crawford and get to know eez contacts. Meanwhile, you two can do what you do best and meet me back 'ere in London in, say ... a week or two."

Both men looked at each other and then at Jacob.

"I guess that would make sense", said Jacob, "Two bags of coin are better than one."

Tobias stopped in his tracks and clapped his hands together. "Good. As much as I like the idea of buying an' selling stuff for extra coin, I gotta tell ya; I'm missing bashing heads for coin."

"You would," said Jacob. "We'll meet with Mr Crawford, and after, let him know that we have other business and that Dupree will be dealing with matters here."

"Oui, pas de probleme …" said Dupree.

Tobias leant forward, his head just above Dupree's. "Come again?" he said,

Dupree raised his hands, palms tilted up, and said, "Ah, no problem, no problem …"

Jacob asked Dupree if this sat fine with him, if he didn't mind that they would leave him in London to sort out buyers, and contacts, on his own.

Dupree just rolled his eyes, mumbled something in French under his breath, waved his hands in front of him and said, "Go, go. Eet is a good idea …"

After they all had seen and spoken to Mr Crawford and explained that Dupree would be dealing with him alone, they parted ways. Dupree had left with Mr Crawford, and Jacob and Tobias had gone back to their lodgings to get their horses to leave London.

"How about a quick one for the road?" said Tobias

Jacob placed his foot in the stirrup and swung his leg over the saddle. Grabbing the reins in his hand, he turned to Tobias. "A quick what?" he asked.

"Drink," said Tobias. "What else??"

Jacob nestled himself in the saddle, pulled on the reins and turned the horse towards the street. "Well, who knows with you, big man? You're a drinker, a womaniser, and a brawler. Could be any one of 'em."

Tobias kicked his heels into the horse, rode level with Jacobs and said, "Do we have time for all three?"

It had started to rain. With no warning, it began to pelt it down heavily. The kind of rain that soaks through in seconds. Both Jacob and Tobias reached to the back of their horses, turning quickly in their saddles. Reaching around while trying to hold their horse steady, trying to grab at the 'greatcoats' that were rolled up and tied off at the back of the saddle. The rain really was heavy and fell hard at such an angle that it hit them in the face. The horses whinnied, their ears flickering and twitching, shaking their heads at the downpour. The two men fought with the reins, switching from left to right as the horses stamped and turned. They had been riding for a couple of hours since leaving London and weren't that far from their destination of Jeremiah's house. But now, the heavens had opened up, and the rain came down hard and fast.

"FUCK THIS …!" shouted Tobias as he struggled to get control of his horse. "LET'S JUST RIDE THROUGH IT …"

Both men sat forward in their saddles, pulled the reins up high and kicked at the horses,

"YAH, YAH! screamed Jacob, as his horse leapt forward and thundered off down the road, with Tobias right behind him. They rode hard through the rain; the ground waterlogged beneath them. Lightning shot across the sky, and moments later, a great rumble and then a loud clap echoed over the land.

"YAH, YAH!"

Both men rode as fast as the horses could carry them, the rain so heavy it blurred their eyes. All they could hear was the crashing of the thunder, the forks of the lightning as it streaked across the sky, and the noise of the hooves on the soaked, wet, muddy ground. This, mixed with the heavy snorting coming from the horses' mouths as they ran as fast as they could along the road, which now had turned into what looked like a shallow raging river …

As they rode, not far now from Jeremiah's, they reached a bend in the road. As Jacob's horse, running as fast as it could, got to the bend, its hind legs slipped on the water-soaked muddy ground and gave way underneath its body. The horse was going so fast that it slid along the ground on its hindquarters, with Jacob clinging to the reins. His feet were pushing hard in the stirrups just to stay on as the horse rounded the bend and managed to get to all four legs without so much as missing a step. Upon seeing this, Tobias pulled back on the reins, bringing his horse's head up, trying to slow it down right at the bend. But his horse didn't just slow; it stopped altogether, sending Tobias over its head and straight through the bushes, landing headfirst in a boggy, water-logged field.

As Tobias hit the ground, his body half-buried in the thick, wet mud and face fully buried, lightning streaked again, followed by an enormous, echoed clap of thunder. His horse reared up onto its hind legs and then took off down the road. Jacob was still holding on to the reins, and his entire body was in a rhythmic motion with his horse, their heads almost clashing with each other. The small dirt track that led down off the road to Jeremiah's house was just up ahead.

Jacob pulled back on the reins to slow his horse and pulled them to the left, taking the horse down the little dirt track, which was now completely flooded. They turned and slowed. The track was under a lot of water, and as Jacob steered his horse towards the house, the water splashed up high as the horse ran through it. The rain suddenly stopped as quickly as it had started. Lightning forked across the sky, but now the rumble came a bit later and sounded fainter, further away. The horse was brought to a trot. Steam shot out of its nose and mouth, and its belly swelled and then shrunk, swelled and shrunk as it desperately tried to take in air to fill its lungs ... Jacob's chest did the same as he gasped for air. All that could be seen around both Jacob and his horse was steam, the hot breath that now swirled around in the cold air.

He brought the horse to a stop and turned in his saddle to see Tobias behind him … But he couldn't. He sat for a minute or so, waiting. 'Any minute now,' he thought to himself. Just then, Tobias' horse came down the flooded dirt track; as it hit the deep water, it slowed almost to a stop. It, too, was breathing heavily, trying to catch its breath.

Jacob sat in the saddle, looking straight at the horse. "Shit," he said out loud. "Where the hell …?"

Jacob grabbed the back of the saddle and stood up in it. "Where the-? TOBIAS …?" he shouted. "TOBIAS! TOBI …………"

Jacob sat back in the saddle, turned on the reins and kicked at the horse's belly. He steered the horse up the track and turned right onto the road.

"TOBIAS ………! TOBIAAAAAAAAASSSSSS?"

He whipped at the reins, and the horse took off back down the road. He was about fifty yards from the bend in the road, and there, to the left, coming through the bushes, was Tobias.

Jacob pulled the horse up to a stop right at where a 'soaking wet, covered in thick mud, with green leaves stuck to him' Tobias stood.

A second later, Tobias' horse trotted passed Jacob and stopped right next to where Tobias stood. It snorted and whinnied and then shook its head.

Tobias stood for a second, looked at his horse, grabbed the reins that hung down and muttered, "Fucking animal!"

Jacob sat and just stared. "How the-?"

Tobias shot up his hand high in the air and said, "DON'T! JUST … don't …!"

Jacob turned his horse around slowly and trotted back down the road towards Jeremiah's house once again. But this time, with Tobias behind him.

The grey, cold, overcast sky had thinned, and bright beams of light shone through the clouds, striking the ground and spreading across it. The dark shadows were being consumed readily and quickly. A now faint rumble could just be heard in the very far distance. As they rode towards the flooded dirt track, the warmth of the now shining sun hit their wet faces suddenly and with welcome. Jacob turned his head and looked behind at Tobias. The sight of his face covered in mud, his clothes saturated, leaving a sheen of smooth, wet mud picking up the sun's light, brought a huge smile to Jacob's face.

Tobias caught sight of this and simply said, "Fuck off."

This made Jacob broaden his smile into a huge grin, followed by a raucous laugh. He laughed hard, his shoulders shaking and his head thrown backwards.

Again, Tobias just said, "Fuck off."

As the sun now beamed through the clouds, making them part and wither away in the sky, the heat was instant, which oddly made Tobias feel colder than when the torrential rain had soaked him. His clothes stuck to his skin, creating a deep chill throughout his entire body. The mud seemed to add to this feeling. He rode about ten feet behind Jacob, his head hung down, along with his shoulders. He was pissed off ...

Jacob had turned into the entrance to the flooded dirt track leading down to Jeremiah's and stopped. He waited until Tobias trotted up next to him.

"Tobias," he said as he stopped. "One thing before we go and see Jeremiah."

Tobias tried to wipe the worst parts of mud off his coat and face.

"You realise," Jacob said, "the last time we was here was to pay off Dupree's debt, and if you remember, Jeremiah wasn't that happy."

Tobias cupped a handful of mud, flicked it and said, "Nor was I."

"That's my point. So, can we just get another job, stay calm, and then be on our way?"

Tobias didn't answer, tapped the reins onto the neck of his horse, and trotted down towards the house.

Jacob did the same and said, "Nice talking to you ..."

Jeremiah sat at his desk, placing different amounts of coins into small bags and then putting them in his safe. He counted out for another bag and heard the loud knocking on his front door. With his finger, he counted out the coins, sliding them across the desk towards himself and dropping them into the palm of his hand. When he had the correct amount, he then opened another small bag and placed the coins inside.

BANG, BANG, BANG.

The door went again. He looked up from his chair, put the bag into his safe, closed the door and locked it. He opened the drawer of the desk, placed the key inside and closed it. With a sigh and groan, he pushed back on the chair and stood up, then walked to the door.

Tobias turned towards Jacob and said, "He's coming. Let me do the talking."

The door creaked open, and Jeremiah was faced with a large man covered with half-dry, half-wet mud.

"Tobias????" he said.

Jacob slipped in front of Tobias with his hand held out, "Good to see you again, Jeremiah," he said.

Jeremiah took the hand and shook it, nodding and laughing. He looked over Jacob's shoulder and said, "Come inside; I have a fire going. You look like you need to dry yourself, Tobias."

Jeremiah led them into the room with the fireplace and told them both to stand there and dry off. "Wait here; you look like you need a drink; you warm your insides."

Tobias stood right in front of the fireplace, filled with deep red burning logs, spitting and crackling, the flames licking the sides of the brick hearth, and rubbed his hands together.

Jeremiah brought in a bottle with three glasses and handed one to each of them. He opened the bottle and filled their glasses. "So, gentlemen, I take it you have come back for another job. I do hope that there will not be a repeat of the last with that fellow … Dupree …"

Tobias downed the drink in one gulp, and before he could react, Jacob said, "You won't have any reason for concern, Jeremiah. We are here to see if you have any work, that's all."

Tobias stood with the glass in his hand, and it filled again.

"Ah, well, in that case, I do," said Jeremiah. "There is a man who, let's say, wants something done about a man who he is quite certain is having carnal relations with his wife …"

"Thinks … or knows …?" asked Jacob.

"Those concerns are not my own. It means nothing to me if he is or is not. My only concern is to pass the job on, ensure the man is dealt with, and take his money."

Tobias drank the second glass of brandy and said, "And what is the job? To rough this man up? Beat him? Leave him with a message?"

Jeremiah stoked the logs in the fireplace, turning them over, causing small sparks to spit out onto the dirty floor and the flames to swirl and flicker. "He is paying for a message - to stay away. A message that will make him listen."

"Then give us the details," said Tobias.

Jeremiah wrote down on a small piece of paper the name of the man, the village where they could find him and the name of the woman.

"What about the money? Where do we get the money from?" said Tobias

"You don't need to collect any money. I will pay you when the job is done."

Jacob drank the rest of the brandy in his glass and said, "So … Do we need any proof of this, like you wanted before …?"

"Do you mean, like a finger?" asked Jeremiah. "You don't need to worry. This job is personal to me; I will know when he gets the message."

Tobias, now nearly dry, gave the glass back, took the piece of paper from Jeremiah and said, "Consider it done. We will be on our way. See you in a day or two for our wage."

Both men made their way to the front door, opened it, mounted their horses and rode up to the main road.

The two men had been riding for about an hour. Just up ahead lay the village where they would find the man on the piece of paper Jeremiah had given them. To the left of the entrance to the village stood a small stone-built church that sat higher than the road. The horses had slowed to a trot. A man was digging a hole down the side of the church. Tobias had noticed him, hard at work, dirt flying off the shovel, making a neat pile at the side, which could have only been a grave.

"Look," he said as he tapped Jacob's arm. "Maybe that's who we are looking for."

Jacob looked and saw the man. "Well, we have to start somewhere; might as well be with him."

Both men turned the horses and trotted up the small hill to the church grounds and steered them to the side of the grave where the man was digging.

"Hello there," Tobias said.

The man bent over in the hole, dug up a shovel full of dirt, threw it out onto the pile, and then bent back down for another shovel of dirt.

"Hello there," Tobias said again.

The man stood up in the hole and threw another shovel full of dirt onto the pile, and again bent back down into the hole.

The door of the small church opened, and a woman stepped out and walked down the small hill into the village. A priest stepped out of the door behind her, stopped a few steps from the door and turned to where the two men on horses stood.

Tobias smirked, turned towards Jacob and said, "What is he, deaf?"

From behind the horses, a voice yelled out, "Can I help you, gentleman?"

Both men turned their heads. There, behind them, stood the priest.

"Please excuse Owen. Unless you are standing in front of him, your words will fall onto deaf ears."

"Ah," said Jacob. "That will explain things."

Both Tobias and Jacob dismounted their horses and introduced themselves to the priest. Jacob beckoned Tobias to show the priest the piece of paper with the man's name on it.

Tobias rummaged in the pocket of his coat and pulled out the paper, unfolded it and held it out for the priest. Pointing with his finger, he said, "We are looking for this man. Do you know where we can find him?"

The priest held the end of the piece of paper. He said, "May I?" and then looked closer at the name. "Ah, Mr Duncan Cook ... Why, yes, he is the local carpenter. May I ask why you are looking for him?"

Tobias took back the paper, folded it up and placed it back into his pocket. "We have some business with him, is all. Could you point us in the right direction?"

Jacob saw a slightly worried look in the priest's eyes. He took his hand to shake it, saying, "Well, thank you for your time. Now, if you would be so kind as to tell us where we might find Mr Cook, we will be on our way. I'm sure you are a very busy man, so we won't keep you a moment longer."

Tobias gave a sharp look to Jacob and then looked back at the priest.

After a few seconds, he turned and pointed down the hill into the village and said, "Go to the end of the road, towards the end of the village. He lives in the house across from the small brook that runs along that way. The only house on that side, you cannot miss it."

"Thank you," said Jacob. "Now, if you will excuse us, we shan't take up any more of your time."

Jacob turned and mounted his horse, and Tobias followed swiftly after.

"Good day to you, gentlemen … And God be with you," said the priest as he watched them ride down the hill and onto the road.

Tobias rode alongside Jacob, their horses moving at a slow trot as they made their way through the village. They passed by small cottages, some with chickens running in the front yards, others with a pig or two. Small children played along the road while women beat out the dirt from blankets. Other than the sound of the children playing and the occasional grunts from the pigs, the village was quiet. A sweet smell filled the air from the abundance of wildflowers that grew along the road and between the cottages.

Jacob breathed deeply, "Ah, now that's a better smell than dirty old London," he said.

As they rode past a couple of large pigs in their sty, Tobias said, "I don't know, my skinny friend, that definitely smells the same…"

All of a sudden, both men pulled hard on the reins, the horses coming to an abrupt stop as two young boys ran across in front of them with short wooden swords, swiping at each other and then running off down the side of a house, disappearing around the back.

A woman called out to them, her hands covered in flour, clapping them to shake it off. "Don't you two run far, now. There's chores to be done before your tea …"

As the horses stood while the boys ran off and the woman shouted after them, Tobias winked at her before continuing down the road. The woman clapped her hands together hard, sending a big plume of flour up in front of her, and then swiftly turned on the spot to go back into her house.

Seeing this, Jacob called after Tobias, his horse a few feet ahead. He laughed and said, "Not every woman takes heed of your charm."

As they neared the end of the village, over past where the small brook ran, they could see a house set back just before some trees.

"Look – there. That must be the house the priest spoke of," said Tobias.

They turned the horses towards the house, rode down and through the small brook, and up the other side towards the house. A small wooden fence, smart and clean looking, surrounded the entire house. Tobias got off his horse, petted its long face, and pushed open the gate. He walked towards the door as Jacob got off his horse and was met with a sudden deep and long growl.

He shot a look to where the noise came from to see, standing with its front legs slightly apart and its head lowered, a huge dog. Its muzzle and nose crinkled to reveal white, sharp-looking teeth. With its fur standing up the entire length of its body, the dog snorted and let out an even longer growl, baring more of its teeth, now showing the red of its gums.

Tobias stood perfectly still, held his hands out towards the dog and said, "Woah there, boy. Woah now … Good dog …"

Now at the gate, Jacob also saw the large dog and stayed on that side of the fence. "Watch yourself, Tobias," he said.

Tobias, not taking his eyes off the dog, still with his hands stretched out, said out of the corner of his mouth, "What do ya think I'm gonna do …? Look at the size of it!"

Thinking quickly and seeing a big stick lying by the fence, Jacob grabbed it and threw it to the left of the dog, landing about ten feet past it. The dog did not move. Still growling, its eyes just quickly looked at where the stick flew by it, and then it fixed its slathering stare back to Tobias.

The dog very slowly edged its way towards Tobias, its sharp teeth on show, and at the same time, Tobias slowly edged his way back towards the gate.

With both hands on the fence again, Jacob shouted to Tobias, "Watch him now! Watch him."

At that moment, Tobias turned as fast as he could and made a run for the gate. The dog darted towards him, running at an angle to Tobias and the gate, cutting off the distance between the two. It jumped up just as Tobias reached the gate and, with its mouth open and teeth jutting out, sank its teeth straight into the first thing that it came into contact with, which happened to be Tobias' right hand. Tobias yelled out in pain as the dog bit down, breaking the skin and sinking into the fleshy part of the side between his little finger and his wrist. As it bit, the dog tried to shake its head, and Tobias tried to shake it off.

"AAAAARRRRGGGGHHHHH!" he screamed out loud.

Tobias kicked the dog, which made it let go with a deep yelp, and in doing so, allowed Tobias to make a very clumsy leap headfirst over the gate. He landed with a thud, and Jacob quickly helped him to his feet. As both men rose from the floor, they were aware straight away that the dog was now next to them, growling even harder than before. It had jumped the fence and was just about to lurch towards them both when a loud whistle sounded. The dog stopped in its tracks, turned and jumped back over the fence and walked to the corner of the house. Still growling, it lay down by a small tree. Both men looked to see a man pointing to where the dog now lay.

"STAY!!!!!!" the man shouted.

Tobias, holding his bleeding hand and Jacob, holding Tobias' arm, both stared at the man.

"Are you alright?" asked the man as he walked towards them.

Tobias held his hand to the man's face and angrily said, "Does it look alright …??"

The man shook his head, apologised and offered for them to go inside his house. Once inside, the man ripped off a piece of cloth, dunked it into a bucket of water and handed it over to Tobias.

"Here, wrap your hand with this," he said.

Tobias took the cloth, made a fist and wrapped his whole hand. Jacob looked around the man's house and could see some tools in the corner. Tools that would be used working with wood. By the back door, he also noticed a scattering of wood shavings mixed with sawdust. The man turned to where he had an open stove. On it was a pot of water, boiling.

"Can I offer you some tea?"

Tobias was busy making the wrapping tighter, didn't look up and said

"Do you have anything stronger.?"

Before the man could answer, Jacob pointed to the corner of the room and asked him, "What are the tools for?"

"I'm a carpenter," the man replied.

Tobias suddenly realised what he was at the house in the first place for. He pulled the paper from his coat and read out a name to the man. "Verity Attwood …"

The man, his back to both men, pouring boiling water into a cup, stopped. Without turning around, the man placed the pot back onto the stove and said, "How do you know that name?"

Tobias clenched his fist, and blood trickled down from under the cloth, "The same way I know the name Duncan Cook …"

The man, still holding the pot, tightened his grip and then, without warning, spun around and threw the boiling water in the direction of Tobias. As the man's arm came around and the pot came forward, Tobias ducked and launched himself to the side. The boiling water flew over Tobias' left shoulder as he just managed to evade it, and it splashed against the wall, spreading steam across it. Duncan then threw the empty pot straight at Jacob, which clattered off his arms as he was quick to cover his face.

Now full of anger, Tobias took two steps towards Duncan and hit him full on the chin sending him flying into the corner where he kept his tools. As soon as he hit the floor, his back smashing into the wall, Jacob was standing over him. He grabbed Duncan by his shirt and lifted him up off the floor. As Jacob did so, Duncan grabbed a wooden mallet from the floor and swung it hard and fast at Jacob's head, hitting him in the neck. Jacob immediately let go of his grip on the shirt, let out a painful cry and jumped backwards.

Tobias was right behind Jacob and threw a right hand over his shoulder, catching Duncan on his ear. Duncan screamed out as the pain from the blow surged through his entire head. As he clutched at his ear, Tobias grabbed him, lifting him clean off the floor and, with a twist, launched Duncan across the room. As he crashed into a chair, smashing it into bits, Tobias ran over, drew his leg back, and kicked Duncan in his stomach. Duncan screamed out, and Tobias kicked him again. And again.

The rage in Tobias was written across his face. Jacob tried to grab him from behind, to stop him from killing Duncan as he lay on the floor trying to curl into a ball. Tobias shrugged off Jacob's grip and then relentlessly began to pummel Duncan's face with his fists. Jacob grabbed at him again, but this time he put all his strength into it and launched himself backwards, taking Tobias with him. After both men struggled against each other, Duncan lay totally still on the floor, and blood covered his face. On his back, with his arms and legs wrapped around Tobias, trying with all his might, Jacob could see Duncan and screamed at Tobias to stop.

Tired and with heavy breath, but moreover, now listening to what his friend was saying, Tobias finally stopped struggling. "Ok! Ok, let go of me … Let go!"

Jacob released his grip, and both men got to their feet. Duncan lay still. No movement.

Breathing heavily, Tobias said, "FUCK …!"

Jacob knelt down next to Duncan and placed his head up his chest. Tobias just stood there.

"He's not dead," Jacob said.

Tobias stood still and let his head fall, staring at the floor. "He threw fucking boiling water at me …" he said, "Boiling fucking-"

At that moment, the door opened, and a woman walked in and screamed!!!

# Chapter Twenty-Two



Tobias walked the horse, with Jacob and Josephine on its back, to the backyard of Jeremiah's house. He helped Josephine down from the saddle and softly told her to go inside and sit by the fireplace. As she walked into the doorway and through the kitchen, Tobias helped Jacob down off the horse. Jacob winced in pain from the wound in his thigh. Tobias put Jacob's arm around his shoulder, gently walked him into the house and sat him down on a chair next to where Josephine stood, her head resting on her arms on the fireplace.

Jacob slumped into the chair, with his wounded leg stretched straight out in front. He placed his hand just above the hole in his leg, squeezed it hard and let out a deep cry, "Arggghhh! Now, that hurts," he said.

Tobias took the knife from his belt, made a slit in Jacob's trousers from the bottom and then pulled at it on both sides, ripping at the material until he could see the wound. The strips of cloth that were wrapped around the top of Jacob's leg were soaked in blood. Tobias removed the strips so that he could see the hole that Gabriel's shot from his pistol had made.

"That needs to come out," said Tobias.

Pale and sweaty, Jacob closed his eyes, threw his head backwards and groaned.

Josephine lifted her head, wiped her eyes with the sleeve of her shirt, sniffed a few times and turned to look at the leg.

"I'm sorry, Jacob," she said. "If it wasn't for Gabriel, you would not-"

Jacob lifted his head and interrupted her as she spoke. "It happened. You're safe, and he's dead. I would give my life for that, so a small hole in my leg ..."

Josephine sniffed again and wiped her eyes once more.

Tobias stood up and turned to the fire. "Jacob's right. You're safe; that's all that matters."

With both hands holding his leg above the wound, Jacob smiled and said, "Well, it ain't all that matters. I've still got a ball of shot lodged in my leg ..."

Josephine, her eyes red with tears, smirked and laughed at what Jacob had said.

Tobias held the knife's blade in the fire, heating it. When it glowed orange, he turned to Jacob and said, "Not for long."

"Shit," came Jacob's reply.

Tobias picked up a small piece of wood at the side of the fireplace from the pile of kindling and gave it to Jacob. "I won't lie. This is gonna hurt," he said.

Jacob took the piece of wood from Tobias and said, "What do you want me to do with this?"

Tobias knelt down, wiped the blood away from the hole to see better and said, "Put it between your teeth; you are gonna want to bite down hard."

Jacob put the wood in his mouth and bit down on it. Tobias placed his finger and thumb on either side of the bloody hole and opened it up. Jacob let out a groan.

Tobias said, "Ok, on the count of three. Are you ready?"

Jacob breathed in deeply, bit down harder on the wood and nodded.

Tobias held the hot knife at the hole and said, "Ok. Ready, 1, 2 ..."

And then pushed the tip of the blade into the hole, twisted it until he felt the shot and picked it out of the hole. Jacob, biting down hard on the wood, screamed a muffled scream as the knife flicked out the shot. Tobias quickly pushed the hole shut and held it closed.

Jacob's mouth opened, and the piece of wood fell into his lap. His head slumped back, and his arm covered his eyes. "FUUUUCK!"

Josephine ripped a piece from the bottom of her shirt and passed it to Tobias, who placed it over the wound. She then tore another strip off, and Tobias wrapped it tight around Jacob's leg.

As Jacob laid back in the chair, intense pain throbbing in his leg, Josephine held him in her arms.

Tobias stood up, looked quickly around the room, and then walked into the study. Seconds later, he came back into the room with a bottle of brandy and poured it over Jacob's leg.

Jacob's head came up fast as he screamed out in pain. Tobias took a swig and then poured more over the leg.

Jacob grabbed at the bottle and took it from Tobias. "Fuck, man! That's enough!" he said.

Tobias pointed at the wrapped, brandy-soaked leg and said, "That will help it - clean it. You will be fine ..."

Jacob swigged from the bottle and drank the rest of the brandy. Letting out a big sigh, he dropped his arm to the side of the chair and let go of the bottle, which hit the floor and rolled under the chair.

"Well," said Tobias, "I'll leave you two here while I go and look for a shovel."

Jacob laid back in the chair and breathed deeply.

Josephine looked up at Tobias with a quizzical look on her face. "A shovel? What for?" she asked.

"To bury your brother," he said. "I'm not going to leave him to just rot in a field. Even he deserves a decent burial."

Josephine stood up and walked towards Tobias. Standing on her tiptoes, she placed her hands on his face and kissed his cheek. Tears trickled down her face as she said, "You're a good man, Tobias. A good man. Thank you."

Tobias walked through the kitchen and out the back into the yard. As he looked around, he saw a shovel, picked it up, and made his way to the field where Gabriel's body lay. It was dark, but the moon was bright enough for Tobias to see. As he reached Gabriel, he looked down at the body. Blood was over his face, and his mouth was open. Tobias took a breath and dug into the ground.

In a short while, he had dug deep enough. He leaned over, grabbed Gabriel's feet and pulled his body into the hole. The body twisted as it fell and ended up face down. Tobias climbed out of the grave, took the shovel, and threw the dirt back in …

After the last shovel, Tobias patted down the dirt. No words were said, and he made the walk back to the house. As he walked, he was reminded of the death of his father just a few weeks before. The difference was that at his father's grave stood himself and Father Almand. A few words were said to send his father's body off. No words were said for Gabriel. Hell would be his home now …

Tobias walked across the field, and standing at the start of the field, stood Josephine.

As he reached where she stood, with her arms folded, she said softly, "He will not sit with my father in heaven, and that comforts me."

Tobias put an arm around her, and they walked back into the house. Not one of them wanted to stay in that house a moment longer. So Tobias helped Jacob to the horse and cart at the front of the house. Josephine took the lamp from the cart, lit it from the fire inside and joined both men back outside. Tobias laid Jacob down in the back of the cart and then drove it back to the tavern.

Jacob's brain woke before his body. He lay still, just his eyes flickering behind closed eyelids. As he started to wake up fully, the wind wooshed and wailed outside, his ears picking up on the sound. As he stirred from a deep sleep, his eyes opened and closed, blinking slowly. Rubbing his eyes and stretching, he was instantly aware of a sharp pain in his leg. He woke and sat upright, startled by the pain, and grabbed at his leg. The bandages of ripped cloth from Josephine's shirt were bloodied. He had slept very deeply and, for that time, had been transported away from the reality of being shot in the leg. Now awake, he was again conscious of the fact. He gently prodded around the area of thy wound, wincing as he did. Sitting in a bed and looking around the room, he knew where he was - back at the tavern. Through the window, he could see the morning sun, just about shining through white clouds with a hint of grey swirled within. The howling of the wind could be heard as it whipped past the walls of the tavern outside. Jacob sat on the edge of the bed, the wounded leg stretched out. He ran his fingers through his messy hair, yawned, rubbed his head, and stood up, testing his weight on the leg. The pain seared through his thigh, but putting his weight on it was bearable. Slowly and with great care, Jacob made his way to the door, walked along the landing, and to the top of the stairs. He looked down the steps that loomed before him, took a deep breath, and then held the banister tightly as he slowly and carefully made his way down. Every single step he took made him wince, letting out painful groans as he went.

Eventually, after what seemed ages, he made it to the bottom step, where he stopped for a second and softly, under his breath, said, "F-uck ..."

The tavern was quiet, not a sound other than the wind. Jacob stood at the bottom of the stairs for a minute and then hobbled his way to the bar. A window was open, the wind banging it open and shut. At the table next to the window sat Josephine.

She sat alone, her head lying in her hands, elbows on the table, just staring into the corner opposite where she sat. Jacob stood at the bar and watched her. She didn't move a muscle - just sat, staring. From where Jacob stood, he could only see one side of her face, the open window behind her, opening and shutting in the wind.

"Penny for your thoughts," he said.

Josephine turned quickly, stood, and walked towards him. "How are you feeling??" she said as she reached him, her arms holding him tight as she embraced him.

"I was about to ask you the same."

Josephine leant back, her hands on both his arms and looked deep into Jacob's eyes, fighting through tears. "I've lost everything. He took it all from me …" she said, wiping the tears from her cheeks. "My father …" Shaking her head and sniffling, she continued. "He took my father, my loving father …"

Jacob placed his hands on her arms, slid down and held her hands. "He's dead now; he can't hurt you anymore."

"Yes, Jacob … I killed him … shot him dead …" Josephine stepped back and wiped her eyes with her hands. "There's nothing left for me here now … It's all gone … There's nothing …"

Jacob looked at the floor and then at Josephine. "You can … You can build a better …"

"A better what …?" asked Josephine. "My father is gone, my brother is …" She brushed her hair off her face and sighed deeply. "Every time I look around this place, I will be reminded … I can't do that, Jacob," she said, shaking her head. "I can't …"

The door of the tavern swung open, and the wind swirled in, scattering leaves over the floor. Tobias entered with an armful of chopped wood.

"By Christ, that wind's picking up," he said as he kicked the door shut behind him, walked over to the large fireplace and dropped the wood onto the floor.

"Cuts right through yer," he said as he picked up a few logs, putting them into the grate over the low burning embers. He bent down and blew at the embers, making them glow orange and a deep red as they came to life, the small flames catching the fresh logs.

Josephine took a pot from behind the bar, filled it with water from a bucket and said, "I'll make us all some hot tea."

"How are yer feeling this morning, Jacob?" asked Tobias.

"It's still hurting, big man. I think it needs new dressing over it; these are a bit bloodied."

Josephine hung the pot over the fire and said, "I'll cut up some new strips from some clean bed sheets I have in the back. Take those off, Jacob, and clean the wound as best you can with some brandy while I fetch them."

As she left the bar, Jacob sat down with a bottle of brandy and gently took off the bloodied dressing. "She can't stay here, big man."

Tobias put some more logs on the fire and turned towards Jacob. "What do you mean?" he said.

Jacob winced as he poured the brandy over the wound. "That's what she was just saying," he said. "She can't stay here anymore. Too many memories for her. She says that there's nothing left for her here."

Tobias turned on his knees to face Jacob. "So where will she go then? What will she do?"

Josephine came back into the bar with the fresh bandages from the bedsheet. "With you both ..." she said as she handed Jacob the strips.

Tobias stood up, walked over to the banging window, closed it shut and turned to face Josephine. "And what about this place?" he asked.

"Well, I shall board it up until I decide what to do with it, Tobias. Right now, after everything, I just cannot bear to stay here."

Jacob wrapped his thigh and tied it off tightly. He poured more brandy over the wrapping and then took a swig himself. He offered the bottle to Tobias. "You can come back with us to London. Can't she ...?" he said as he turned to get the bottle back from Tobias.

"No reason she can't," replied Tobias.

"Good, then it's settled. We can stay here for a day or two while Jacob's leg gets better and board this place up, ready to go," said Josephine. "Now, let me make some tea."

# Chapter Twenty-Three



BANG, BANG, BANG.

Tobias hammered in the last nail of the board on the final downstairs window. He dropped the hammer into the wooden bucket with the nails inside and stood back, looking at the tavern that was now all boarded up. Josephine stood behind him, eyeing up the place she had been born in, grew up in, and worked in her entire life.

Tobias, noticing tears forming in her eyes, put a big arm around her and said, "Are you sure this is what you want, little sister?"

Josephine leaned her head on his broad shoulder and wiped her wet eyes. "Yes … Yes, I'm sure. Things will never be the same now."

Tobias hugged her tighter with one arm and kissed the top of her head. "Well, I can promise you this much: you will be safe with us."

Josephine looked up, stood on her tiptoes and kissed Tobias on his cheek. "Thank you."

Jacob stood in the doorway, holding onto a crutch crudely made from a rather bendy branch. "I see you're all done, big man. I'm sorry that I couldn't of been more help to you."

"Well, my skinny friend," said Tobias. "You can drive the cart back to London while I have a sleep in the back."

Jacob nodded. "I can do that," he said.

Josephine went back inside, gathered her belongings and placed them in the back of the cart. She wrapped cuts of beef, bread and apples, filled two leather flasks with ale, collected the five bottles of brandy that were left, and put those in the cart. Tobias nailed the doors shut as Josephine and Jacob climbed onto the cart. He picked up the bucket of nails with the hammer, put them in the back of the cart and climbed in.

"Well, take one last look," said Jacob and then whipped at the reins.

As the cart slowly moved along, Josephine looked at the place she called home. Suddenly, she grabbed Jacob's hands and said, "Stop! … Wait!"

She jumped off the cart and ran back towards the tavern, running past it to the small chicken run. She opened the gate, stepped inside and shooed at the chickens. They ran around her in all directions and then out of the gate. Josephine took the bucket of feed and scattered it over the floor, and then ran back to the cart. She climbed on, tapped Jacob's arm and said, "Now we can go."

Jacob whipped at the reins again, and the horse moved forward to the road. The cart trundled up onto the road. Josephine looked behind one more time.

Tobias made himself comfortable in the back before closing his eyes and saying, "Wake me when we get to London …"

After a few hours, Jacob could see the outline of London in the distance. The sky was overcast, and there was a chill in the air. To his left, way over, he could see the River Thames with ships going up and down of all sizes. Josephine was asleep, her head on his shoulder. The sound of the cart's wheels as it trundled along had sent her off.

From behind Jacob came Tobias' voice. "A blind man could know when London is within sight. The smell of shit hits you …"

"It sure does, big man," said Jacob.

As they got nearer, Josephine stirred, rubbed her nose and then sat up. "Lord above," she said, holding her nose. "What is that awful smell?????"

"That's London," said Tobias. "It comes and goes."

Jacob shifted in his seat, rubbing his leg. "Depends on what way the wind's blowing," he said. "Once we get into London itself, especially near the docks, you won't notice it as much."

Tobias laughed. "Yeah, then all you can smell is piss."

Jacob shook his head and pointed as the docks could be seen from the road. "Look … Can you see?" he asked Josephine. "All the ships? Bringing sugar, fruits, meat, spices, cloth, tea, coffee and furs. You see? All the colours and smells …"

The cart passed by the docks and entered the city. Josephine was immediately aware of the size of it and the number of different people of all colours, shapes and sizes, rich and poor. The amount of people on the streets, bustling and walking in every direction. Children were running about, and she saw all kinds of animals. She was completely astounded by it all: the different colours, cultures, and noise. London was indeed a living, breathing city. There were more people in that instance as the cart trundled through the street than she had ever seen before in her whole life.

As they drove down the street, she could see men in tall hats with canes walking with women with their breasts half exposed, wearing dirty dresses. Women had their arms filled with linen and clothes; men were drunk in the street, and people, including children, were selling every and anything from food to cloth, trinkets and treasures galore. Her heart beat fast, and her eyes widened, taking in all around her. Even the buildings, some old, some new, and some being built, amazed her. How tall and big they looked, being three and four stories high. There were inns and shops, coffee and tea houses. There was too much to take in as her eyes flitted from one thing to another. Suddenly the cart stopped, and Jacob pointed to the sign hanging from the wall. 'ROOMS FOR RENT.'

"That's where we have rooms to stay," he said.

Tobias jumped off the back of the cart, jolting it as he did, and stepped around to the side to help Josephine down. He turned to

Jacob and beckoned him to get off as well. "You get the rooms, and I'll take the cart around back."

Jacob shifted across the seat, and Tobias helped him down.

As Tobias got up into the cart, he called after Jacob and threw him the bendy branch crutch. "Don't be forgetting this; we don't want you falling now, do we?"

Jacob caught the crutch and slapped it onto the hind leg of the horse, causing it to dart off, with Tobias clinging on to the reins, trying desperately to gain control.

"Don't you fall off now!" cried Jacob after him.

Josephine followed Jacob into the building, where he paid for rooms for the week for all three. She was handed a rather large key by the owner and told to follow him.

Tobias had taken the cart around to the back and unhitched the horse. He placed it into the stable, gave it food and water and then collected Josephine's belongings and took them to her room.

The door was open; Josephine looked out of the window down below into the street, watching the scene.

Jacob sat on her bed, patting it and said, "They are quite comfortable to sleep in, not like your beds at the tavern, but they will do."

Josephine was more interested in the bustling street below and just nodded.

Tobias walked through the door and put her belongings on the bed. He then slapped Jacob on his thigh, to which he winced and let out a small cry in pain as he grabbed at it.

"That's for the horse," said Tobias and then turned towards Josephine. "Well, what do ya think of it? Of London?" he asked.

"I can't wait to see more," she replied.

Tobias helped Jacob to his feet, put the crutch in his hand and walked towards the door.

"Well, we can all have a wash and then get ourselves a good drink over at Maggie's. She owns the inn across the road a ways."

Jacob hobbled to the door as Tobias walked through it. He then turned back to Josephine. "Settle in, and we will come and fetch you in an hour."

Josephine picked out some clothes from her belongings and nodded as Jacob closed the door behind him.

An hour later, Jacob knocked on the door and heard Josephine call out, "I'll just be a minute."

Moments later, the door opened, and Josephine stepped out. She was met by Jacob, and Dupree, who held out his hand, bowed his head and said, "Miss Josephine, you look as beautiful as ever."

Josephine blushed, said thank you and shook his hand. Jacob told her that they would be going across the road to Maggie's inn. They walked down the stairs and out the door.

"Where is Tobias?" she asked as she looked around.

"Ee eez already in there," said Dupree. "Eez always in there, with Madame Maggie."

"Well," said Jacob. "Let's go join him."

Dupree opened the door of Maggie's inn, bowed and waved his hand, gesturing for Josephine to enter. "After you," he said.

She smiled, nodded her head and said, "Thank you, Dupree."

Jacob walked in and led Josephine to a table where she sat down with Dupree. At the bar stood Tobias talking and flirting with Maggie, his huge hands wrapped around hers as he bent across the bar to kiss her cheek. He felt a tap on his back and turned around to see Jacob.

"Ah, my skinny friend; about time you turned up." And then, spinning around, he said, "There she is … Josephine. Josephine, come here and meet the lovely Maggie."

Maggie poured a jug of ale and gave it to Jacob. Tobias put his huge arm around Josephine as she came to the bar and said, "Maggie, Josephine. Josephine, Maggie."

"Nice to meet yer, my love … What's yer poison???"

Josephine looked confused for a second until Maggie, upon seeing this, laughed and said, "I mean, what'll you be drinking?"

"Ale," came the reply.

Maggie smiled, poured another jug, put it on the bar and said, "My kind of woman." She looked at Tobias and said, "I like her already …"

A smile spread across Josephine's face as she lifted the jug and began to drink the ale. She finished it in one go, placed the empty jug back on the bar and wiped the froth from her mouth. Jacob stood and raised his eyebrows. Tobias smirked from the corner of his mouth, nodding his head. And Maggie, with both hands on her hips, said, "Well, well … I like her even more now!"

As the night went on, all four of them sat at the table and drank. Maggie kept bringing them drink after drink. And they laughed and talked louder and louder. The time had gone by fast. Maggie closed the door behind the last few people who had left and locked it after them. She brought two bottles of brandy from the bar and put them on the table.

"Mind if I join you now?" she said.

Tobias pushed himself and his chair out from under the table and slapped his hand on his lap.

"Why, of course, my little darling," he said, "You can sit right here."

They all carried on drinking, talking and laughing. Josephine's thoughts were far from her brother and from the troubles that had befallen her a few days before. She felt happy being with Tobias, Dupree, and, of course, Jacob. She felt good deep inside herself. With a feeling of new beginnings and a new life, her heart lifted, and her troubles sank. She poured herself a glass of brandy, stood up and held the glass high in the air.

"To a new start," she said.

All of them held their glasses up and together said the same, then threw their heads back to drink …

===== The next morning =====

It was mid-morning, and the rain fell heavy and hard onto the roof of Maggie's inn. Water dripped onto the head of Tobias as he snored loudly. Maggie had been meaning to get the roof fixed for a while now, but it only ever really leaked in places when the rain was indeed heavy. Today was one of those days. She lay next to Tobias, her head on his large, hairy chest, moving up and down with every breath he took as he snored. She stirred as the water hit Tobias' head and splashed onto hers as her face nestled into his neck. She frowned and blinked her closed eyes, licking her lips as the water splashed and as she stirred from her sleep. She opened her eyes slowly, opening and closing them for a minute as she woke. The water splashed her face again. Her eyes, now fully open, blinking and trying to focus, stared at the rain hitting the window. Water splashed her again. She lifted her head, stretched, yawned, and then turned to face Tobias as a loud snore whooshed in her ear.

Jacob woke from a thud to his back and the side of his head. He was immediately aware of being on the floor. He sat upright as soon as he felt the thud. And hit the top of his head. He ducked and held it as a sharp pain seared through it. "Ouch," he said.

"Good morning."

Jacob rubbed his blurry eyes to see Dupree sitting at a table. He looked around to see that he was on the floor of Maggie's inn. He stood up, reaching to steady himself on the table with his hand.

Dupree ran his fingers through his beard and scratched his chin. "Oh, ma tete," mumbled Dupree.

Jacob rubbed his eyes again and then his face, looked at Dupree and said, "What?"

Dupree covered his eyes with his hands. "Zee head … she eez sore …"

Jacob took a deep breath, held it for a few seconds and then breathed out. He nodded at Dupree and then slowly shook his head from left to right. "How much did we drink last night, Dupree??"

"Well, mon ami, by zee look of the empty bottles of brandy and jugs of ale, quite a lot."

With his back to the bar, Jacob suddenly scanned the room. "Josephine," he said. "Where's Josephine?"

Dupree pointed to behind where Jacob was. Jacob turned around to see Josephine lying on her side, sprawled over the bar. Her hair had fallen down, covering her face and hanging down the bar. He walked over to her and gently shook her shoulder. She groaned and turned onto her back.

"Josephine," he whispered. "Josephine …"

Her eyes opened, and she stared straight at Jacob. He stood for a moment, looking back. She blinked, closed them for a second, and then opened them again. Then she sat bolt upright, swinging her legs around and hopped off the bar, leaning back onto it.

"Ohhh," she said, holding her head, leaning forward and swaying a little. "Ohhh …"

Jacob gently rubbed her shoulder and said, "Let me get you some water."

He walked to where a wooden barrel of water was kept behind the bar. He grabbed a small jug, dunked it in the barrel, filled it, and then offered it to Josephine. She took the jug and gulped down the water, put it on the bar, and swept back her hair.

All three looked towards the ceiling as they were suddenly aware of a scraping and banging noise coming from the floor above their heads. And then, "Uh, uh, uh, uh, uh ohhh!"

Jacob looked at Josephine, who looked back and then shied away.

Dupree shook his head and said, "Mon Dieu. Ee eez like zee rabbit …"

Josephine smiled and then burped. Then covering her mouth, she ran to the backyard of the inn, clawing at the door to open it. Both Jacob and Dupree looked at each other as they heard her being sick.

Jacob refilled the small jug from the water barrel and stepped out the back where Josephine was doubled over, one hand holding her hair off her face and the other hand leaning against the wall of the inn.

"Here, some water for you," he said, holding it out behind her.

Josephine let go of her hair and reached behind to where he held the jug, taking it from his hand. "Thank you," she said without turning around.

Jacob walked back inside. As he walked back in, Maggie was behind the bar, standing at the barrel, drinking from the large ladle that hung from its side.

"Morning," she said as she turned to see Jacob.

Before Jacob could say 'morning' back to her, Tobias stood up from behind the bar with a jug of ale and swiftly drank it. "Ahh … hair of the dog that bit ya," he said.

Jacob shook his head and sighed. Tobias wiped his mouth and stood behind Maggie, grabbed her waist and nuzzled her neck. Josephine stepped through the doorway and sat down opposite Dupree.

"You feel better now?" he said. "Eet eez better out zan in, no …?"

Josephine pushed her fingers through her hair, licked her lips, and just nodded.

"I think we could all do with some breakfast, soak up all that ale in our bellies," said Maggie.

"That sounds like a good idea," said Josephine. "I'll help you make it."

"Thanks, many hands make light work. Follow me, my love, into my kitchen out the back, and we can get started."

Tobias slapped his stomach and then rubbed his hairy chest. "Mmmmm," he said. "Can't beat a nice bit of grub to fill a hole first thing."

Dupree patted his own stomach and licked his lips. "Yes, yes, a nice egg or two."

All of a sudden, there was a knock at the door.

"Who could that be?" Tobias said as he sunk a cup into the water barrel, filling it up.

The door knocked again …

Jacob stood up, walked to the door and opened it. He then smiled with his hands out in front of him. "You're back!" he said as Solomon walked through the door and greeted them all.

Maggie and Josephine came from the kitchen with a breakfast of eggs and cured ham with a large loaf of bread and placed it on the table.

"You've returned, Solomon, and earlier than you said," said Tobias, shaking his hand.

"Sit, sit … and just in time for some breakfast … You hungry??" Maggie asked.

"I could find room for a couple of slices of that there ham," said Solomon.

Josephine sat down at the table, cut two thick slices of the ham and passed the plate to Solomon.

"Hello," she said. "I'm Josephine. We haven't met."

Solomon took the plate, wiped his hand and shook Josephine's gently. "Solomon's the name, miss, and I'm happy to say we have now."

Josephine felt herself blush as she shook his hand and stared at the big smile that had spread across Solomon's handsome face. Jacob did not notice this as he was cutting a slice of bread, but Maggie did as she handed a plate to Dupree.

Tobias poured a jug of ale and put it in front of Solomon. "Drink, eat, and tell us why you are back earlier than you said."

Solomon took a bite of the ham, chewed it for a second and then washed it down with a swig of ale.

"I came across a very bountiful ship not two days from here, full of goods that you will all find agreeable to your wants. I came here straight away to let you know and, of course, to sell them to you, or strike up a deal with you."

Jacob, Tobias and Dupree all sat up to listen to what Solomon had to say.

"Ok," said Jacob. "What deal do you have in mind?"

"Well, let's finish this hearty breakfast, then I shall take you to my ship. And then we can make a deal …"

# Chapter Twenty-Four



Verity slumped to her knees next to where Duncan lay, his face a bloody mess, his body still. Her screams now turned into wailing cries. She shook at Duncan's body, shouting his name. Duncan moaned deeply and then coughed and spluttered, bringing blood up onto his chin and chest.

"OHH, oh, Duncan … Duncan, my love, can you hear me?" she said, taking his face in her hands and wiping the blood from his face. "It's me. Verity. Can you hear me?"

Duncan opened his eyes and, coughing, said in a feeble voice, "Ver- Verity, Verity …" Then, suddenly and with speed, he shot up to his feet and pulled her behind him, facing the two men. With his arm holding Verity behind him, he bellowed at them. "WHO ARE YOU? … WHAT DO YOU WANT????"

Tobias clenched his ham-like fists, but before he could make any sort of move towards Duncan, Jacob thrust an arm across his chest and stepped forward.

"We were sent here to give you a message, Duncan Cook," said Jacob. "To stay away from a Mrs Attwood, another man's wife. To make sure you get the message."

Verity quickly stepped out from behind Duncan's grasp, with fury etched over her face,

"Who the hell sent you?" she said aloud. "That weasel of an ex-husband of mine …??"

Both Jacob and Tobias stood, looking at each other, confusion on both their faces.

Verity continued. "No … No, not him. Hasn't the stomach for it himself … No, but his brother, though, he has, hasn't he? Another weasel of a man … Jeremiah!!!!!"

"What are you saying?" asked Tobias.

Duncan stepped forward, wiped his face from blood and said. "What she is saying is that she is not married. Not anymore. But will be again, very soon, to me."

Even though this was just another job for Tobias and Jacob, it did not sit easily with them. Not at all.

Jacob tried to say something to them. "Look, we … We just came here for a … It's what we do for mon-"

"Just get out," Verity said, holding Duncan in her arms. "Go! Go and collect your money, leave us alone."

Both Jacob and Tobias stood for a few seconds; no words could be said.

"GO …. GO NOW!"

As both men left the house, the door closed as quickly behind them. They walked to their horses, mounted them, and trotted down the road and through the village. As they got clear of the houses, they kicked at the horses and galloped off down the road, leaving the hamlet in the distance behind them.

"So," said Tobias, "he has a brother …"

Jacob shuffled in the saddle, shook his head, and turned his head. "That's why Jeremiah said not to collect any money, that it was personal to him. The message was from him."

Tobias rode, staring ahead, his mind elsewhere.

Jacob shook his head again. "That was a beating because Jeremiah's brother had been jilted by his wife for another man. And so Jeremiah wanted the man to suffer for it."

"Why did he have to throw the boiling water at me?" said Tobias. "I lost my head; anger took over my whole body …"

"He didn't deserve that," said Jacob. "She said her ex-husband."

"I was full of rage … Couldn't stop hitting him," said Tobias looking at his knuckles.

Jacob shook his head once more and then told Tobias that he didn't agree with Jeremiah sending them to do his brother's dirty work. He said that he felt guilty because it didn't sit well with his conscience. It was one thing to have to beat up on a man who did not repay his debt or to scare a man, but what they just did wasn't at all right in Jacob's mind. Tobias agreed.

They carried on to Jeremiah's house. Both men agreed they would collect payment and then leave.

"That was difficult," Tobias said as both men left the dirt track from Jeremiah's house.

"I know," said Jacob, pulling on the reins to turn the horse right, onto the road. "Especially when he gave us the money and then smiled out of the corner of his mouth."

Tobias clenched his huge fist and shook it in front of his face. "I should of just broken his jaw."

Jacob nodded. "This time, I agree with you, big man."

"It's not too late," Tobias said, bringing his horse to a halt.

"Let's just get back to Dupree, and put this whole thing down to experience," said Jacob.

After riding for a while, they came upon the now familiar sights of London. They rode through the streets, and Tobias stopped at Maggie's inn.

"Time for a quick drink before we head back to the rooms and find Dupree," he said.

Jacob stopped his horse just passed the door to the inn, turned it around and jumped off, tying it to the post. He looked up at Tobias, who had tied his horse and was at the door.

"You sure it's just a drink you're after??"

"Well to start with," laughed Tobias. "And then … who knows?"

Maggie was clearing some glasses from a table, and Tobias walked up behind her and slapped her arse. She spun around to see his big frame looking down at her.

"Oh, you're back, are you?" she said. "Ain't seen yer for a few days."

Tobias put his big arms around her waist, picked her up and planted a kiss on her lips.

"Why? Missed me, 'av yer?" he said with a big smile.

Maggie pulled at his arms and wriggled from his grip on her waist. "'Ere, leave off, will yer? I've customers to attend. Ain't seen yer for a few days, an' you come bowling in an' put yer big hands all over me!"

As soon as her feet touched the floor, she turned on her heels and walked toward the bar. Tobias slapped her on the arse again, making her jump a little with a smile on her face.

She stepped behind the bar and asked what he would be having.

Tobias put both hands on the bar. "Two jugs of ale to start, my lovely."

Jacob stood next to him and nodded to Maggie as she poured the ale. "Hello again," he said.

Maggie put both jugs in front of the two men. As soon as she did, Tobias picked one up and drank the entire jug in seconds, spilling froth down his chin and shirt.

"AAAAAAHHH," he said as he wiped the froth away with his sleeve. "Fill it up again, please."

Maggie said hello to Jacob and filled the jug again. "Thirsty, was yer?" she said as Jacob took a mouthful from his jug.

Tobias picked up the second jug of ale, winked at her, and said, "Aye, I am, and not just for your ale, Maggie, my darling."

Jacob rolled his eyes as he placed the jug on the bar, looked at Maggie and with half a smile, slightly shook his head. Maggie looked at Jacob and raised her eyebrows with a crooked smile.

From behind them, a hand was placed upon each of their shoulders, and a familiar voice spoke.

"Gentlemen, you are back. And so soon."

Dupree slipped between them and tapped on the bar. "Ah, sweet Maggie, zum brandy for my dear friends and I."

Maggie bent down, grabbed a bottle from under the bar and put it in front of Dupree.

"Did you hear that?" she said, looking at Tobias. "A true gent, this one … sweet, he called me … Didn't come in and start grabbing my arse, did he?"

Tobias gulped from the jug with one hand and with the other arm, put it around Dupree's shoulders and hoisted him up off his feet, squeezing him as he did. And then let him down again. "And he never will," he said, winking at her.

Dupree grabbed the bottle from the bar and told the two men to take a seat at a table. "Come … We 'av many zings to talk about."

All three men sat and talked. Dupree explained that in the couple of days they had been gone, he had secured deals with a few of the most successful traders and merchants within the docks of London with the help of John Crawford. And he had restocked with goods so that they could travel back towards Brendan's house to sell the goods at the market he held and put some coin in his hand, as promised. Without Brendan's help in the first place, they would not be in the position that they found themselves in. Both Jacob and Tobias agreed, and Dupree added that by the time they had visited with Brendan, Solomon would have returned to the docks. They could take whatever he plundered from his time at sea and begin to set up their business properly. This would be profitable for all involved. They now had links to build up trade as merchants. Solomon would provide goods at a cheaper rate; other merchants would buy from them at a cheaper rate, and the rich would buy at any rate they so chose to sell them, especially furs and silks and spices. Plus, they also had the link at Brendan's market. Their future certainly looked fruitful.

"Come, gentlemen … Drink up," said Dupree. "We 'av much to celebrate."

Jacob knew that the life of a merchant would be a profitable one. Most merchants had to battle against many things to make their coin. One, in particular, was from their goods coming across the sea. High winds and terrible storms claimed many a ship, sunk many a crew and with them, the goods. This was accepted, to a degree, as just a way of life. But another major setback on the crossings from the new world to England was pirates. Large companies enlisted paid help in the form of Privateers. These men, who were once pirates themselves, were used to hunt down the feared ships that bore the black flags of pirates. This, to the pirates, was also just a way of life. But for Jacob, Tobias and Dupree, they had chosen to make a pirate part of their business. Solomon was very good at stealing from the smaller ships. His schooner was ideal for getting close to larger ships than his; the speed of his schooner enabled Solomon to do so. And the privateers were hired for the larger ships, galleons, which held large quantities in their hulls. The haul for Solomon wasn't as big, but the risk wasn't either. He could be more frequent than the pirate galleons and, with a smaller, faster ship, more successful. With all these men working together, the link they had with each other meant more opportunities for coin. The future did indeed look fruitful …

Dupree raised his glass to the two men, made a small toast to their future and then placed a hand on each of their shoulders.

"Tomorrow, ve shall ride out to Brendan's. My cart, she eez full. In fact, eet isn't big enough to carry all the goods in one go. I zink zat we may 'av to buy a bigger one."

Tobias pulled the bag of coins from the job they had just collected that day from Jeremiah and threw it onto the table. "Well, that should cover the cost of a bigger cart, my friend. We can go from Brendan's and see my old friend, Joseph, the blacksmith. Maybe he can build us a cart with an iron cage."

Jacob drank the glass of brandy, nodded as he did, and then said, "That's a great idea, big man. So it's settled, then. Tomorrow, we ride, but right now, we need a good night's rest."

Dupree agreed and stood up to leave with Jacob. They both walked to the door, but Tobias remained seated. Jacob opened the door and then turned towards him.

Tobias was watching Maggie cleaning glasses behind the bar as she watched him. He looked straight at Jacob, winked, and said, "I shall see you two in the morning."

The following morning, Dupree and Jacob woke early and gathered a few things for the journey to Brendan's house. They placed everything in the cart, and then Jacob saddled his and Tobias' horse. He grabbed the reins of Tobias', mounted his own, and rode around to the front of Maggie's inn with Dupree following behind. Dupree stepped down off his cart and held onto the two horses as Jacob banged on the front door of the inn.

"Let's hope he is awake and ready," said Jacob as he turned to face Dupree.

Dupree nodded, stroking the face of Tobias' horse. "Oui, and not doing other things," he said, pointing to the upstairs window.

Jacob raised his fist to bang on the door again, and the door opened before he could.

"Morning," Tobias said as he walked through the door and out onto the street.

A second "Morning" came from behind him as Maggie stood in the open doorway.

Both Jacob and Dupree said good morning back, with Dupree tipping his hat at Maggie.

Tobias turned and planted a long kiss on Maggie's lips, holding her waist, her arms hung around his neck, standing on tiptoes as she did.

"Well, we shall be off now, my love. See you in a couple of weeks or so."

Tobias took the reins of his horse, stepped up onto the stirrups and sat in the saddle. Jacob mounted his, and Dupree climbed up into the cart. Tobias blew a kiss as all three men took off down the street.

Maggie waved goodbye as the cart trundled off down the road and out of London.

Tobias and Jacob rode alongside Dupree as they left London behind them. They had a very long journey to take to get back to Brendan's, at least two days of riding.

A few hours had passed by, and as they came to a bend in the road, a fallen tree blocked the path.

"Woah," Dupree said as he pulled on the reins, bringing his horse to a stop.

Jacob and Tobias also brought their horses to a stop. The tree had fallen across the road, totally blocking it.

Dupree stood up in the cart for a better look. "Merde!!!!!!" he said, as there was no way to pass.

Jacob climbed down off his horse and studied the fallen tree. It was a very large tree and looked very heavy. Tobias jumped down and stood next to Jacob.

"We'll pull it," he said.

"With what?" said Jacob.

Tobias reached into the back of the cart and pulled out a length of rope.

"This ... We can tie it to the trunk and then to the saddle and pull it aside using the horse."

"Good idea, big man, but how are we going to tie it around the trunk? There's thick hedges on either side, and the branches make it difficult."

Tobias scratched at his head and then his chin. Then he pulled the axe from his belt. "With this," he said, holding the axe in the air. "Watch ..."

Tobias started chopping at the branches to make a clearing for the rope to be tied around. Jacob grabbed at some branches, bending them out of the way to make it easier.

Then from behind them, they heard Dupree's voice. "Gentlemen ... Gentlemen..."

Without looking behind them, Jacob said, "Just a moment."

Dupree said it again, louder. "GENTLEMEN!"

Jacob turned his head, and just as Tobias was about to bring down the head of the axe to another branch, Jacob stopped him. "Shit! Look," he said.

Tobias turned around. Dupree was sitting in the cart, a pistol at the side of his head. Three masked men, all armed, were holding pistols in each hand and aimed at Jacob and Tobias.

The man on the cart had a pistol pushing against Dupree's head and, in the other hand, had another aimed at both of them. The masks were black and covered the top half of their faces, with two holes for them to see through. They were dressed completely in black from head to foot. The two men on the ground stepped forward towards Tobias and Jacob, and the sound of four pistols clicked as the hammers were pulled back and cocked. The man on the cart tapped the barrel of the pistol on the top of Dupree's head.

"OFF ..." he said. "STAND AND DELIVER."

Under his breath, Jacob muttered the words, "Fuck! Highwaymen ..."

Dupree jumped down and stood by Tobias. Jacob started to speak but was cut short by the man on the cart.

"Don't say a word," came the authoritative voice. "This is a robbery. We are taking your cart and anything else you have on you."

Tobias stepped forward, and as he did, so did the man pointing both pistols at him. "Try it, and it will be the last thing you ever do."

Tobias stopped and grimaced. "Are you sure you want to do this? Think about it. I will give you a chance to leave."

The man jumped from the cart and walked towards Tobias. Without missing a step, he brought up one of the pistols and struck at his head. Tobias caught the man's arm to stop him. The other man aiming at Tobias stepped forward with his arm stretched out and let off a shot with the barrel of the pistol right at Tobias' ear. 'BANG!'

Tobias whipped his head to the side and then let go of the man's arm.

A ringing noise roared through his ear as the man who had fired said, "Try that again, and the next one will be in your eye."

Tobias, his hand pressed against his ringing ear, smiled.

Jacob held his hands out in front and waved at the men to calm themselves. "Take what you want," he said, "and be on your way."

The man who tried to pistol-whip Tobias tapped the outside of Dupree's coat with the pistol.

The metal barrel hit something. And then the man said, "We will be gone as soon as you hand over what's inside your pockets. Starting with you, old man."

Dupree put his hands inside his coat, pulled out a silver pocket watch on a silver chain and handed it over. "Zat eez all I 'av, monsieur."

The man took the watch, held it up to his eyes and said, "That will do nicely." Then he told the man who fired the shot to check the other two. He patted down both Tobias and Jacob and opened their coats to check again.

"Nothing. Just this, covered in dry blood," he said as he waved the handkerchief that he had pulled from Tobias' inside pocket, throwing it to the ground. Two of the men climbed into the cart, keeping their pistols pointed.

The other man stood right in front of Jacob, his face nearly touching his. "You wouldn't be holding out on anything, would you?" he said.

Jacob, now up close, frowned as he looked right into the eyes of the man. "No, you have everything," he said softly.

"Good, good," he said as he backed away, still aiming both pistols at the three of them.

The other two men had turned the cart around in the road; one held the reins in one hand, pointing a pistol with the other. And the other man knelt at the back of the cart, with both pistols aimed at all three.

Jumping up onto the back and sitting with his legs dangling off the back, the man waved both pistols and said, "You have just met The Dick Darkling Gang … We bid you a good day."

As the cart sped off into the distance, Dupree snatched the beaver tail hat from his head and threw it to the ground, screaming out in French and kicking at the dirt. "MERDE!!!!!!!!!!!"

Tobias swung the axe and slammed it down onto a thick branch with such force, cutting it clean in half.

"Bastards! Robbing, thieving bastards!" he said.

Jacob sat back against the fallen tree and grasped the back of his head, rocking back and forth.

"What are we going to do now?" Dupree said, bending down and picking up his hat off the ground.

Tobias lifted the axe high above his head and slammed the head into the trunk, causing it to be stuck. Jacob looked at the axe, sighed deeply and stood up, rubbing his head.

Tobias tugged at the axe, trying to release it from the trunk he had slammed it into. It didn't budge, held in tightly by the trunk. "ARRGGHHH …!" he screamed out, as he pulled and pulled until the blade popped out.

Dupree dusted off the dirt from his hat and shook his head, turned and said, "So …?" He held his arms in the air. "Vot now?"

Jacob walked past Tobias to address Dupree, "Nothing," he said. "Well, not right now, anyway. There's nothing we can do right now. But, we have a name, though, don't we? Dick Darkling."

Tobias swung himself around, waving his axe, his face contorted with anger. "And when I get my hands on him and his gang …"

"Yes, big man," Jacob said as he placed a hand on his shoulder. "We will find them, find Dick, and reclaim back what is ours. But now we will have to return to London and stock up again. This time, we make sure we are ready - with rifles and pistols. And before we get to Brendan's house, we will take a detour to your friend, Tobias, and seek a cage to be built."

Tobias nodded his head. "Yes, Joseph will build one for us, but first, we will have to buy another cart, a bigger one."

Dupree just stood still and stared down the road.

Jacob tapped him on his back and said, "Come, help me get our horses. You can ride on the back with me. We need to get going, get back to London and sort out some things."

Tobias was suddenly aware the horses were not in the road anymore. He looked desperately looked around either side of the road, into the fields and, to his relief, spotted both beasts munching on some grass a hundred yards into the field.

"There they are," he said, pointing across the field.

Jacob reached out and grabbed the reins, patting the horse on its back and walked it towards the other. Holding both reins, he walked back towards Tobias and Dupree, making their way across the field. Tobias grabbed the saddle, put a foot in the stirrup and mounted his horse. Jacob held a hand out to Dupree as he helped him up onto his horse. All three men made their way across the field and onto the road and started the journey back to London.

# Chapter Twenty-Five



Solomon wiped his mouth of crumbs from the chunk of bread he had just eaten and washed it down with a jug of ale. He patted his stomach, looked around at everyone and said, "Well … that filled a hole. Thank you. Now, let's go and see what goods I have for you down at the docks."

Maggie stood up and picked up a few of the plates. "Well, I better get started on clearing this away and get ready to open up. You can stay and help if you like," she said, looking at Josephine.

The men stood up, ready to leave with Solomon.

Josephine stood as well and said to Maggie, "Actually, I would prefer to go down to the docks. I've never seen a ship before, or in fact, a dock."

Solomon took another swig from the jug, wiped the froth from his mouth and held out his hand. "You are more than welcome to see my ship, miss. And are invited to come aboard, if you like."

Josephine took his hand, smiled and said, "I like."

Solomon opened up his arm for Josephine to take hold and said, "Then you shall."

As they all walked down the bustling street towards the docks, dodging people with things for sale and children running around, Jacob poked at Tobias' ribs. "Look," he said, pointing in front to where Solomon and Josephine walked, arm in arm.

Tobias smiled a huge smile, put his arm around Jacob and said, "Are you jealous, my skinny friend?"

Jacob shrugged off his arm. "Don't be stupid."

"Then why poke me?" asked Tobias.

"I'm just saying; she don't even know him," said Jacob.

Tobias laughed and patted Jacobs back. "You're jealous," he said.


Solomon led Josephine down the wooden steps to the docks and to his ship. As she passed by all the people busy about their day loading their carts and woven baskets and unloading all the various goods from the abundance of ships and small boats, she was giddy with all the colours and smells of all the different kinds of food, spices, materials and furs. All the reds, greens, yellows, silvers and gold colours. She had never left where she lived in her entire life. Josephine had been raised, educated and worked in the tavern. She had gone to the local villages but never further afield. She had never really experienced anything other than what her life was, with her father and brother, at the tavern. She had come across many, many people of all different kinds who had passed through and taken a bed for the night. But her life had very much revolved around the tavern.

Her entire life had rolled merrily along for as long as she could remember. Until now … her life had changed since that very first meeting of Jacob and Tobias almost two years ago. She immediately had a connection with Jacob and made a friendship with him, as well as a lover. She had fallen in love with Tobias like a brother. She didn't really have that before. Her whole life was the tavern, her father and her brother. And now she found herself with none of that. All that had happened in the past weeks was like a dream - a nightmare, in fact. Her father was gone. Her brother was also gone. And now, she was away from her home; the tavern boarded up. Her life was now … not her life.

As she stood next to this huge black, handsome man, a pirate, with a pirate ship in front of her, Josephine felt calm. Safe even. The noise of the ship moving in the water, the low creaking of tight wood in time with the movement of the small waves. She could see out across the water as it led onto the open sea. The sun flickering, seagulls flapping the sound of their shrieking as they flew and swooped all around. Something suddenly came over her. A sort of knot formed in the pit of her stomach, causing her to take a deep breath.

She turned around, Jacob and Tobias now behind her. "Isn't it beautiful …?" she said to them, looking out to sea. "I wonder what is beyond it all?"

Solomon stepped onto the plank to board his ship, turned and held out his hand. "A whole world, beautiful and full of life, just waiting to be seen."

Josephine grabbed a handful of her dress at the front, lifting up the bottom and took his hand, stepping onto the plank.

Tobias took a bite from the apple that he had swiped from a basket moments before. "All I can see is water."

Josephine boarded the sloop, its rigging gently moving and creaking with the wind cast off from the sea, and walked to the bow. Cupping her eyes from the glare of the morning sun, she looked out towards the open water. The stretch of the River Thames with its winding banks as far as her eyes could see. The shimmer of the sun wobbled and flickered as the water seemed alive, in constant movement. A gentle breeze pushed and pulled at her auburn hair, the sun lighting up the colour even more. She looked out at all the other boats and small ships lined up along the banks, coming in and out of the docks. The men on board were busy and bustling, working the sails and pulling ropes. She heard the shouts and calls of the men working together.

Solomon watched her for a moment as she stood breathing in the salty air, a smile etched upon her beautiful face. "Downriver is where you will find her," he said, now next to Josephine.

"Her?" she replied.

"The open sea," he said, smiling. "She is both beautiful and brutal. Calm and ferocious. Tranquil and terrifying. She can take you to paradise or to the very depths of herself. She is to be respected and feared …"

Josephine breathed deeply and closed her eyes, feeling the warmth of the sun on her face. "She sounds wondrous, Solomon."

"Yes, she is that … She is that …"

Dupree stood a few feet behind them, holding onto a rope that hung from the rigging.

"That's not my memories of the sea," he said. "Eet was a terrible journey from France zose many years ago. Freezing cold winds, waves as high as the sky, battering and belting zee small ship which sailed me 'ere. I remember zee crossing vell. Scary … in fact, I can recall zat ven I first stepped onto England's soil, I kissed zee ground and zanked God I vas still alive."

Solomon turned to Dupree. "As I said, old man, she can be cruel …"

"Well, she is calm right now," said Josephine.

"Zat is not zee sea, mademoiselle, zat is just zee river. Zee sea, she eez huge."

Josephine brushed her hair from her face. "I would very much like to see her one day."

Solomon put his foot up to the rail and his elbow on his knee. "You can sail with me whenever you like, miss Josephine."

Jacob felt hot all of a sudden and asked Solomon what goods he had on board. Solomon opened up the hatch and led him down into the hull. There, stacked up everywhere, were the goods he had plundered. Tobacco, tea, coffee, and sugar … And that was the prize right there. Barrels and barrels of sugar. Over the last few years, sugar had been brought over from the new world, America, and how people latched onto it. The sweet taste made everything taste better. People used it for many things, and Dupree knew that it was very profitable. In fact, he knew the name that had been given to sugar: 'white gold.' A smile spread over his face, this would be easy to sell on, and there was a lot of it.

The four men talked and came to an agreed price to take all that Solomon had. If he could get his hands on these types of goods, then money could be made for all involved. Why pay the cost of dealing with merchants when they now had a very good source to buy from? The risks were higher, especially for Solomon. Dupree knew many eyes would be on them in London and that the penalty for piracy was death, also for those associated with pirates. But, the risk set against the reward was too much to pass, and they all knew it. Dupree suggested that from now on, their business should operate out of London. They could come to London to do business but not to deal with Solomon. Also, Dupree knew that he could get a better price back towards Chelmsford and Ipswich, in fact, anywhere in Essex.

Josephine had come away from her home. Away from the memory of the tavern. The place where she had been born and raised. She had come with them to London just to get away. Now, standing on board this sloop, breathing in the salty air, meeting Solomon, listening to him, the stories he told, and the adventures he had experienced - it was a world away from what she knew. The life she had. The death of her father and what that all had led to - her killing her own brother. Her head was filled with thoughts about what she had been forced to endure, made to do and what she had lost. All of it had changed her ...

Here and now, she could feel it deep inside her very soul. Perhaps the adventures she listened to excited her, making her think and feel in a way never before. Her heart pounded, and her head raced. She felt faint but also strong. Dizzy, but as sturdy as the mightiest of trees. Here in front of her, stood Jacob. A man she had met just two years ago and had fallen for his charms. His soft, gentle nature with her and his shy, bashful way towards her. But also his strength, both physical and mental. And, of course, how handsome he looked.

From the moment she had met him that day in the tavern, that first glance, those first spoken words, she knew that she found him attractive. A bond had formed with him - not only with him but also with Tobias. This was the reason she had sent them the message to help find her father's killers in the first place. Because of that bond … But now, she knew she had changed. Not how she felt for Jacob and not how she looked towards Tobias, but she could feel it grow within her. Filling her with something she had not felt before. She looked out at the water, and it made her feel … alive. The unknowing. What lay beyond it?

Josephine suddenly felt small. Her entire life had been working in the tavern. It was all she had ever known, which had been fine to her. She had loved her life with her father and brother and never thought of anything more. She had been forced to become a woman at a young age when her mother died. She was forced to grow up quickly, and she never complained or worried about it. But, these last few months had taken that world of hers and turned it upside down.

She now knew that what she wanted was out there, beyond the water, over the horizon, across the sea … And Solomon would take her there …

# Chapter Twenty-Six



===== September 1713, Robbed and back to
London =====


Dupree held on tight to Jacob as they rode back to London.

Tobias had a face like thunder; he had never been robbed before. No one had ever dared. His size and look were enough to be safe from any such thing. "I can't believe it," he said angrily.

"Let it go, big man. There ain't nothing we can do about it now."

Tobias, his face screwed up and his nose wrinkled, let out a loud roar. "AARRGG!" He was so vexed over the highwaymen robbery that he held the reins so tightly his knuckles had turned white.

"I tell you this, Jacob, I will find them, and when I do-"

Dupree rolled his eyes as he looked at Tobias. "And 'ow are ve going to find zem??? Ve don't even know vot zay look like …"

Tobias looked straight ahead as they all picked up speed, London in sight, and didn't answer.

"I know one thing," said Jacob. "I'll not forget those eyes; the brightest blue I've ever seen."


They approached London in silence, the sound of the seagulls shrieking to the left of them as they passed the docks and entered the city, bringing the horses to a fast trot. As usual, London was alive with the bustling bodies going about their business. They turned right into the road that led them to Maggie's.

Tobias suddenly responded to what Jacob had said a few minutes ago. "Blue eyes??"

Jacob looked back at him. "Yeah, the brightest blue."

"I didn't notice any blue eyes," replied Tobias as they pulled up outside the inn.

Jacob swung his leg over the horse's head, leapt off, and then helped Dupree down.

Tobias sat in the saddle, "How did you notice the man's eyes? We were being robbed; all I could see were masked bastards holding pistols to my head."

Jacob tethered his horse to the post, pulled an apple out of the saddle bag and held his hand out for the horse to eat. "That's because I notice things in any situation, and just as well I do, big man."

Tobias footed the stirrup, swung himself off, and hitched his horse. "Well, there can't be too many people with eyes as blue as you say," he said.

Jacob opened the door of the inn and walked inside, followed by Dupree.

Tobias patted his horse and also pulled out an apple to feed it. He stepped inside the inn and walked to the bar where the other two stood. Jacob turned with a jug of ale in his hand and offered it to Tobias.

"This is needed," Tobias said as he put the jug to his lips and gulped down its entire contents, leaving a thick layer of froth stuck to his mouth.

Maggie had already filled a second jug, anticipating what Tobias would do, and placed it on the bar. "Thirsty, I see," she said. "Again …"

Just then, both of the other jugs came down hard onto the bar as Jacob and Dupree wiped at their mouths.

Maggie eyed both men with a slight look of bewilderment on her face. "Well … Something must of happened for you all to need a drink so badly. That and the fact that you are back as quick as you all left …"

Tobias slammed the second jug down. "We were robbed," he said, "Bloody robbed! In broad daylight, no less …"

Maggie began to fill all three jugs again, sinking each into the large barrel filled with the ale. "Robbed?????" she said, putting the first back on the bar. "How …? I mean, who …? Who would rob you???"

Jacob quickly grabbed the jug before Tobias could and took a mouthful. Tobias gave him a sharp look as he did. Maggie filled a second jug and placed that on the bar. Dupree, just as quickly, grabbed it and looked up at Tobias to see the same look he had given Jacob.

"Bloody highwaymen …" said Tobias, leaning on the bar, ready to grab the next jug.

"Ooh, yes, I've heard that a small gang have been holding up carriages outside of London," she said thoughtfully as she poured herself a glass of brandy. "A month or so back, Mr Riley had mentioned it when he came in. He had been travelling in a carriage with a couple, and they had come across the devils."

Jacob wiped his mouth and broke off a piece of bread from the loaf that Maggie had placed on a plate. "Who's Mr Riley?" he asked, chewing on the bread.

Maggie put three more glasses on the bar and started to pour in some brandy. "Mr Riley … He owns quite a few of the stalls down at the market, sells cloth and such like. Anyway, he often comes in for a drink and a bite. Lovely fella - on his own since his wife passed. Well, he told me that he had been robbed, but lucky for him, he only had a few shillings on him at the time…."

"Well," said Dupree, "zey 'av robbed us, not only of all our goods but also zee cart as vell. And my silver pocket votch …!!!"

"If only you had warned us of that, Maggie," said Tobias.

"I never paid it no mind, especially with you. I mean, look at the size of yer. Who would even dare rob you?"

"Well, they did, and we have been."

Maggie filled the jugs again and left the brandy bottle on the bar. "Well, you must be hungry after all that, fellas; I have just made a meat pie. Do you want any?"

All three of their eyes lit up at the sound of a freshly made meat pie. And so Maggie went into the kitchen to fetch it. The three of them sat down at the nearest table and slumped into the chairs.

Maggie brought out a large steaming hot pie and placed it in front of them. Under her arm was a piece of paper.

"Oh, Tobias, this came for you. A priest came in the hope of seeing you in person, but when I told him that you had left for Chelmsford and I didn't expect you back for a week or so, he wrote this on a piece of paper for you."

Tobias took the paper and opened it up, written on it were the words:

> TOBIAS, YOUR FATHER IS VERY ILL.
> I HOPED TO SPEAK WITH YOU IN
> PERSON AND BRING YOU TO HIS
> SIDE. I PRAY THIS REACHES YOU
> IN TIME.
>
> FATHER ALMAND

Jacob could see a look of concern etched across his face as he read the note. "What is it, big man???"

Tobias read the note again, then held it in his hand and looked at Jacob. "It's ... It's my father ... He is very ill ... I must go and see him."

Tobias held out the paper, and Jacob took it and began to read. "I'm sorry, Tobias," he said.

Tobias looked sullen and sad as Jacob handed the paper back. "I guess I should expect this. He has just been a drunk ever since my mother died - never recovered from it."

Maggie placed her hand on his shoulder, leant forwards and kissed his cheek. "I'm sorry, my love," she said.

Just then, the door burst open, and a very exhausted looking young lad entered the inn. His face was as red as a summer sunrise. Panting and clearly out of breath, he said, "Please, can any of you help me? I'm in desperate need of finding someone."

Maggie walked over to the young lad. "Now, now," she said. "Sit yourself down, boy, and catch your breath. Who is it you are after?"

The young lad pulled a small pouch from around his back and opened it up. From inside it, he pulled out a letter and waved it in his hand. "I'm looking for two men, miss," he said, panting.

"Come now, boy. Take a deep breath and calm yourself," said Tobias as he stood from the table.

Jacob spun around in his chair and faced the boy. "Do you have the names of the two men you are looking for??"

The boy gulped, swallowed, tried to gain control of his breath, and then held the letter out. "Yes, sir," he said.

"Well then, speak up."

"Jacob Hammond … and Tobias Johnson …"

Tobias and Jacob turned to each other and then back to the young lad.

Jacob walked to the boy with his hand out. "Then look no further. You have found us. What does this concern?"

The young lad held out the letter. "My instructions were to find you and give you this, sir."

Jacob took the letter and opened it. He started to read. As he read, he slowly walked across the floor.

"Well, what does it say???" said Tobias.

Jacob continued to read without looking at or answering him. He had walked over to the bar and then, still holding the letter, slumped his hand down to his leg. He turned to face Tobias.

"Well? … What is it, man?????"

"It's from Josephine … Her father … He's been murdered!!!!!!!!"

Tobias snatched the letter from Jacob's hand and began to read. As he read, he shook his head. "No … No … It can't be … George … is dead ….!!!!!"

Jacob ran over to where the young lad stood next to Maggie, squatted down and grabbed both his arms. "How long ago did Josephine give you this letter, boy??" he asked with a raised tone.

"Two days ago, sir," the boy answered quickly and shaking.

Jacob turned from the boy, his head in his hands and elbows on his knees. "Fuck! … Fuck!"

Tobias fell silent and slumped back into a chair. Dupree sat, switching his eye between them both; no words could he conjure.

"We must leave at first light," said Jacob.

Tobias slowly looked up, "Yes … We must go to her at first light."

Jacob took the letter from his hand and put it inside his pocket. Then he turned, grabbed the brandy from the bar and swigged straight from the neck.

"No, Tobias," he said, handing him the bottle.

"You must go to your father's side; there is no time. You should be with him; if you do not go, you will regret it for the rest of your life, and so shall I for not making you."

Tobias nodded and shook his head at the same time. A numbness filled his large frame. He took a swig from the bottle and rested it in his lap, staring into nothing.

Jacob gently tapped him on his shoulder and said, "We will meet each other at the tavern in a couple of days."

Tobias stood up and took a deep breath. "Then I shall leave tonight. Give myself a head start."

Jacob looked into his eyes and could see that there was no talking him out of this decision. He had seen that look many times since their first meeting nearly two years ago.

Tobias corked the bottle and walked towards Jacob, putting both hands on his shoulders. "You stay safe, my skinny friend. See you at Josephine's."

He then walked past Dupree and gave him a nod as he walked up to Maggie, put his arms around her and kissed her goodbye. He opened the door of the inn, and before he walked through it, he turned to Dupree. "Look after my Maggie for me, old man, and yourself, my friend." He then turned and left.

Jacob sat in the chair opposite Dupree and shook his head. Dupree had only met George briefly, but he had got to know Josephine through Jacob and Tobias. He felt sad and terrible for her and also, right now, Jacob.

"You should get a good night's rest, Jacob," said Maggie. "You will be wanting to make haste at first light."

Jacob agreed, nodded his head and kissed her cheek. "Thank you, Maggie," he said,

"No need to thank me, my love. You just get yourself off and, at first light, get to Josephine. She is going to need you now, more than ever."

The following morning, at daybreak, Jacob said his goodbyes and mounted his horse to set off for the tavern. The sky, even though it was becoming daylight, was overcast, and it had started raining. He made his way up the road and turned left onto the main road that would take him out of London.

The rain battered against his face as a torrid downpour was being driven in every direction by a strong wind …

!!!!! THE END !!!!!
To be continued…………